TWICEBORN ENDGAME

MARINA FINLAYSON

FINESSE SOLUTIONS

Cover design by Karri Klawiter
Formatting by Polgarus Studio

Published by Finesse Solutions Pty Ltd
2017/12

Author's note: This book was written and produced in Australia and
uses British/Australian spelling conventions, such as "colour" instead
of "color", and "-ise" endings instead of "-ize" on words like "realise".

National Library of Australia Cataloguing-in-Publication entry:

Finlayson, Marina, author.
Twiceborn endgame / Marina Finlayson.
ISBN 9780994239129 (paperback)
Finlayson, Marina. Proving; Book 3.
Paranormal fiction, Australian.
A823.4

CHAPTER ONE

Naturally my sycophantic lizard of an ex-husband had chosen to hole up with our kidnapped son at the Park Hyatt, with its million-dollar harbour views. The graceful white sails of the Sydney Opera House curved against the sky just across the busy waters of Circular Quay, with the larger harbour spread out beyond it. At this time of night the lights on the rich northern shore twinkled like a fairyland. If there was a more perfectly located hotel in Sydney, or a more expensive one, I hadn't heard of it.

Nothing but the best for Jason. Even before I'd known he was a dragon his taste for luxury had been obvious. The dragon bit just made it more understandable. Beats me how he'd ever settled for a small suburban life with Lachie and me, even for a couple of years. No wonder he'd kept disappearing on those "business trips". He was probably off living the high life again. Playing happy families was a novelty that soon wore off.

Car doors slammed as we got out on Hickson Road. Dave had found a parking spot just down from the hotel. He was a small guy with a big heart and fully human, or I would have suspected there'd been magic involved. Were there such things as parking fairies? Even at nearly eleven o'clock at night, a parking spot in the heart of Sydney was hard to come by.

Steve got out and stood next to me, eyes still on his laptop screen. He dwarfed Dave, though that wasn't saying much. He was half-Maori and built like Schwarzenegger on steroids; he dwarfed most people. The laptop looked like a toy in his massive hands. He was human too, though I wasn't asking any questions about the legality of the tracking app or whatever piece of computer wizardry it was that held his attention. It had gotten us this far, so I didn't care. The phone that Lachie had used to call me half an hour ago was in the Park Hyatt, according to Steve, and that was all I needed to know to get my son back.

The rest of us weren't human, though we looked it at the moment. Delicate little Luce was actually a wyvern, and even in human form wasn't someone you wanted to meet in a dark alley at night, despite looking like a petite Chinese doll. The surly brute hulking next to her was Garth, and that advice went double for him. He wore his hair short, military-style, and his constant state of alert spoke of a life lived on the edge. I'd already experienced the joy of being attacked by him in his wolf form, and let me tell you, that was not an experience I wished to repeat. And that was in spite of the fact I wasn't exactly the tame soccer mum I appeared on the outside.

I certainly had been—only a few weeks ago, too—but now there wasn't a name for what I'd become. "Hybrid" didn't really cover it. "Half-human, half-dragon" made no mention of the fact that two separate souls, or consciousnesses if you preferred something less metaphysical, had fused to create the person who now called herself Kate O'Connor.

I was just as likely to call myself Leandra, dragon queen, these days, which wasn't as confusing as it sounded, though it sure had been a rough transition, and certainly not what I'd planned to do with my life. But the original Leandra hadn't given me any choice when she'd colonised my body to save her own miserable life. Dragons were like that. Selfish megalomaniacs, the lot of them.

And now here we were, trying to look inconspicuous on a Sydney street while we waited for the rest of our party to join us. Guess their parking fairy wasn't as effective as Dave's.

"It hasn't moved for a while," said Steve, still watching his screen.

"Probably a wild goose chase," Garth muttered. The glass was always half-empty with the big werewolf. He shifted restlessly, and his normally grey eyes flashed yellow as he checked the street. His wolf was eager for release. When he turned that golden gaze on me I shivered at the intensity in his eyes. "He must know we'd find him."

"Maybe not." I refused to accept that we could fail to get Lachie back. I'd spent seven months in hell already, believing him dead. Nothing was going to keep me from my son now. "His number was withheld. He wasn't to know our resident computer geek had ways to hunt him down anyway."

Steve grinned at the compliment, but he deserved it. Tracking the phone had been the last thing on my mind at the time, having just survived an assassination attempt and seen the would-be murderer escape with my precious son. Lachie had managed to sneak his father's phone and call us. Luckily he'd spent a bit of time lately with Mac, and he knew the pink-haired werewolf's number off by heart, since I'd lost my phone in the madness of the last week and hadn't yet had a chance to buy another. Steve had tried to trace the call while we spoke, but Jason had intervened before the call had lasted long enough, at which point I'd given in to a temper I would have found unacceptable in my son, and hurled poor Mac's phone against the wall.

Fortunately the screen was the only thing that shattered, and Steve was still able to work his computer magic and uncover the origins of the call.

Four others joined us at last, all new thralls. Young men, strong and lean, which seemed to suit their previous mistress's tastes. I hid my disquiet at the way their gazes fell on me and stuck, as if I were the sun around which their worlds revolved. That was pretty much how enthralment worked. They'd been enthralled to Elizabeth, my late and unlamented dragon mother, for so long they would have been left gibbering idiots at her death if I hadn't enthralled them myself. But that necessity didn't change how I felt about it. Their adoring gazes creeped me out. No one should have such power over another.

Now we were a party of nine, all big imposing men in dark clothes except for Dave, myself and Luce. She wore black too, as usual, but only those who knew her found her imposing. Others were fooled by her size and her pretty face. If they survived the learning experience, they didn't make the same mistake twice. Wyverns fight like the devil, whatever shape they're wearing, and if she wasn't in trueshape, rending you with her spurs or paralysing you with her fear breath, she'd break all your limbs with her martial arts skills as a human.

And I looked like some hobo they'd picked up on the street, still in the torn jeans and dirty shirt I'd worn when I'd pretended to be Kasumi's prisoner earlier in the day, back when Elizabeth was still dragon queen not only of Sydney but of all Oceania, and I was her soon-to-be-dead daughter.

Now she was dead and I was queen, though anything less regal-looking would be hard to find. My auburn hair was scraped back into a messy ponytail and my face was still pale from blood loss. I rubbed at a smear of blood on my bare arm. My royal image was the last thing on my mind with Lachie gone. It had been a huge relief to discover he was with his father. Kasumi could have taken him anywhere, done anything to him. Instead, he was alive and, much as I hated Jason, I knew he could keep our son safe, at least for a little while. But I had no intention of leaving him with my ex any longer than I had to. Jason's ambitions meant he kept dangerous company. Lachie might be safe for the moment, but I knew that moment had an expiry date.

"Let's move," I said.

We were attracting attention clumped here on the pavement across from the arched entry to the hotel. We didn't look like partygoers or workmates out for a drink. The silence of the men and their serious faces had already caused a few passers-by to cross the street to avoid us. We looked like the kind of trouble no one wanted to run into at eleven o'clock on a Friday night.

Luce led the way and we fell in behind her. I walked next to Steve and peeked at his screen. It showed a blinking red dot on a grid of Sydney's streets: the Park Hyatt, lit up like a Christmas tree.

"How precise is that thing?"

He glanced at me. "I can get us within a metre. Big Brother is watching. Scary, isn't it?"

"What's that?" I pointed at a number on the screen.

We entered the gleaming foyer and the receptionist looked up enquiringly.

"Altitude." He glanced at the high ceiling above us and paused a moment, obviously calculating something in his head. "Probably the … third floor?"

"Let's go," said Luce from his other side.

She motioned Dave to wait with two of the thralls in the foyer, and the rest of us headed for the bank of elevators on the left. Dave nodded and led the thralls to a dimly lit lounging area, where he began a methodical survey of all the people in sight, most of whom were lingering over drinks. If Jason came through, he wouldn't get past without being spotted.

On level three the hall glowed with a soft, muted light, and the carpet muffled our footsteps as we followed Steve to the right. The walls were panelled in a dark brown, with artworks tastefully displayed at intervals along the corridor. Everything was in toning shades of brown: carpet, walls, doors and even the artworks. All of the rooms were on our left, on the side that faced those fabulous harbour views; the other side of the corridor had only narrow windows which overlooked the street we'd parked on. The only sounds were the gentle hum of air conditioning, and the faint chatter of a TV from behind one of the doors we passed.

Steve's footsteps slowed as we passed a rather phallic sculpture, and he pointed soundlessly to the door of Room 330. Like the others we'd passed, it was tucked into a small alcove. Garth slipped past him and laid his head against the door, listening. He moved fluidly, graceful for such a big man. A long moment passed while we stood like statues abandoned in the corridor.

"Can't tell if they're still there," Garth murmured. "The TV's on, but I can't hear anyone moving around."

"Can you smell anything?" Luce asked.

He shrugged. "Jason's been there. Lachie too. Don't know how recently, though. Guess we'll just have to suck it and see."

Luce nodded and the two thralls drew their guns. Garth stepped back to give himself room, then aimed a savage kick at the door. Werewolf strength was handy like that. It sure beat having to carry a sledgehammer. The door crashed back against the wall, no match for Garth's power.

Somehow I'd ended up at the back of the group as we surged into the room, and I strained to see over all the taller shoulders hulking in front of me. The curtains were drawn, and the room was dark except for the glow of the TV screen, but it was soon apparent the place was empty.

I flicked on the light, disappointment pressing like a weight on my chest. My saner self had known it would have been too easy, but still I'd hoped to find Lachie here. I needed to hold him, to be certain he wasn't hurt, or frightened. My fists clenched with frustration as I leaned back against the wall, letting my eyelids sag shut. His terrified screams as Kasumi carried him off still rang in my ears, and I started to shake. Adrenalin had got me this far, but I'd been stabbed and poisoned only an hour before. Now everything started to hurt again.

"Check the room," said Luce, but I could tell by her tone she didn't expect to find anything useful either.

I opened my eyes in time to see one of the thralls cross to the desk by the windows. The glittering harbour lay spread out below, the Opera House looming opposite. He yanked open the top drawer.

"Hey, here's the—"

A blast shook the room. The thrall flew through the air like a rag doll cast aside by a petulant giant and slammed into the wall. The windows blew out and the rest of us were knocked to the floor. Winded, I fought for breath, trying to make sense of what was happening as pieces of the desk sprayed the room like so much kindling. Some massive splinters were flung with such force that they embedded themselves into the walls.

Luce was first on her feet, while I still lay there, my abused body throbbing. She hurried to the downed thrall. Flames licked at the curtains, and somewhere in the corridor outside a fire alarm began to shrill.

I staggered to her side, my head ringing, and looked down. Clearly there was no need to take the man's pulse. Half his head had been blown off.

Steve cleared his throat nervously. His normally dark face was ashen. "I guess he found the phone."

"Bring his gun," Luce ordered the other thrall. "Let's move."

Garth's arm snaked around me, hard as iron. His golden eyes blazed with a protective fury. "You're bleeding."

"Am I?" I raised my hand to my face and brought it away bloody. "Must have been a splinter. It's nothing."

"It's not nothing. You've lost enough blood already today." His warm hand cupped my face, inspecting the wound. He was so close I felt his breath on my skin, and a wholly inappropriate shiver pierced me. This was not the time. Not the place.

He felt the shiver and his grip tightened. "What's wrong? Are you hurt?"

Shifters like us healed with supernatural speed, but my body was already on overtime after dealing with a knife to the heart earlier in the evening. My hands found the hard muscles of his chest without my even meaning to, instinctively seeking his support. It felt natural, right, to sag against him.

"I'm fine."

So not fine. My son was gone, that poor man had just died, and now my stupid dragon libido had decided that werewolf was on the menu, despite the fact that I already had a boyfriend in Ben. My new self suffered desires and violent surges of emotion that I could barely control at times, which only made an already difficult situation all the more nightmarish. How do you cope with a world gone mad when you can't even trust *yourself* any more?

"That bastard," he growled. Even the damn growl turned me on. It was so primal. "I'll kill him."

"It's my fault," said Luce, hustling everyone out the door and back towards the lifts. Doors were opening all along the corridor, people calling out worried questions. "I take full responsibility. I should have expected a booby trap from Jason."

"Why should you? Who would have thought he'd have the time? We were barely half an hour behind him." Weary. I was so weary. I just wanted to be home safe with my baby. The smell of smoke was strong in the corridor, and behind us I heard the faint crackle of flame. Instead I was here, trapped in a nightmare that seemed unending, fighting someone else's war.

The ceiling sprinklers turned on as we reached the lifts. Voices were raised in shouts of alarm all along the corridor. Somewhere a child began to cry. The thin, hiccupping sound reminded me of my own child, though he hadn't cried like that since he'd been very small. When he'd first started school he'd had a recurring nightmare about being chased by a black teddy bear. Would Jason remember that he liked to sleep with his door open, so the room wasn't completely dark?

"Take the stairs," Garth muttered, his hands all over me, holding me up, holding me together. I felt like crying myself. Sometimes this new life was almost more than I could bear. "Let's get away from these people."

It was true, people were staring. I could feel the wound in my cheek knitting together already, but there was no disguising the blood, and I wasn't the only one looking the worse for wear.

"What's happening?" A woman stepped wide-eyed into our path. "Is it a fire?"

Garth pulled me toward the fire stairs, shaking her off. "Get out of here, lady. Can't you smell that smoke?"

Then the heavy door slammed shut on her worried face with a hollow thud that echoed in the concrete stairwell. We plunged down the stairs, a party of five that had gone up as a party of six. I hadn't even known the dead man's name.

One more casualty in the terrible bloodbath of the proving.

CHAPTER TWO

Ben still wasn't back when we returned to Elizabeth's palace. Or my palace, I suppose, since she was dead and I was now queen. It was nearly midnight as we climbed the curving road toward its blazing lights. I'd never seen such a mansion before, much less owned one. Perched high on a hill with ocean views out the wazoo, everything about it screamed money, from the marble floors to the chandeliers dripping crystal high overhead. Elizabeth's taste in furnishings ran to antiques, and her walls boasted a few old masters. It was like walking through an art gallery or a museum. Not quite my cup of tea, but if I ever needed money, I could live off the proceeds of the sale for the rest of my life. Probably my grandkids could too. It was hard to think of it as mine yet, though it was probably the best thing about my inheritance. The main part of what Elizabeth had left me was a tangle of problems.

"You all right?" Garth asked as I started the long climb to my bedroom. The staircase was massive, as imposing as everything else in this house, and the first floor seemed a long way away to my tired legs.

"Fine." Hey, apart from my missing son, my missing boyfriend, and enemies lining up to kill me in all directions, what did I have to worry about? Life was just peachy.

He didn't say anything else, just stood in the middle of the marble foyer and watched me all the way up the stairs, his brows drawn in that familiar brooding look. It was a relief to escape to the privacy of my own room, where I didn't have to put on a brave front any more.

If only Ben would turn up, or at least send word, that would be one worry off my list. He'd disappeared the previous night, off on a mission of his own, leaving a note to say he'd be out of contact for a while and not to worry. Not to worry! Considering he was human and injured, that was a bit of a joke. He had no shifter powers to aid him on whatever idiot quest he was on, just a gun and his native stubbornness. When someone like Ben says *don't worry* it usually means they're off doing something highly dangerous and/or illegal. Events had kept me well and truly distracted, what with the attack on my house, our own assault on Elizabeth and my remaining sister Alicia, plus Kasumi's assassination attempt and the kidnapping of Lachie. It had certainly been an action-packed twenty-four hours, but I'd still managed to sneak in plenty of fretting over whatever Ben was up to. Knowing him, it was probably both stupid and dangerous.

Still, sufficient unto the day are the evils thereof, and all that. No need to borrow trouble, there was still plenty coming my way. I peeled off my disgusting clothes and had a shower to wash off the blood and grime, but I didn't feel any cleaner. That would take a lot more than soap and water. It still bothered me that I hadn't even known the name of the man who'd died tonight.

Leandra had been like that. She'd cared so little for her thralls that she'd had trouble telling them apart. They were no more than interchangeable lumps of meat to her, their only value in the service they could provide.

That wasn't me. I refused to become like the other dragons. I stared at myself in the bathroom mirror. Troubled green eyes stared back. The wound on my cheek had completely healed already. A pink scar on my breast showed where Kasumi had plunged the dagger into my heart tonight, but by tomorrow that too would be gone. Dragons were fast healers.

Just as well, since people tried to kill them so often. Maybe they should consider a rethink on their personal relationship strategies. Alone in the sumptuous marble-lined bathroom, a sudden longing to be human again filled me. Back then my bathroom had had a couple of bare patches where tiles had fallen off the walls, and a water stain on the ceiling, but I hadn't even known that shifters were real. I'd trade a lot of luxury for the certainties of life in those days. Dragons and werewolves and goblins had been creatures you read about in stories, not people you met on the streets of Sydney.

And now I was one. Stupid bloody Leandra.

I turned out the light and climbed into the massive four-poster bed, but sleep refused to come. Would Jason keep our son safe? His record of doing that wasn't exactly glowing. Valeria had hurled my little boy off the top of the Sydney

Harbour Bridge when he'd been in his father's so-called care. Now Jason had thrown in his lot with the Japanese queen. How was I going to get my son back before she decided that Lachie was more use to her as a tool to hurt me, never mind that he was the son of her new ally?

I shifted uneasily on the pillow. There'd have to be a honeymoon period, where she'd be pleased with her new alliance. Maybe a week. Maybe more. Surely I had a few days, at least, before the situation went that far. I swallowed hard, my throat suddenly dry. My curly-headed boy had been through so much already. He was tougher now, but I longed to hold him in my arms all the same. He tried to act grown-up, but he still liked a cuddle at bedtime. A story too, though he could read perfectly well himself. And Jason hadn't had the patience for such things even when we were married. Busy with his new alliance, would he make time for his son?

I rolled over, staring at the hulking shapes of unfamiliar furniture in the dark. I had so much to do tomorrow, decisions to make and plans to set in motion if I were to have any hope of surviving what was coming. And I had to survive, for Lachie's sake.

Beside me the bed was empty, the sheets cold where Ben should be lying. My feelings about him were … mixed, and it wasn't even as simple as Kate-feelings versus Leandra-feelings. Our friendship had turned into something more only recently, but already the initial euphoria was fading in the face of his reaction to my new dragon status. It was a hard thing to look at the face of the person you thought loved you and see only revulsion. I'd thought he would get over it. I was still me in many ways. Trying to be, anyway. But if anything it was getting worse.

And then there was the pure Leandra rage at his calm assumption that he knew best. That he had the right to wander off as he pleased on his own mad quest to find the goblin mage Blue Monroe, despite my insistence that we didn't need any goblin magic. I was trying hard to talk myself out of that rage, because I knew the old Kate wouldn't have felt like that, and it only seemed to prove his point that I'd become too dragonlike. But still it persisted, seething away under the surface of my concern for him, until I couldn't tell whether anger or relief would win out when he finally reappeared.

At five o'clock in the morning I gave up and got dressed. I wandered downstairs to see who else was about, and spent fifteen minutes cross-examining the two thralls on duty in the comms room as to their names and complete personal histories. I also discovered the dead man had been known to his mates as "Wazza", was a mad-keen Eels supporter, and liked Mexican food, the hotter the better.

The lights were on in the kitchen, and I followed the sound of voices and the smell of coffee brewing and found Dave and Luce and two more of the new thralls getting ready for their shift. I gave them the third degree too before they hurried off to their duty.

Luce eyed me over the top of her coffee cup. She wore her usual black pants and long-sleeved top, despite it being the middle of summer. "You can't save everyone, you know."

"What do you mean?" I sank into a chair at the big table, feeling grumpy and defensive.

She nodded at the door the thralls had disappeared through. "Those guys, me, Dave—all of us—we're all expendable. You need to think like a dragon if you're going to make it through this."

"Speak for yourself." Dave set a steaming cup of coffee in front of me. He had big hands for a smallish guy, but he handled the delicate cup with the same competence as one of his knives. One of those hands gave my shoulder a gentle squeeze. "I'm not expendable. None of the rest of you bastards can make a decent cup of coffee to save your lives."

Luce gave him her usual poker face, refusing to be diverted. "Obviously I'd prefer not to be expended myself, if it comes to that. But the point is, we are resources." She turned serious brown eyes on me. "You can't afford to be getting all attached to people, or the proving will break you. The only certainty we have here is that people will die."

"I think that's been pretty well demonstrated already," I said, a little tartly. "But the day I stop caring about that is the day you may as well kill me too. I am *not* the Leandra you knew."

Just as I wasn't exactly the old Kate either. Damn, this shit was complicated. I was certainly coping better with all the death and mayhem than I ever would have before. There was a dragonish ruthlessness that hadn't been part of Kate's makeup. But I was still human enough to feel that people mattered. Everyone was the centre of *someone's* world. I'd known what it was like to lose the person you loved most. My world had ended the day Lachie died, and I only came back to life when I discovered he wasn't dead after all. I would never forget the all-consuming pain, the despair, the black void that had swallowed my heart. I could never see death the way Leandra had, as an unfortunate necessity in her plans.

Luce shrugged. "I'm just trying to help. A little distance is not a bad thing."

"I'll bear that in mind." It certainly seemed to work for her. She wasn't exactly the warm cuddly type. "Since you're here, we may as well go through what needs to be done. How about some breakfast, Dave?"

My new super-healing powers certainly seemed to require a lot of fuel. I was always starving lately.

Dave grinned at me from the other side of the long serving bench that separated the main room from the cooking area. That side was his, and when he was working no one else was allowed there, though he'd made an exception once or twice for Lachie. The two of them had formed a snack-sneaking conspiracy against me. "Bacon and eggs?"

"Perfect." Who would be sneaking junk food to Lachie now? Was he even being fed properly? I swallowed the familiar pangs of worry and tried to focus on what Luce was saying.

"I've already anticipated some of your commands," she said. "I have people watching the airport and the major hotels, plus others checking all Jason's known addresses."

"He's not likely to go to any of those."

"No. Not likely. But we'll check anyway."

"What about the wolves? Have they turned up anything?"

"Not yet."

"No sign of Kasumi?"

"No." Luce's lips thinned. She had shared Garth's opinion of the kitsune woman. "Jason said she'd gone back to Japan, and I think it likely he was telling the truth. We checked the passenger manifesto of last night's flight to Tokyo. Her name wasn't listed, but who knows? She could have been on it, but we can't be sure."

I nodded. Kitsune were impossible to detect if they wanted to remain hidden. Not even their own mothers could have told them apart from whoever's face they wore. It was a skill that had allowed me to defeat my mother, the reigning queen, and my sister, both of whom had a lot more resources than I did. Funny how a kitsune on your side tended to even up the odds.

Sadly, I'd also learned that their skills could be put to use in less positive ways, such as pretending to be someone else and then putting a knife through the heart of an unsuspecting victim and kidnapping their son. Definitely a mixed blessing.

However, dwelling on the past wasn't going to get us anywhere. It certainly wasn't going to bring Lachie back. I had to focus.

"Do you know of any way to unmask a kitsune?"

Luce had been bound to Alicia the whole time Kasumi was with us, so I hadn't had the benefit of her considerable experience. I looked hopefully at her, but she shook her head.

"I've never had much to do with them. They rarely travel outside Japan. The goblins might know, but you know what goblins are."

Yep. Unreliable, and liable to charge you a fortune just to tell you the time. After borrowing your watch.

"Well, never mind. We have a coronation to plan."

One delicately arched eyebrow rose in surprise. "A coronation? What about your new sisters?"

That had been yesterday's bombshell. Just when I'd thought the proving was over I'd discovered the existence of seven new sisters. Seven more people I'd have to kill if I wanted the throne. No, that wasn't right. I couldn't give a rat's arse about the stupid dragon throne. I hadn't even known it existed until recently. Seven more people I had to kill if I hoped to ever be left alone to live in peace with my son.

"What about them? As far as I'm concerned, Elizabeth had five queen daughters. We've fought it out to see who should succeed her like good little queenlings, and I'm the last one standing. Therefore, the throne is mine. If she chose to lay another clutch of queen eggs later and rear them in secret—and we only have the word of traitors on that; they could be imposters for all we know—then that was her choice. But since she's dead, as far as I'm concerned any plans she might have had for them die with her.

"I hold the throne, and I refuse to recognise that they have any claim whatsoever."

Luce's gaze was cool. "They won't care if you recognise them or not. You'll still have to kill them."

"Perhaps." I hadn't given up hope of finding another way. "But I don't see the point in legitimising their claim by accepting a second proving. Let's invite the overseas queens and get the damn crown on my head already, before they all decide they want to annex the place. I need to at least appear to be in control."

"Even if you're not," said Dave, coming to remove my empty plate.

I smiled up at him. "*Especially* if I'm not."

Luce and I spent the next hour going over the arrangements for the coronation. I could get Mac to handle the details for me. She was still feeling guilty about Kasumi impersonating her to attack me, though it was hardly her fault. Giving her something to do would keep her mind occupied. By the time Luce and I had finished, the sky had begun to lighten and the currawongs warbled in the trees.

"Give the prisoners some breakfast, then bring them to the throne room," I said.

The throne room had had a thorough cleaning since the bloodletting yesterday. Elizabeth's ostentatious throne had been removed and replaced with a more modest chair. I didn't care for the dragon assumption of superiority over every other living being—and besides, it was impossible to get the blood completely out of the fabric. It would need to be reupholstered. Greeting guests while seated on the blood of your murdered mother just didn't seem right, even if the old bitch had deserved it.

My own, very human, mother would probably do some bloodletting of her own if she found out that I'd been keeping Lachie's miraculous return from the dead from her. I felt terrible that she and my sister both still mourned him, but the idea of making all the necessary explanations of the current situation seemed even more overwhelming than having to take on seven new sisters and the overseas queens combined. Besides, if I told them he was alive I'd have to tell them he was in Jason's clutches. I wanted to wait until I had him back safe and we could celebrate properly.

Not that there weren't plenty of other things clamouring for my attention. Like the matter of what to do with Elizabeth's former household, now eating breakfast in my dungeons. In a normal proving, they would simply serve the new queen once the old one died, but there was nothing normal about what had happened here. Usually the incoming queen didn't behead the old one. Nor were there usually seven extra claimants nobody had ever heard of before—although I knew some, at least, of Elizabeth's staff had not only heard of them but had aided in keeping them secret. Loyalty was going to be hard to come by, but I had to know who I could trust.

Garth and Luce joined me as I settled myself on the "throne", standing one on either side of me like a pair of mismatched bookends. The room was long, enormous by any standards, but big even for this mansion. It had been designed to impress, funnelling guests down its imposing length to cower before the queen on her dais. One side was floor-to-ceiling glass, with French doors opening onto a paved terrace nearly as big as the throne room itself, and offering a view of sparkling blue ocean and a curve of white sand below.

"Ready?" asked Luce.

I nodded, and she signalled a thrall to throw wide the double doors at the far end of the room.

In marched an odd assortment of shifters, their auras glowing in many colours, from the blue of a lone griffin through the greens of the water shifters to the many earth tones of the goblins and other earth shifters. Alicia's two leshies were among this last group. Dragon red was conspicuously absent.

I looked them over. Some I'd seen before, like Bear, the leshy who'd freed Gideon Thorne yesterday. He scowled in my general direction but didn't meet my eyes, probably afraid I'd capture his will again. He was lucky I didn't do worse: Thorne was a powerful dragon, the spymaster of the previous queen. Now, thanks to Bear, he was free to continue his scheming against me.

Others were household staff who hadn't been involved in the fighting yesterday, several humans among them. In all there were about forty people under the watchful eye of all my new thralls. The shifters wore silver handcuffs to prevent them accessing their powers, and the guards had the whole group covered with assault rifles. The fear in the room was palpable.

I'd be scared too, in their position. Any other dragon would probably fix the problem by telling the guards to open fire. Luckily for them I wasn't any other dragon.

I rose, drawing every frightened eye in the room. "By right of proving, I am now your queen." In spite of myself, the words touched something deep within me. Leandra had waited so long to say them. But this wasn't how she'd dreamed this scene would play out, with her original body lost and her soul twinned to mine.

A few of the prisoners stirred, but no one dared argue.

"I need loyal subjects, not backstabbing traitors." And definitely no double agents. The battle ahead was going to be hard enough. "Therefore I have an offer for you." *Special introductory offer! Hurry, last days!* It was Elizabeth's money I was spending, so I had no problem being generous. "Anyone who wishes to leave my service is free to do so. You will be given a plane ticket to any other domain you name. My servants will see you aboard the plane."

The expressions on the faces in front of me ranged from incredulous through darkest suspicion all the way to the first glimmerings of hope. The leshy Bear looked frankly disbelieving.

"You'll let us go?" he said. "Just like that?"

"But my family's here," said a voice from the crowd.

"In that case, you face a difficult choice," I said. "You can arrange for your family to join you overseas, of course, but this domain will be forever off-limits to you. I won't have you running off to support Thorne and his pretenders to the throne. If you want to oppose me, you'll have to do it long-distance. Anyone who is found in this domain again will be put to death."

I put some power into that threat, so it resonated with them. I sure as hell didn't want to ever make good on it, but they had to believe I'd do it.

"What's to stop you killing us the minute we say we don't want to work for you?" Bear objected. Naturally he wouldn't consider working for me. His head was way too far up Thorne's backside to change sides now.

I crossed my legs and smiled sweetly. "Nothing, of course. I'm the queen; I can do what I like."

At least that's the way it had always worked, with very few exceptions. No wonder dragons were so unpopular. Pack of bloody tyrants.

"Nevertheless, the offer is genuine. You can choose not to believe me, but I warn you, anyone who stays will have to submit to questioning under a compulsion, so I'll soon find out if you're lying. And in that case I may not be so lenient. So choose wisely."

"Well, I'm not staying," said Bear. He drew himself up to his full willowy height and thrust his chin out, as if daring me to smite him on the spot. For him I could almost wish I was the smiting type. I'd be in a much better position if he hadn't engineered Thorne's escape.

Luce gestured him out of the pack, and he marched to one side like Joan of Arc heading for her funeral pyre. I fully expected him, at least, to try sneaking back into the country. His devotion to Thorne's scheme was strong.

But that was a problem for a future date.

"Who else is joining Bear? Come on, don't be shy."

No one moved for a long moment. Finally a goblin crossed to the other side of the room, and his defection set off a chain reaction. Soon there was barely half left, all human except for the two leshies that had been Alicia's, and a lone selkie woman.

"Corinne!" Bear said to her. "What are you doing?"

She stared straight ahead and said nothing, her cheeks flushed with bright colour, her aura pale and trembling.

"You'll be sorry when we take this bitch down."

Garth crossed the floor in quick strides and backhanded him across the face. Bear staggered and threw me a venomous look. Shame looks couldn't kill. I would have been a lump of dead meat and all his worries would have been over.

"You might have trouble taking anyone down from the other side of the world," I said mildly. "All of you can give your intended destinations to my security officer. You'll be locked up until your flights can be arranged."

I motioned to Garth to take them away.

"You're lying!" Bear shrieked as he was herded towards the doors. "You're going to keep us in chains forever."

Garth hit him again, just for good measure. I probably should have objected, but my dragon side was rather enjoying watching the leshy suffer. Dragons made bad enemies.

When the doors had closed behind them, I turned to the remaining people. It was a smaller group than the one that had left. It didn't look like I was ever going to win any popularity contests in the domain, at least while there were still any other options for shifters to cling to. Was it really that bad that I was half-human? Clearly other humans didn't think so. I found it telling that all the humans among Elizabeth's staff had chosen to stay on. I guess it didn't make much difference to them which dragon butt sat on the throne. Maybe they even liked the idea that the shifter world was getting so shaken up.

I sent two thralls to bring chairs for my new guests, and waited until they were settled comfortably. Well, "comfortably" probably wasn't the right word. I could almost smell the fear in the room. They sat rigid in their chairs, bodies stiff with tension, as if they expected me to turn dragon any minute and devour them.

Trying to appear non-threatening, I slumped down in my own chair. "Don't look so worried. I hardly ever eat people." All I got were a few sickly smiles. "Okay, let's get this over with, and then you can all relax. It's not too late to join the others if you've changed your mind."

Nobody moved, so I called forward the first of the two leshies who'd come with Alicia and Luce yesterday. "Let's start with you. What's your name?"

"Yarrow." His eyes were the green of new grass in spring, and they held my gaze unwaveringly, even as he felt my will invading him.

"That's an unusual name."

It was harder to compel a shifter than a human, and the stronger the shifter, the more difficult it became, which was why I'd chosen to leave the humans until last, and start with the shifters while I was still relatively fresh. Plus I wasn't exactly in top condition after the events of the last few days.

"My mother was an unusual woman."

Well, there were a few of us around.

"Yesterday I killed your mistress, Alicia. How do you feel about that?"

"Guilty." His fabulous green eyes stared adoringly at me, completely under my spell. His aura, which was a muddy green like khaki, throbbed in time with my own heartbeat. That wasn't disconcerting *at all*. He was a very easy subject for compulsion, as if he were eager to join with me.

"Guilty? Why? You couldn't have saved her."

He shook his head. "Guilty because I don't feel bad that she's dead."

"Oh? Why's that?"

"I didn't like the way she hid behind us and let us take the hits meant for her. As if her life was worth more than ours."

She'd been a shocking coward, that was true, but such disregard for anyone else's safety or comfort was hardly peculiar to Alicia—it was pretty standard dragon operating procedure. *I'm all right, Jack, and bugger the lot of you.*

"So why did you work for her?"

"Most of our clan did. We liked the living conditions."

She'd had an estate in the Blue Mountains that backed onto the bush. Terrible fire hazard, as it turned out, but the wilderness and seclusion were leshy catnip. Up there the only sounds were bellbirds in the trees, the only smells the citrus tang of lemon-scented gum, or the fresh aroma of moist earth after rain. For a forest-loving species like leshies, it was heaven on earth.

"You could have chosen to stay out of the proving altogether."

His green gaze was direct. "So people say, but in practice it's almost impossible for the stronger shifters. Dragons want allies and they don't like taking no for an answer."

Well, that was certainly true. Time to wrap this up. I could feel my concentration wavering already.

"And how do you feel about working for me?"

"To be honest, I'd rather go home and leave you dragons to fight it out, but that wasn't an option. I'm certainly not leaving Oceania. My roots are here. So it looks like I'm stuck with you."

Not exactly the ringing endorsement I'd been hoping for. "Will you follow me loyally?"

"That madman Thorne will send the place to hell in a hand basket if he gets his way. You are the best chance we have of finding peace again."

That was slightly better news for my bruised ego. I released him with relief and sat back, trying not to let my dizziness show. Two more shifters and eight humans to go. I might have to pace myself.

The next leshy, Carter, turned out to be the brother of Adam, the leshy who'd saved Ben and me during the battle at Alicia's house. He was more enthusiastic in his support, knowing that I was an enemy both of Alicia, who'd put Adam in harm's way, and of Jason, who'd killed him.

That left the selkie woman, Corinne. Hopefully she'd prove weaker than the two leshies, as my head was pounding from the strain of holding them to my will. I probably shouldn't even be trying to do something like this after the injuries I'd sustained yesterday. I rubbed at my chest where the scar still showed. It ached, but dully, like a wound that was three weeks healed.

"Corinne."

She looked up at me. Her eyes were huge and brown, and her aura roiled like a storm at sea, the rich deep green of the troubled ocean.

"There's still time to change your mind," I reminded her. The internal confusion her aura betrayed made me question her commitment, but she shook her head.

I took a firm grip on her will and she relaxed like a puppet whose strings had been cut. Her mind felt as alien as the leshies', but where theirs had thrummed with earth energy and the joy of growing things, entering hers felt like sliding under a dark wave, cool and enveloping.

"Will you support me loyally and wholeheartedly, following every command I give you?"

Best to keep this short. I could feel my will slipping away into the mysterious depths of her mind, dissipating like foam on the ocean.

She nodded dreamily. "Yes, mistress."

That was good enough for me. I pulled myself together and got out of there before I drowned. What an intriguing mind. I'd never even met a selkie before, much less compelled one.

I wondered what a kitsune's mind would feel like. If I'd tested Kasumi's loyalty like this when she'd turned up on my doorstep offering to join me, Lachie might still be here. Perhaps her mind would have been as slippery as her body, changing form and hiding the truth of what she was. But I'd been too human then to even think of such a thing, and with wolves as the only shifters on my team, no one else had thought of it either. Luce would probably have suggested it, but Luce had been trapped with Alicia.

No use beating myself up about it now. I wouldn't be surprised if Kasumi had been able to fool me anyway. She was a consummate trickster. She'd had me convinced she was the best thing since sliced bread, right up until the moment she'd put a dagger in my heart and taken off with my son. Now getting him back depended on me not stuffing things up again. To be a ruthless and suspicious dragon, not a trusting human.

I needed a break—or at least a cup of coffee. Even dragons liked coffee. I turned to Garth and was about to suggest he take a quick trip to the kitchen when the double doors opened again and a familiar figure strode in.

"Ben!" Okay, it turned out that relief beat anger after all. Just. Knowing that the stupid, pig-headed man was still in one piece was better than a cup of coffee any day.

He gave me a quick one-armed hug. Stubble scraped my lips when he kissed me. He looked tired and he held his bad arm against his body as if it were hurting him.

"Where the hell have you been?"

His grin widened. His eyes were the same rich brown as the selkie woman's, but he was one hundred per cent human. I knew. I'd checked every inch.

"I brought you a present."

"Roses? Chocolates? Gideon Thorne's head on a stick, perhaps?"

He shook his head, making his dark curls bounce. If he didn't get a haircut soon he'd start looking like Michael Jackson in his *Thriller* period.

"Better. I found Blue Munroe." He turned, sweeping his good arm through an extravagant arc like a magician unveiling his trick, and two thralls marched Blue Munroe, goblin mage extraordinaire, through the door behind him.

Maybe "marched" wasn't the right word. The goblin reeked of alcohol, and one whiskery cheek rested uncomfortably on the shoulder of the thrall to his left. His whole body listed that way, as if caught in an invisible wind, and he seemed to be having trouble focusing. The wind was probably called Johnnie Walker, judging by the smell.

Bright orange hair hung in a tangled mat across his face. Blue blinked owlishly in a futile effort to clear it out of the way.

"Hello, Kate," he slurred.

I sighed. Sober, Blue might be a good find. If he could be persuaded to co-operate, a little goblin magic could be handy. Drunk, however—and Blue was almost always drunk—he was no use to anyone.

"Where on earth did you find him?" Ben was looking a little grubbier than usual himself, though on his handsome face stubble was a much more attractive addition than on the bleary-eyed goblin.

"It was more *under* earth," he said. "I had to pull a few strings, or I'd still be searching."

Blue's eyes had sagged closed while we talked. He now appeared to be asleep on his feet, his weight resting on the thrall who held him. The poor man stared straight ahead, trying to pretend a stinking and none-too-clean goblin was not, in fact, drooling on his shoulder.

"What are we going to do with him?" I could hardly drag my eyes from the damp spot spreading on the thrall's crisp white shirt.

"Step one is get him sober. Step two—who knows? He's a goblin mage. Use your imagination."

CHAPTER THREE

An hour later the police were knocking on my door—just another one of the fabulous bonuses of my new lifestyle. My old friends Detectives Hartley and Franks had managed to track me to my new home, probably courtesy of another anonymous tip-off to the police hotline. There was no shortage of shifters eager to cause trouble for me. I could practically smell the suspicion coming off them as they entered.

"Nice place." Detective Hartley's sharp eyes swept over the antique furniture, the high decorative ceilings, the luxurious swags of velvet draped over the floor-to-ceiling windows, then came to rest on me. She had a way of looking at you that would have made even the most innocent person feel guilty, as if she had assessed you and found you wanting. "You been here long?"

She knew I hadn't, but that was her style, always trying to catch you out with seemingly innocuous questions. Last time she'd interviewed me, I'd been living at Arcadia on one of Leandra's properties, a large house set on several hectares.

Elizabeth's house left it for dead, grandiose enough to qualify for the name "palace". Only someone seriously wealthy could afford to live in a place like this.

"Just got here," I said. "My aunt died unexpectedly, and I've come to settle her affairs."

"Who's your aunt?" Detective Franks asked. His eyes were small and close together, which gave him a shifty look. "She must be rich."

"She is. Or was, rather." I looked down at the carpet. I wasn't going to pretend to be heartbroken at the loss, but a little sadness was probably expected. Especially if the story was going to be that we were so close she'd left all her wealth to me. I had people drawing up the relevant documents even as we spoke: fake birth certificates and other ID, as well as a comprehensive will. "You might have heard of her. Elizabeth Appleby."

Detective Hartley nodded. "Sorry for your loss. I don't like to intrude at such a sad time, but we have some more questions for you."

"Have you found my husband?"

I'd set her on Jason's trail last time we spoke, with a light compulsion that would have long since worn off. Messing with people's minds was never a great idea, particularly if those people were police officers. Others tended to notice if detectives suddenly developed weird obsessions, or started acting in illogical ways. It could ruin careers, and I didn't want to be responsible for that. Sure, they were a pain in my arse with their questions, but they were only trying to do their job.

"No. Not yet."

Did she realise she frowned every time she looked at me? I felt a twinge of guilt. In other circumstances I would have liked Detective Hartley. She was thorough and dedicated, with a healthy cynicism, the kind of person who makes a good friend but a bad enemy. Not an easy person to fool. The poor woman was probably still wondering why her memories of certain recent events flat-out contradicted the notes she'd made on them. For an orderly mind like hers it must be particularly galling not to be able to trust your own recall. I wish I could have come up with some other way of dealing with the problems my own stupidity had created, but I'd been caught between a rock and a hard place, with no time for finesse.

"Actually we wanted to talk to you about something completely different," Detective Franks said.

"Where were you last night between ten and eleven p.m.?" Detective Hartley asked.

My first instinct was to insist I'd been home all night, with the whole household to back me up, but instinct was what had got me into such a mess last time. They wouldn't be asking for no reason.

Her voice was mild, as if she only had a vague interest in my answer, but I wasn't fooled. They were already suspicious of me over Valeria's death, and then there were the infamous "dragon wars" outside my old house at The Rocks that the Internet was still buzzing about. Denials weren't going to wash with them.

"Why?" I hedged. "Am I under suspicion for something else now?"

"Answer the question, please." Hartley was too old a hand at this to give me any clues.

"I was out with a group of friends."

"And where did you go with this group?"

Damn it, I'd probably hesitated too long already. An innocent person would be gushing about the scary explosion at the hotel they'd visited, not prevaricating about whether or not to answer. If they were here asking, they already had something that placed me at the scene. Maybe Jason had tipped them off, trying to cause trouble for me. Tit for tat, I guess, since I'd set him up with the cops too.

"We were going to go to a nightclub, but we stopped at the Park Hyatt on the way. Did you hear about the explosion there?"

They exchanged glances. Did I sound too eager now?

"You were going clubbing right after your aunt died?" Detective Franks sounded as if he found the idea offensive.

Shit. Why was I such a bad liar? "Well, I wasn't really in the mood, of course, but my friends thought it might cheer me up."

"I see." Detective Hartley wrote something in her notebook. "Yes, we did hear about the explosion. We were hoping you might be able to tell us more about that."

"Why would you think I'd know anything about it?" I let indignation colour my tone. It would be so much easier if I could just compel this all away, but I resisted the urge. I had too much respect for Hartley to screw her over again if I could possibly avoid it.

"I don't know, Ms O'Connor, let me think." Detective Hartley held up her fingers and ticked her points off on them. "One, you lied to us about your movements on New Year's

Eve, and the fact that you did know the murdered woman, despite initially denying it."

"I told you, that was all my husband's fault."

She ignored me. "Two, there's some kind of shoot-out at your home in The Rocks, plus footage of a dragon and some other weird creatures being involved. Three dead bodies there, to add to the one we fished out of the Harbour on New Year's Eve. And three, last night there's a mysterious explosion at the Park Hyatt, with another death, and we have CCTV footage placing you at the scene just a few minutes before the explosion."

"You've got to admit that looks suspicious." Detective Franks glared at me out of his little piggy eyes. Guess he was playing bad cop today. Must be a nice change for Detective Hartley; that was usually her role. "And now your aunt's dead too."

I didn't have to admit anything of the sort. "Are you suggesting I killed my aunt?"

"Not at all," said Detective Hartley, with an impatient glance at Franks. "But you're obviously very rich. Even richer now your aunt's dead. This place, the terrace at The Rocks, that big property out at Arcadia. You must be one of the wealthiest people in Australia."

The wealthiest, more likely. Not that I was going to tell her that. "What of it? Is it a crime to have money?"

"Rich people think differently," said Detective Franks. Bad cop time again. "Act differently. As long as they're achieving their goals, they don't tend to notice the fallout. They don't care what happens to the little people." He was describing dragons to a tee. Ironic, really, considering how hard I was trying *not* to act like a dragon. The urge to swat him like the insect he was was becoming harder to resist. "We're just wondering what your goals might be, and why you keep turning up in connection with these incidents."

Okay, I needed to turn this around. I had too much to do to spend time squirming on their hook.

"It doesn't matter how rich I am, Detective Franks, I don't go around blowing up hotels. I'm not a terrorist." I took a deep breath. "My goal is to get my son back. My husband has kidnapped him."

The big detective's hairy eyebrows crawled up his forehead in surprise. "This is the son you told us about last time, that your husband faked his death?"

"Yes. I only have one son. An associate of my husband's snatched him last night."

"Why didn't you contact the police? And why did you lie to us just now and say you were going clubbing?"

"My husband threatened me. He said if I told the police anything I'd never see Lachie again."

"So what were you doing at the Park Hyatt? Not going clubbing, I gather." Detective Hartley leaned forward in her chair, like a bloodhound sniffing out the truth. Well, they do say the truth will set you free. Truth might serve my cause better than lies now.

"I knew my husband had been staying there. I went to get my son back."

Okay, so there was truth and there was truth. I had to be careful now not to give her too much or she'd end up investigating me instead of Jason. I didn't want to come across as the deranged mother prepared to do anything to save her child. Even if it was true.

"So you go to the Park Hyatt to meet your husband."

"Not to meet him, no. He didn't know I was coming."

"You planning on roughing him up with those big guys that got in the lift with you?" Franks suggested.

"Just moral support."

I tried to remember if there was a camera in the lift. Probably. I hadn't been thinking of such things at the time. Would they have footage of us getting out on the third floor? Of entering the room? My palms started to sweat. Dammit, I hated talking to the police.

"And which room was your husband staying in?" Detective Hartley's voice was still mild. Somehow that was more threatening than Franks's posturing. Maybe she was playing bad cop after all.

"I don't know. My son managed to contact us without his father knowing. He said it was on the third floor, but he didn't know the room number. But when we got out of the lift the hallway was full of people running, and smoke, and there'd been some kind of explosion. It was chaos. I couldn't find Lachie."

Actually, it wasn't talking to the police that was the problem. It was the *lying* to the police I hated. But what else could I do? I could hardly tell them what had really happened, could I?

"But you tried? You went into the room where the explosion was?"

"No. We couldn't get close. The fire … it was too hot."

"Do you think the explosion had anything to do with your husband?"

"Yes, I do. I think he found out Lachie had called me. It was his way of warning me not to try to get Lachie back. He's a dangerous man, Detective. You have to help me."

"Do you have a recent photo of your son? And of your husband? We'll need you to come down to the station and make a full statement."

"I can't do that. He told me not to go to the police. If he even finds out you were here today …" I put some mental pressure behind my next words. No matter how I tried, it always seemed to come down to dragon compulsions in the end. I was keeping too many secrets to stick to the straight and narrow path. "You'll have to keep this quiet. I can't be involved. You have to find him."

She nodded, that familiar glazed look in her eyes.

"And when you find him, call me. He's a dangerous man. You'll need my help."

In her current state, she didn't question that. I gave her a photo of Jason, and she didn't even notice there wasn't one of Lachie too. There was no need to get the police too involved. Hopefully the impulse to call me would stick, even if she didn't quite remember the reason for it, and I'd be able to swoop in and snatch Lachie back without any of the police getting hurt. They'd be no match for a dragon, but they could be useful in locating one. So why did I feel like such a monster for using them?

CHAPTER FOUR

Probing the innermost secrets of someone's mind is hard work, even for a dragon, if you're not at full strength, and I was still recovering. Add a police interview to that, and by the time I'd finished interviewing my new staff I wasn't fit for anything but bed. Dr Ben and Dr Luce conferred, then prescribed plenty of rest.

"I have things to do. Lachie—"

"Is safe with Jason for the moment," said Ben. "I don't like it any more than you do, but we *will* get him back. And it will be easier if you're not about to collapse."

Luce turned me firmly in the direction of the stairs. She would never have dared with Leandra, but since her stint as Alicia's virtual slave, Luce had returned even more determined to control everything and everyone around her. I could sympathise. No one liked being someone else's puppet. I'd had some pretty bad experiences myself recently, when Leandra had been trying to steal my body. That didn't mean I was going to let Luce boss me around. I was top dog in this relationship.

Asserting my superiority might have to wait until I felt less like a limp dishrag, though.

"You have to admit," Luce said, "whatever Jason's other faults—and they are legion—he's very protective of Lachie. He staged the kid's death just to hide him away from Valeria and … you." She shook her head. "Leandra-you, not Kate-you. I'm still having trouble adjusting to that."

You and me both, sister.

"He didn't do such a great job of protecting him when Valeria was threatening to throw him off the roof of her house," I objected. "Or when she decided to drop him off the top of the Harbour Bridge."

The fact that Jason was supposed to be her ally hadn't stopped Valeria from using our son as a pawn in her game against me. He was only safe with his father for as long as it took Jason's new mistress to see Lachie in the same light. How long did we have?

"Those were unusual circumstances."

"And aren't these unusual circumstances?" Worry for Lachie nagged at my exhausted mind, insisting I should be doing something, anything. I was his mother; he needed me. *Get up. Move. Save him.*

Ben put an arm around my shoulders, and I couldn't help sagging against him. "Nevertheless, you're no use to anyone like this. You need rest."

He urged me up the stairs, and I allowed myself to be led to the bedroom. Despite my protests, in my heart I knew they were right. There was still time before Lachie was at risk, and I would be no use to him like this. It would require all my skill to pick my way through the maze of problems that confronted me. I couldn't afford to stuff this up. Gratefully I sank into the soft white cloud of my pillow and let oblivion take me.

So it was the next morning before the planets aligned and Blue was sober and I was able to string more than two words together in a coherent thought.

We met in the throne room, on Luce's advice.

"A show of strength," she said. "Goblins won't do anything unless they can see what's in it for them. You need to appear powerful."

"He helped us before." Goblin mages had their own defences against dragon manipulation, and I knew I couldn't compel him. I hadn't wanted him here, but since he was, I hoped for some co-operation.

"That wasn't for you, that was for Garth. He owed Garth a debt, and now that debt is repaid. I doubt he'll be so accommodating this time."

I considered the big werewolf. As usual, his grey eyes followed me. He watched me almost as keenly as the thralls did, though in his case it sent a thrill of pleasure through me every time I met his gaze across the room. He never had explained what that debt thing was all about.

Still, there was always money. It was old-fashioned, but money was still a great motivator. I had plenty of it now, and there was nothing goblins liked more.

"He wasn't keen on coming in," Ben said, interrupting my train of thought. Probably best not to spend too much time staring at the werewolf when he was around anyway. "I had to be quite *persuasive*."

I threw him a startled glance. Though I'd known him for years, he'd managed to keep some sides of his personality well hidden. Like the whole delight-in-beating-up-recalcitrant-goblins thing. For that matter, he'd kept the goblins themselves and all the rest of the shifter world a secret too, so I should hardly be surprised. I really didn't know him as well as I'd thought.

Without meaning to, my eyes slid back to Garth. Him, on the other hand, I'd only known for a short time. But he kept nothing hidden. What you saw was what you got.

With an effort I wrenched my thoughts back to the problem of the goblin. "Bring him in, then."

The big doors swung open and Steve marched our goblin "guest" in. He looked a lot more alert than last time I'd seen him, and he didn't flinch away from the light streaming in the long wall of glass that ran down the side of the throne room. The eyes behind his little round John Lennon-style glasses were still bloodshot, but less bleary. He had on clean clothes, too, though they were a little big. Probably borrowed from Dave, who was closest to his height, though built on more solid lines than the scrawny goblin.

His eyes flicked around the room as he advanced. He nodded to Garth, lounging with Mac by the French doors to the terrace. Garth returned the nod but said nothing. He scowled when his gaze fell on Ben, standing beside my chair.

"Nice place." His gaze took in the whole of the imposing room and settled on me in my chair on the dais. "You've moved up in the world."

"You could say that. I hear you're back to living in caves again."

"Nothing wrong with a nice cave. Just the thing for a goblin on his own."

"And where's your clan chief these days? Still on the Gold Coast, is he?"

"Living it up at the casino, I heard," said Ben. "He's a high roller. Limousines, women, parties every night."

"Half the clan's up there," said Luce. She was positioned on my other side, her arms folded across her chest. She regarded the goblin with disdain. "They've got a whole floor of the hotel to themselves."

Blue scowled at her.

"Seems a shame they've got all that money, and you're the one living in a cave, when it was your magic that earned it."

"Money doesn't buy happiness, you know." The goblin's tone was sharp. "Look at you—got all your mother's millions now, but are you happy? And you can't seem to afford more than one chair."

He looked around the empty throne room pointedly.

"Garth, bring a chair for our guest," I said, as if noticing for the first time that he was still standing.

"That's better," he said when he was seated. "Now, what does a person have to do to get a drink around here?"

"We're thinking of your liver, Blue," said Ben.

"My liver doesn't need anything from you except a bottle of scotch and a few ice cubes."

"Sun's not over the yardarm yet."

"It tastes just the same whatever the bloody time of day." Blue had a pointed nose that made him look, even in human form, rather sinister, though it couldn't seem to manage to hold up his glasses properly. They kept sliding down, and he kept pushing them back up. Bloodshot eyes, lank orange hair and a surly expression completed the less-than-attractive picture. "Are you going to give me a damn drink or not?"

"Not. I brought you here to discuss how you can serve your queen, not to watch you get drunk."

He snorted, an unpleasant nasal sound. "Who says she's the queen? Heard there were a few other contenders for the job."

My temper flared. He hadn't been this insolent last time. What was his problem?

Without any conscious effort, full-sized dragon claws erupted from my fingers. Long as swords and just as sharp, they were enough to make Wolverine jealous. I tapped my claws together and watched Blue squirm in his seat.

"That's not the way this is going to work," I said. "The clans have always sold the works of their magi to anyone willing to pay. I'm buying, and you *will* provide what I need."

"I've left my clan."

"I don't imagine Chief Trimboli is very happy that his little money-making goose has flown away. I'm perfectly happy to negotiate with him instead of you."

Blue might be a drunkard, but he wasn't stupid. "So you'll give me back to him if I don't do what you want?"

"That's a very negative way of looking at it. Think of it this way: you make me happy, you get to keep the whole payment for yourself."

He shot me a vicious look, but his shoulders slumped in defeat. He knew he was caught. "You dragons are all the same. What do you want me to do?"

"How about we start with something easy, like changing someone's appearance?"

I didn't really know what I wanted him to do. Not for the first time I wished Kasumi were here, even though she'd turned out to be a backstabbing traitor. Or frontstabbing, I suppose. Right up until she'd thrust that knife into my chest, she'd been the most fabulous resource, with her amazing ability to perfectly mimic the appearance—and even the aura—of anyone at all.

Come to think of it, a goblin seeming probably wouldn't help. I knew from experience that they didn't affect the aura of the underlying wearer. I'd come across my first goblin seeming in this very room, when Elizabeth was still queen and my sisters and I were meeting for the first time at the Presentation Ball. The ball was meant to introduce the candidates for the throne to the shifters of the domain, but it had set a new record: fastest time ever from presentation to the first death. Valeria's griffin lieutenant had worn a seeming and slipped into the ball in disguise, but the fact that her aura had still betrayed her as a griffin, despite the spell that changed her appearance, had saved me from the bomb blast that killed my sister Monique. The discrepancy had raised alarm bells with the ever-watchful Luce, who'd gotten me out of the room just before little bits of my sister spattered all over it. Monique had been the first sister to die in the bloody succession war of the proving.

The only one I hadn't killed myself.

I glanced involuntarily toward the French doors leading onto the terrace. I could still feel the scrape of stone against my face and hear the terrible blast ringing in my ears. I'd gone sprawling across that terrace in an undignified heap, but at least I'd lived. The damage, of course, had been repaired long ago, and all I could see out there now was blue sky and sunshine.

"Just a general change, or are you looking to impersonate someone? 'Cause I'd need part of them for that. Plus it costs more," he added.

He used his middle finger to shove his glasses back up onto the bridge of his nose again. It looked like he was giving me the finger. Probably intentional.

"How about we pay you by not handing your sorry arse back to your clan?" Luce suggested.

Blue shot her a killing look, but I waved her to silence.

"Look, Blue." I leaned forward, letting my claws disappear. "You're the expert. I want my son back. You tell me what I need, and you will be well and truly compensated."

"Where is he?"

"I don't know."

"Well, that's your first problem right there, isn't it?" He jumped up. Out of the corner of my eye I saw the ever-protective Garth stiffen, ready to leap to my defence, but Blue made no move toward me. "Can't rescue the poor kid if you don't know where he is. I'll need to scry for him. You got something of his? Something personal, I mean. Blood or hair is best."

"Is that all you need?" The prospect of finding Lachie had me suddenly as energised as the goblin. "When can you do it?"

He strode toward the French doors. Garth moved to block his way with an enquiring look at me, and I waved him back. We followed the goblin out into the sunlight. Already the stones of the terrace radiated heat; it was going to be another hot day. Below, the beach glittered in the sun and the shrieks of small children playing at the water's edge drifted to us on the wind.

Blue took the wide stone steps down to the garden and made a beeline for the central fountain. It featured mermaids and mermen waving tridents, surrounded by pouting fish that spat water when the fountain was turned on. At the moment nothing disturbed the pool of water around the central statues except the occasional goldfish. Blue parked his bony butt on the fountain's stone edging and took off his shoes. His feet were as long and narrow as the rest of him, and his toenails were filthy.

"Right now, if you like," he said.

"You need bare feet to perform magic?"

"Nah. I just like to feel the grass."

He wiggled those hideous toenails and I turned away, sending Mac to Lachie's room for his hairbrush. The pink-haired werewolf had spent plenty of time playing Lego with Lachie and, even though he'd barely moved into this house before he'd been snatched, she knew where it was.

Sure enough, there were so many hairs caught in his brush it looked like it had a nest of spiders living in it. I pulled one curly brown hair free, careful not to disturb any of the others. Hair, nail clippings, bloody handkerchiefs—even snotty ones— were all grist to the goblin mage's mill, and I didn't want him having any more than he needed.

I passed the hair to Blue, and he turned and dropped it in the still waters of the fountain's basin.

"I'll need a knife," he said. "My own would be preferable,"—he shot an accusing look at Ben—"but any knife will do."

Garth stepped forward and pulled a throwing knife from inside his shirt. Trust the big werewolf to have a knife on him. His love of edged weapons was almost as great as his love for *Star Wars*. He said nothing, but there was a new alertness to his stance as he passed the weapon across. When he stepped back he positioned himself so that his large body shielded mine from the now-armed goblin. I knew that wasn't an accident.

But Blue showed no interest in stabbing me. Instead he turned the knife on himself, drawing the sharp blade across a skinny arm that bore the scars of many previous occasions. Strange that the scars remained. Most shifters only scarred from really savage wounds. Supernatural healing was one of the perks of an otherwise often dodgy lifestyle.

Blood dripped into the water as Blue muttered under his breath, too softly even for my sharp dragon hearing to catch. It spread across the water's surface like a bloom of red algae, thick and viscous, instead of dissolving and disappearing as I'd expected.

Blue's arm began to shake. He'd gone deathly pale. Beads of sweat stood on his forehead and dripped from his mat of orange hair. He swayed, as if he might topple into the water, and I stepped forward. Garth stopped me, his big hands closing on my upper arms.

"Don't touch him. You'll break his concentration."

"Is he all right?" He hadn't lost that much blood. Why did he look like he was about to pass out?

"Goblin magic is hard on the mage," Luce murmured. "Just watch."

Blue laid the knife on the stone beside him, and Garth wasted no time in retrieving it. The blade was as clean as if it had never been used, and it sparkled in the sunlight. Blue's arm had stopped bleeding and he cradled it against his chest. He leaned forward and placed his other hand above the still-spreading bloodstain, not quite touching it, but so close an ant would have had trouble fitting through the space between.

I folded my own arms across my chest. I hated not knowing what was going on. The blood made me uneasy. There hadn't been that much. How could it now cover more than half the fountain's basin? It crept around water jets and past lilies whose bright green pads made an eye-popping contrast to the crimson stain, as if it were alive. It gave me the horrors.

It's just blood, for God's sake. It can't hurt you. No one said a word as the red stain continued its march across the fountain's wide basin. When at last the final stretch of clear water had been conquered, Blue cried out in the harsh goblin tongue and plunged his hand into the foul water.

There was a blinding flash. Someone swore, and several of the thralls reached for their guns. I blinked the after-effects from my vision and saw that the blood was gone. Shapes moved in the depths of the pool now.

I leaned forward, straining to see against the glare of sunlight on the water. Blue was still muttering under his breath, and the shapes resolved into a picture. The surface of the water flickered like a badly tuned TV screen. Interrupted by water lilies and bits of plumbing, faces came into focus. People moved in a large room whose background faded into darkness. Lachie was there, and Jason too. I clenched my fists. Pity this wasn't a portal. I'd reach right through and punch that smug face if I could.

And then I'd grab my boy and hold him tight. He looked like he needed it. Tiny in a large armchair, he sat with his legs curled beneath him. He was hunched over, as if trying to make himself smaller. His little face was pinched with worry as his eyes moved between his father and the others in the room, following a conversation we couldn't hear.

"Can we get sound?" I whispered to Luce. I'd wring Jason's neck when I got my hands on him. How dare he put his ambitions before Lachie's welfare? Lachie should be safe with me, playing with his Lego, his biggest worry whether he could manage to sneak a cookie from Dave without me noticing.

She shook her head, her eyes roving over the scene. Probably memorising every detail. Luce was good at details; that was part of the reason I'd survived this long. Just as well, too—I was too distracted by that look on my baby's face to pay as much attention as I should have.

"Who's that?" she asked. The central fountain took a huge chunk out of the picture. We could see the legs of two people sitting on a couch, but the rest of them was cut off. "I wish they'd move."

A couple of men I didn't know were also in the room, standing by the wall. They were short but solid, and their faces were completely blank, as if they stood the world's most boring guard duty. Though they stood in the shadows, no aura lit the area around them, unlike the faint red glow surrounding Jason, so they were human.

The most interesting thing about them was that they were Japanese. I glanced back at the legs of the seated figures. One was a woman. Now more than ever I needed to see her face.

"Blue. Can you zoom in a little?"

"I'm not a bloody camera." The goblin's voice sounded strained. He moved the hand that was still in the water, ever so slowly. Tiny ripples quivered through the bottom of the picture, but the viewpoint began to shift. The picture followed the moving hand like a dog on a leash. A window came into view.

The room was high up. We could see the tops of buildings and glimpses of roads far below. Lachie was the most brightly lit thing in the image, as if the spell focused on him as much as I did, and the edges of the image blurred and faded. Jason disappeared as the viewpoint continued to move slowly across the scene. More of the world outside the window came into the frame, with a familiar harbour, and the beginning of a very recognisable sweep of iron girders.

"They're still in Sydney, then," Garth said, with satisfaction in his voice, as the Harbour Bridge slowly revealed itself.

And then the woman came into view. Even in the blurriness of the goblin's image I recognised her. She was one of the most famous shifters in the world.

Daiyu, queen of Japan.

CHAPTER FIVE

Silence fell on the garden, broken at last by the goblin's nasal laugh.

"You should see your faces." He grinned as he shoved his glasses up to their normal resting place again.

Garth snarled, as if he'd like to jam those damn glasses somewhere sideways. The thought held a certain appeal.

"Bad news, is it?" Blue continued. "Has she come to steal your crown?"

He lifted his hand and shook the blood-red water from it. The picture in the pond dissipated as the flying droplets struck it.

"I think I liked you better when you were drunk," I said.

The goblin's smile widened. "Well, that's easy enough to fix. Just point me at the nearest bottle and I'll get on with it."

"Nobody told you to end the scrying," said Luce, indicating the now-clear water.

"Sorry, love, couldn't hold it much longer anyway."

This was the most cheerful I'd ever seen the goblin mage. His good mood seemed in inverse proportion to the black expressions around him. He lounged on the stone coping of the fountain, his gaze flicking with obvious pleasure between all the grim faces surrounding him.

Bastard. A wholly dragon rage swept over me, an urge to smash his grinning face into ruins. I drew a deep, shuddering breath. Seeing Lachie so miserable made me want to lash out and hurt someone. He'd looked so pale, as if he was suffering from one of his headaches. I'd bet anything that Jason wouldn't remember that tablets made him gag, and he had to have soluble painkillers instead.

"It doesn't matter," I said to Luce, forcing myself to concentrate. Worrying wouldn't help Lachie, only action would. I needed to be more than his mother now. *Focus, Kate.* "We know they're in the city. It shouldn't be too difficult to track them down."

I even had the police helping with that now. No, the problem would be what to do once we'd found them. Dragons were very hard to kill. Lately that had been working to my advantage, since I'd faced more than my fair share of attacks. It took something so catastrophic that the body's supercharged healing powers couldn't cope with it, like a beheading or a bomb blast. Dragonfire would do it if the victim was in human form, but no dragon was going to stand around in human form long enough to be blasted with dragonfire. Certainly not a dragon as old and cunning as Daiyu of Japan.

That left poisoning, and there were only two poisons known to be fatal to dragons. One was bane leaf, which Jason had used to kill Leandra in her original body, and the other was even harder to come by, which was saying something, since bane leaf was so rare it was just about extinct. The second poison was called du, and the secret of its manufacture was known only to the Chinese queen—who was Daiyu's sister.

The queen of Japan wasn't Japanese at all. She had been locked into an exhausting proving for the throne of China with her last remaining sister when an opportunity had come up to assassinate the queen of Japan. Problem solved: now there were two thrones available for the two warring sisters. I don't know how they had settled who took China and who took Japan, but Daiyu had moved in before the true Japanese queen's body had even had time to cool, and the coup had been presented to the other queens as a fait accompli. Celeste Rousseau, who ruled all of Europe from her throne in France, had made a rather half-hearted attempt to unseat her, but it had come to nothing, and Daiyu had remained unchallenged since.

Not that I particularly *wanted* to kill Daiyu. Or at least, I hadn't until now. When all she'd done was try to manipulate her way to my throne, it hadn't been personal. Now that I'd seen her so close to my precious son, killing her seemed like a damned good idea. If it wasn't for her and her scheming, Lachie would still be safe with me. I could hold him until his headache went away and distract him with silly stories, like I used to do when he was little. He wouldn't have to sit in a room full of strangers and worry about what was going to happen to him.

And so we were back at the whole *kill or be killed* thing, like the proving but with the heat turned up a notch. Fantastic. For such a supposedly superior race, dragons sure had a primitive grasp on diplomacy.

"So can I go, then?" Blue asked. "You can find them without my help. I'll just take my gold and head back to my cave, and leave you people to get on with your little war."

"What, afraid Chief Trimboli will find you if you stay above ground too long?" Ben said, a jeering note in his voice that sounded completely unlike him. "That could still be arranged unless you co-operate, you know."

"I *am* co-operating! What more do you people want?"

"What I *want* is my son back. What I want is to defeat all these damn enemies that keep popping out of the woodwork." I held the goblin's gaze, and kept a firm grip on my temper at the same time, though the delay chafed at me. I wanted to run to Lachie *now*. Intellectually I knew that would achieve nothing, but my heart didn't want to listen.

Focus, Kate. I clung to that like a mantra, armouring myself against the tide of frustration that threatened to sweep me away. *You can't help Lachie if you fall apart now. Time to be a dragon, not a mother.*

Behind his glasses the goblin's eyes were huge. His vision must be shocking. "What I want is for you to help me achieve all this. As you said yourself, I'm a rich woman now. I can make it worth your while."

"Well, what *I* want is to stay alive, since we're chatting so frankly. And getting involved in a dragon war isn't the best way of achieving that. Doesn't matter how much gold you pay me if I'm too dead to enjoy it, does it?"

Luce fixed him with a hard stare. "I have Chief Trimboli on speed dial. Just say the word and I'll press the button."

He looked at me, then Ben, then Garth, and back to Luce. Every face was stony. His bravado collapsed and he slumped down on the edge of the fountain again.

"Fine." He sounded as sulky as a three-year-old. "Whatever. What *else* do you want me to do?"

"I'll let you know. In the meantime you can stay here."

"So I'm a prisoner?" His cheerful mood had evaporated.

"More of a houseguest." One that would have to be closely watched. Letting a hostile goblin mage roam free in your house wasn't a winning plan.

From the corner of my eye I saw Steve coming down the steps from the terrace, but the goblin held most of my attention.

"I'll need some things from my cave," he said. "You can't make magic from nothing, you know."

"Make a list and we'll send someone out to get them."

Steve offered a shallow bow, more for the goblin's benefit than mine. I didn't like to stand on ceremony. Having people bowing to me felt wrong.

"Mistress, a herald."

"Where's the message?"

His hands were empty.

"The herald comes from the Japanese queen."

Speak of the devil. My anger surged again. This woman stood between me and my child. I had to breathe deeply until I had mastered myself again.

Messages from royalty required the herald to hand the message directly to the person addressed. I glanced at Ben, who shrugged.

"I'll go and check it out."

Ben knew all the local heralds, having been one until recently. I waited while he and Steve went inside. In a moment they returned, escorting another man between them. He was average height, with sandy brown hair and a growth of stubble that hadn't made up its mind yet if it wanted to be a beard. There was a sharp intake of breath from the goblin, still seated on the stone coping of the fountain. Now he was sitting up straight, looking almost eager.

"This is Ken Thomas," said Ben. "He's an old friend."

The herald went down on one knee and offered me the usual thick beige envelope. I glanced again at Blue. What was his problem? He'd had such a look of anticipation on his face for a moment there, as if waiting for a show to start. He stared back, now all butter-wouldn't-melt-in-his-mouth.

Had Ken hunted him down for a job he didn't want to perform, just as Ben had? But that smile had a gloating quality to it, as if he knew something I didn't.

I turned back to Ken and studied him for a moment. His herald's charm, a tiny silver representation of Hermes, messenger of the gods, hung in full view on his chest. As far as I could tell, it was genuine, but Ben would have checked that.

Besides, Ben knew him. I met Ben's gaze, unaccountably troubled by that look on the goblin's face and his involuntary gasp. It was fairly safe to assume at this point that anything that would please the goblin probably wasn't good news for me. I wasn't exactly his favourite person at the moment.

"How old a friend? Like Nada?"

He frowned. Nada had been no friend of ours. But she *had* worn a goblin seeming to the Presentation Ball. Fortunately Ben was smart enough to make the connection.

"I haven't seen Sarah in ages," he said to the man still patiently kneeling at my feet. "I hope she's well?"

Ken's eyes flicked to the side. Chitchat in the middle of a delivery was an odd departure from the usual routine.

"Fine, thanks," he said after a moment.

In reply, Ben launched himself and drove the herald to the ground. I leapt back, nearly landing on Blue's lap. The man wriggled like a fish on a hook beneath Ben. I saw something flash silver in the sunlight as his hand came up, but then Steve and Garth joined the fray, and he was no match for their combined muscle.

Ben climbed to his feet and brushed grass off his clothes. "You okay?"

"Fine." It hadn't been me rolling around on the grass. His face was pale. He'd probably hurt his bad arm with that little manoeuvre. At this rate it was never going to heal properly. "Who's our visitor?"

Garth had the man flat on his face, his arms pulled back at a painful angle, with one of the big werewolf's knees in his back. Steve's gun was out, aimed directly at his head. The herald—or whoever he was—lay still. Sensible guy.

"I don't know, but it's not Ken. I'm sorry, he had me fooled. I should never have let him in."

"Who's Sarah?"

"Ken's wife. She's been dead for years."

"Oh." So someone had had the same idea as me—a goblin seeming. Jason had probably called in the real Ken on some pretext and managed to swipe a hair. "Is he armed?"

Ben gave me a reproachful look. "We searched him before we brought him out."

"Search again," I said to Garth. What was that flash I'd seen?

To my surprise—and to Garth's—the man began to struggle. Garth punched him in the side of the head and he lay still again. Garth didn't believe in pulling his punches. When he punched someone, they stayed punched.

"He's clean. Just a ring." He pulled a black signet ring from the man's unresisting hand.

"Give me that," said Luce.

I cocked an eyebrow at Blue, who'd lost that anticipatory smile. "Well? You saw something, didn't you? How could you tell he wasn't the real deal?"

Blue had probably just saved my life. He'd be kicking himself later.

He pushed his glasses nervously up to the bridge of his nose. "Don't know what you're talking about."

Liar. I could tell by the way his gaze shifted away. On an impulse, I reached out and snatched those annoying glasses off his face.

"Hey!"

I put them on and looked down at our captive. My turn to draw in a shocked breath.

"Bloody hell. It's Kasumi."

"What?" Garth clenched his big fist, eager to punch her again.

"Let me see," said Ben.

I passed him the goblin's glasses. "That's amazing." He had a good look at everyone present. Smart man. I should have thought of that. Then he glared at Blue. "You've been holding out on us. How do these work?"

"Goblin glass," he said sullenly. "Always shows true. Haven't you ever noticed how many highborn goblins wear glasses? It's not because they're short-sighted, trust me."

I suppose that made sense, given the ability of goblin spells to change a person's appearance. You didn't want imposters sneaking up on you. But this wasn't a goblin seeming. Kasumi was a kitsune, one of the fabled fox people of Japan, and mimicking the appearance of others was one of her natural abilities. Interesting that the goblin glass could see through that deception as well. I'd never known that was possible, but then, Leandra hadn't known much about kitsune. They were rarely seen outside Japan.

I folded my arms and contemplated the goblin mage. He'd had these all along and never mentioned them. What other tricks was he keeping up his sleeve?

"I guess we know what your first job will be now." I took the glasses back from Ben. "I'll need about a dozen pairs of these."

"Impossible! They take weeks to make."

"You'd better get started, then. I'll keep these ones as a down payment."

"Perhaps some ointment would do? That's quicker to make, but you would have to keep reapplying it."

Ointment? There were fairy tales of people who'd rubbed magical ointment on their eyes and been able to see fairies all around who'd previously been invisible. The trouble was, I wasn't sure I trusted Blue enough to rub anything he gave me into my eyes.

"Glasses," I said firmly.

I put them back on and looked down at Kasumi again. Seeing the stubbly-faced man disappear, to be replaced by her familiar wide face and dark, red-tipped hair, was disconcerting.

"Let her up," I said to Garth.

"I can't believe you had the hide to show your face here again," he growled.

She shook him off and climbed to her feet, ignoring Steve's gun. She was a small woman, solid and powerful looking. Her short bob swung loose around her face, red tips as bright as ever.

"Believe what you wish, wolf."

He growled. They'd never liked each other. "I should have hit you harder."

"Look at this," Luce said.

She held out the signet ring—only now it had a sharp needle-like spike protruding from it. A drop of some thick liquid glistened on the needle's tip. She pressed a hidden catch or button on the side and the spike withdrew again.

"What's in the ring?" She glared at Kasumi as if she'd like to use the poison on her. "Bane leaf?"

"No." Kasumi's gaze was level as it held mine. "We know that doesn't work."

Because she'd already tried that on me. In fact, this was the first time I'd seen her since she'd stabbed me in the heart, fully expecting that the poison on her blade would kill me. And then she'd abducted Lachie. Rage pounded in my head, and bloodlust sang in my veins. I could smash her to pieces with a smile on my face.

It hurt even more because I'd thought she was my friend.

"Du, then, I assume." It was the only other poison that killed dragons.

Kasumi shrugged, but didn't answer. I could hardly stand to look at her. She'd taken my son. Had she hurt him? I would tear her apart.

Luce held the ring as if it might grow fangs and bite her. Perhaps it could. Du was fatal to wyverns too.

"Let's inject her and see what it does to kitsune," suggested Garth in a menacing rumble.

"Maybe we can swap her for Lachie," Ben murmured, a quiet voice of reason among all the hostility.

But Kasumi heard. "Don't be ridiculous. Daiyu finds him too useful in controlling Jason to give him up."

"Not even to save her loyal kitsune?" Ben didn't look convinced.

That made Kasumi laugh, though it wasn't a happy sound. "Daiyu knows I'd be first in line to kill her if I could. There's no such thing as a loyal kitsune any more."

I frowned. The bitterness in her tone had the ring of truth about it. I fought down my rage and tried to think logically. If she'd managed to kill me … what would have happened to her?

That was an easy one. Garth, or Luce, or Ben—just about anybody in this garden—would have killed her on the spot. She hadn't come here expecting to walk away. So why commit to a suicide mission if not for loyalty to her queen?

"What hold does Daiyu have over you?" Was I being a fool again? But I'd been so sure Kasumi had wanted me to succeed, had even liked me personally. Maybe she'd only turned on me because she had to.

She hesitated, then seemed to come to a decision. "The same hold she has over every kitsune. Not that there are many of us left any more. She's seen to that. She holds all our hoshi no tama as surety for our obedience. If one of us disobeys her, all will die."

"That's crap," said Garth. "We've seen your stupid star ball. You had it with you when you were pretending to be on our side."

The hoshi no tama was the heart of the kitsune's magic. Without that glowing golden ball she wouldn't have been able to take Ken Thomas's form.

She didn't look at Garth. "She sent me here to destabilise your proving, and remove all the claimants if I could. She knew I needed my hoshi no tama for that."

"Then why didn't you just run away once you got it?"

Now she looked at him, a look of withering scorn. "Does your pack mean so little to you that you'd abandon them to certain death so that you could be free? I have children. A husband. A father. She holds their lives in her hands. One wrong move from me and my son and daughter would have their throats slit in their sleep."

I looked down. I couldn't bear that look of desperation in her eyes. More than anything, that convinced me she was telling the truth. I knew what that felt like. Nothing was more important than your children's safety. It must be tearing her apart to know they were in constant danger.

"What will happen now that you've failed to kill me?"

"I suppose it depends what you do to me. If I die she won't take action against my family."

"And if you live?"

"You'd better kill me. If you don't I'll keep trying to kill you until I succeed." She shrugged as if she didn't care either way, but I wasn't fooled.

"Why don't you join us? Help us defeat her, and your family will be free."

"I can't." Her dark eyes held a weary sorrow. "She keeps the hoshi no tama of every kitsune in a special case. It is always locked, always guarded. The minute I move against her, she will destroy them. A kitsune cannot live without her hoshi no tama. It would be the end of our whole race. If I raise my hand against her, they will all die. Even if someone else kills Daiyu, they have standing orders in Japan that in the event of her death, all the kitsune are to be slaughtered. Not only can I not move against her, but I must actively work to keep my bitterest enemy alive lest all my family die like dogs. It is a most effective trap she has me in."

"We could steal the case." God knows how, but we'd pulled off some pretty wild schemes together before. It would be worth it to have Kasumi at my side again. The advantage it would give me against my new sisters would be phenomenal.

Kasumi shook her head. "I don't even know where the case is. Somewhere on her main estate, most likely. But even if we could steal it, we'd have to steal all the kitsune out from under her nose at the same time, or she'd just have them killed. They're defenceless without their hoshi no tama. There is too much that could go wrong. I cannot risk it. I'm sorry, Kate. I wish it could be different." The old warmth was back in her eyes for a moment. "But I can't risk it, not even for you."

Deflated, I looked away, back over the now-clear water of the fountain. I caught a flash of orange as a goldfish slipped under a lily pad. The yellow lily rocked ever so slightly, its beautiful petals turned up to catch the sun.

I'd have to lock Kasumi away, then. Probably chain her in silver, too. She was dangerous, perhaps the most dangerous shifter I knew, even more so than a dragon. It would be like keeping a time bomb ticking away in the dungeon, always wondering when it was going to explode. But what else could I do? I couldn't kill her. She'd saved my life more than once. We'd been friends. And two little fox children waited in Japan for her to come home.

"Where is your family?"

"Tokyo. At her main estate."

"And the other kitsune? They're in Tokyo too?"

"At the moment. Daiyu likes to have them all easily accessible when she's out of the country, just in case."

"Good. That will make things easier."

Hope blossomed on Kasumi's broad face, and she drew a deep shuddering breath.

Ben gave me a suspicious look. An almost identical one had appeared on Luce's face. "What things?"

I smiled brightly at him. "I've always wanted to go to Japan."

CHAPTER SIX

"I hope you know what you're doing." Ben stood with his good arm around me as we watched Kasumi's motorbike roar down the drive. He still favoured the other one, though he refused to wear a sling. "She's a dangerous woman to leave roaming around. She said herself she wouldn't stop trying to kill you."

"Until the kitsune hostages are freed," I reminded him. "Then we'll have a secret weapon."

"If you live that long," said Luce, a sour note in her voice.

"Have a little faith. I'm not so easy to kill."

"Maybe not if you stay here. The security on this place is the best of the best. Let me go to Japan, if you insist on this madness."

"Luce, give it up." She'd been trying to talk me out of it since I'd floated the idea, but her arguments didn't hold water. The only chance we had of pulling this off required a whole lot of compulsions, and that meant dragon involvement. And I wasn't exactly getting knocked down in the rush of dragons volunteering to join my cause. I would have to go.

"Do you think Daiyu will believe Kasumi didn't get a chance to see you?" Ben still stared out the window. He looked tired and weighed down with worry.

I slipped an arm round his waist and leaned against him for a moment. He smelled of pine forests and fresh air, with a hint of honest sweat. It was hot outside, and we'd only just come in from the garden.

"You worry too much. Why shouldn't she believe it? She already thinks I'm an abomination. It's hardly a stretch to think that I wouldn't have the dragon-born manners to personally accept a communication from another queen."

"As long as she doesn't compel the truth from Kasumi." His frown deepened.

"Hush." I stood on tiptoes to kiss him. "She's not going to compel her. She's got Kasumi tied up so tight it will take a miracle to untangle her." A miracle I was determined to provide. "Didn't Kasumi deliver everything she wanted before? She has no reason to suspect her. Stop dreaming up problems that don't exist. We have enough real ones to deal with."

He looked down at me, that frown still lingering. "Like your new plan to somehow sneak into Tokyo and free a bunch of people you don't know, and who have no reason to trust you, from the probably unbreakable security of the queen of Japan?"

"That's the one. Genius, isn't it?"

He and Luce both sighed loudly, and I couldn't help laughing, though it wasn't really funny. He was right, it was a crazy thing to attempt, and it wasn't as if I didn't already have some major problems to deal with. Seven of them, actually, all thirsting for my blood. But I couldn't see a way of getting Lachie free of Daiyu's clutches without risking his safety unless I had someone on the inside helping me. Jason was clearly not an option, which left Kasumi. I could only work with the tools I had. And freeing Lachie was my number one priority right now. In the back of my mind a clock was ticking. How long did I have before Daiyu tired of waiting for my throne and decided to use Lachie against me?

We were kicking around ideas for how we might actually pull off the genius plan when Steve entered, an odd look on his normally cheerful face.

"How's the repatriation going?" I asked.

Steve had been overseeing the deportation of our prisoners, under Luce's guidance.

"About halfway there," he said. "Only ones left are the ones who chose North America. That flight's leaving tonight." He hesitated. "You're not going to believe this …"

"What?"

"That Ken Thomas guy is back."

Luce was instantly alert. "The real one? You're sure?"

Surely Kasumi wouldn't try the same stunt twice.

"We checked him with Blue's glasses. Seems to be."

"Who's his message from?"

"Gideon Thorne, he says."

Ben stood. "I'll go."

He strode out, trailed by Steve, and I raised an eyebrow at Luce. "What could Gideon Thorne possibly have to say to me?"

"An offer of fealty?"

I snorted. In my dreams. More likely a death threat.

Turned out we were both wrong. The envelope Ben handed me didn't contain a black dragon scale snapped in half, as I'd expected, but an innocent sheet of expensive paper, hand-lettered in a beautiful flowing script.

"It's an invitation."

Ben craned over my shoulder to read it. "To what?"

"To the Presentation Ball. Cheeky bastard."

"Presentation Ball?" Garth's grey eyes snapped with anger. He'd followed Ben in, back from organising a group of thralls to retrieve Blue's supplies. "As in Presentation of the Candidates?"

"Yep." I read from the sheet. "Leandra Elizabeth is invited to present herself to the people of Oceania and her fellow candidates for the throne at a ball to be held on the twenty-fourth day of January blah blah blah. He thinks he can initiate a second proving."

"You can't go," said Ben. "It's a trap."

"You think?" I reined in my temper with an effort. No point snapping at Ben. I laid an apologetic hand on his arm and said more mildly: "Of course I'm going. It's perfect."

"Perfect for what? Getting yourself killed?"

"Honey, I may be safe sitting in this compound with all my guards, but I can't *do* anything. I've got to get out there and make things happen, or we'll be trapped in this house until we all die of old age."

And that could be a bloody long time, in my case.

He grunted in frustration and threw himself into an armchair. "What kind of things can you make happen in the middle of your enemy's stronghold, surrounded by people who want to kill you?" He scrubbed a hand over his face and through his curly hair, leaving it even wilder than before. "I'm having trouble seeing how this can work to our advantage."

I sat down too, and started ticking points off on my fingers.

"First, it's an opportunity to get all my sisters together in one place."

Garth bared his teeth in a wolfish grin. "Beats hunting them down one by one."

I grinned back. His bloodthirstiness appealed to the dragon in me.

"So they're all together," Ben said. "How are you going to kill them? There'll be more security than bloody Guantanamo Bay."

I frowned at him, one finger still up in the air. "I never said I was going to kill them. Second, I'll have access to Gideon Thorne." I paused, contemplating the second finger with pleasure. "Him, I am going to kill."

And they were words I could never have said a few weeks ago. Truly I wasn't the same woman I'd been before Leandra hitched a ride. Garth's eyes glinted with anticipation, and I felt a thrill run through me.

"What do you mean, you're not going to kill the sisters?" Luce interrupted my bloody dreams of taking Thorne down, the black werewolf at my side. I noted she didn't say "your" sisters. Luce was even less willing than me to accept the existence of these new threats. She'd rather die than admit they might have any claim on the throne we'd fought so hard for. "They'll sure as hell be trying to kill you."

"I haven't ruled out the possibility, but it's a last resort."

"Don't go soft. They'll have been brought up to fight for the throne, just like you. You'll never get them to sit around and sing 'Kumbaya' with you instead. That's not who they are."

"We don't know who they are, Luce. For crying out loud, they're not even twenty years old. If I was their age and someone offered me a one in eight chance of survival on one hand or the chance to enjoy my full five-hundred-odd-year lifespan on the other, I might have to at least think about it."

She rolled her eyes. "You don't think like a dragon any more."

Except that in so many ways I did. Why was my head full of Garth and blood when I was supposed to be in love with Ben? Something in the big werewolf called to me in a way Ben didn't, and it didn't help that everywhere I turned he was there, his intense blue-grey gaze following me.

"You say that like it's a bad thing. Maybe that's why I'm still alive."

There was a short silence. Luce folded her arms and stared out the window at the long curving driveway and the terraced gardens leading down to the massive front gate. God knows what she was thinking. Probably wishing she had the real Leandra back.

I focused on Ben, refusing to let my eyes be drawn to Garth, though I knew he was watching me.

Ben scrubbed at his face wearily. "Was there a point three?"

"What? Oh." One: sisters all together. Two: kill Gideon Thorne. Three? I scrambled for some more good news. To be honest, silver linings were pretty hard to come by these days. "Point three—point three, we have Blue."

"He could make us a seeming." Garth's eyes lit with enthusiasm. "Maybe of that idiot Bear. Thorne trusts him, he might let his guard down—"

"Don't encourage her," Ben snapped. "This is a really stupid idea. We'd be outnumbered and surrounded. It's suicide."

"Someone's got to encourage her." Garth folded his arms, making his muscles bulge, and gave Ben a disdainful look. "Because she's right. She's not going to win this war by hiding away. She's got to get out there and grab that bastard Thorne by the balls before he has the chance to screw us over."

Well, this was a turn-up for the books. Garth was usually the first one to argue when my safety was concerned. I shot him a grateful look and saw a glimmer of yellow in his eyes as he glared at Ben. His wolf wanted out.

Ben got to his feet and returned the glare with interest. "There's got to be a better way of doing that than turning up on his doorstep practically gift-wrapped. How's a damned goblin seeming going to protect her?"

"*I'll* protect her," Garth growled.

"I don't need anyone's protection. I'm a dragon, not a bloody fairy princess. And I'm going to this ball." Enough with the male posturing! They were acting like a couple of teenagers.

"Don't worry, Kate, no one's going to forget you're a dragon."

The viciousness of Ben's tone shocked me. "What's that supposed to mean?"

"Why even bother asking anyone's opinion when you know you're going to do whatever you damn well want anyway?" His brown eyes were colder than I'd ever seen them. "Typical bloody dragon."

Oh, God, not this again.

"Yes, I'm a dragon, Ben." I couldn't bear the look in his eyes. As if he didn't even like me, much less love me. "And that's not going to change. This is the life we're stuck with. There's no going back."

Without another word, he stalked out of the room. No going back. But maybe there was no going forward for us either.

CHAPTER SEVEN

As Elizabeth's closest living relative—at least as far as the funeral director was concerned—I rode in the official limousine, accompanied by Ben, Garth and Luce. The fact that I'd helped kill her, while ironic, wasn't considered relevant. This was the benefit of using a funeral home that dealt with shifters on a regular basis.

There was very little talk on the way to the service. None of us were in mourning, but relations between Ben and myself were still strained. Luce stared out the window, and Garth alternated between watching me and glaring at Ben, which didn't help the taut atmosphere in the car. It was a relief when the limo turned in at the gates of the crematorium and stopped. In front of us stretched a line of cars, barely moving, that wound all the way up the hill towards the chapel.

"Never thought Elizabeth had this many friends," Garth muttered, scowling at the congestion. Parked cars lined the roadside. Some were even piled haphazardly on the lawn, stowed in whatever little nook the driver could find between the bushes.

"It's marvellous what money can buy," said Ben, in that clipped, faintly hostile tone that was becoming the norm for him.

He looked like a lawyer today, dressed in a dark business suit and red tie. I'd never seen him so formal before, and it was a good look on him. It was just a shame the coldness in his dark eyes spoiled the effect.

Shame about the searing hot day outside too. We'd all be broiling once we stepped out of the air-conditioned limo, even me in my sleeveless black shift dress.

The car crawled up the hill. Well-groomed ladies tottered along on their heels, easily keeping pace with us, accompanied by grey-haired men in suits. Society matrons rubbed shoulders with shifters of every stripe as everyone who was anyone turned out for the funeral of Elizabeth Appleby, investment guru and philanthropist. This was one shifter death we couldn't brush under the carpet. Elizabeth had been big in the mundane world too.

"Half these people probably didn't like her any more than we did," I said. "They're just here to be seen."

It took us ten minutes to reach the open area in front of the chapel. It was only open because the security guards had kept it clear, shepherding people and cars away. They hulked together like a line of front-row forwards, their auras glowing a deep troll-brown.

One of them opened the door of the limo as we pulled up, then stepped back respectfully. He nodded to me as I got out, and I nodded back. These were a Hunter Valley clan, and their loyalty was to the throne, regardless of who was the current occupant. Since that was me at the moment, I knew they'd die to the last man to protect me, which was oddly comforting, even though I wasn't expecting any trouble today. Funerals were traditionally an unofficial ceasefire.

Of course dragons were traditionally a bunch of backstabbing traitors too, so Luce and Garth were well prepared. Even Ben was carrying a gun underneath that handsome suit. Most of my staff were here, the thralls at least all armed to the teeth, plus we had the trolls on security and most of the Sydney pack circulating discreetly among the mourners. The funeral director had also arranged for some regular human security, given how many people were expected here today.

Looking around at the mass of bodies, I figured he might have underestimated. Extra seating had been set up outside, with cameras broadcasting the service to huge temporary screens, since there was no way more than a tiny fraction of all these people would fit into the chapel itself.

Life had been much simpler for shifters in the pre-modern age. It would have been so much easier just to set her corpse on fire and be done with it, but these days there was paperwork and the expectation of a decent funeral when a society figure died. Bodies of prominent people couldn't just disappear. The manner of her death had been covered up, of course—beheading was hardly common any more—but there would be all sorts of awkward questions if a coffin were not produced and farewelled with due ceremony. Much as I might have liked to torch her and scatter her ashes to the winds, I had to turn up for this farce instead. Which really got up my nose when I had so many other, more pressing, matters clamouring for my attention. Singing hymns for a woman who'd done her damnedest to kill me was not going to get Lachie back any faster, and that was top of my to-do list.

There wouldn't be too many tears shed for Elizabeth, despite the size of the crowd. Anyone who was anyone in Sydney society had turned out, probably more from curiosity to see who'd inherited all that lovely money than any affection for the deceased. Even the prime minister would be here. He'd been a "close personal friend", apparently. More likely the grateful beneficiary of millions in campaign dollars, but whatever. It showed Elizabeth's clout if he could make time for her funeral in the middle of what the papers were calling "the monster crisis".

Two trolls flanked us as we entered the chapel and made our way down the aisle to our front-row seats. Shifter auras glowed in a rainbow of soft colours on either side, brightening the sea of mourning black. Some of the society ladies wore hats, and one even had a short black veil, which I thought was going a little too far. Enough pearls to sink a ship circled leathery old necks, and discreet diamonds winked from the earlobes that peeked out from their perfectly blow-waved hair. So much elegant appropriateness made me wish I'd worn a bright red dress, or turned up in bare feet.

Still, drawing attention to myself wasn't part of the plan. Luce had already fielded a couple of requests for interviews, explaining that I was too deep in mourning to be able to speak to the press at the moment. A few cameras had flashed as we walked from the car to the chapel door, but I doubted many of those photos would see the light of day. Elizabeth wasn't sexy enough to have gossip columnists covering her funeral; the reporters were more likely from staid financial publications. Any articles that resulted from today's activities were more likely to focus on what would happen to her various companies than speculation on the unknown woman who'd inherited her large fortune. Best to keep it that way. I had enough to deal with already.

Elizabeth's coffin was almost invisible under the mound of flowers the funeral director had provided. There must have been a thousand red roses cascading over the sides of the dark mahogany casket where it stood in solemn isolation at the front of the chapel. The smell was overpowering to a sensitive shifter nose. I glanced sideways at Garth, stationed against the right-hand wall of the chapel, his powerful arms folded across his broad chest. He sneezed once, then returned to resolute scowling at all and sundry.

I shouldn't have looked at him. As if he felt my eyes on him, his gaze found mine, and I felt that surge of longing and lust that was becoming all too familiar. What was wrong with me? We hadn't known each other that long, and the first time we met he'd been trying to kill me. How had he managed to worm his way so far into my heart so fast?

I looked away, my body buzzing from the intensity of that grey gaze. Ben was at my side; I should be focused on him. We were going through a rough patch, but Ben was a great guy. *So is Garth*, my heart whispered. I only had to meet his eyes and my stupid heart skipped a beat. So much feeling in those eyes: everything that Garth was, laid bare. Stubborn, infuriating, loyal and compassionate. *So is Garth. And he is fierce and strong, and he glories in your dragon.*

Though I was facing the front, I knew when the prime minister entered by the sudden buzz that swept through the congregation. The usher showed him to a seat in the row behind me, and I banished all thoughts of hunky werewolf and nodded politely. The prime minister didn't know me from a bar of soap, but I bet he was hoping to change that. Just thinking of all Elizabeth's lovely money slipping away would be enough to make a politician weep.

The chaplain stepped up to the microphone, which squealed as he began the service. I let my attention wander to the various dilemmas that awaited me and only caught the occasional word. The prime minister made a short speech, but it was the usual polite talk, all about Elizabeth's "great contribution to society" and how deeply she would be missed.

Right. The only person who might possibly miss her would be Gideon Thorne, and he hadn't dared show up.

Deep in planning for my Japanese excursion, I gradually became aware of noises from outside. Garth was still at his station, but his eyes kept flicking to the closed double doors at the back of the chapel. Even the chaplain faltered a little during the closing prayer, distracted by the sound of many voices. I looked around for Luce, but she was nowhere to be seen.

At last the chaplain finished. Bach played while the coffin slid out of sight and the curtains closed. Pity we couldn't see it actually slide into the cremator and start to burn, but I guess it didn't matter. She was most definitely dead, and I knew she wouldn't be coming back.

The chaplain came over to shake my hand and offer his condolences, then he gestured me to lead the way out. The prime minister leaned forward and offered his hand too.

"I'm very sorry for your loss." His handshake was so firm it made me wonder what he was trying to prove. He had a reputation as a "manly" man. Seemed like he wanted to make sure everyone knew it. "Mrs Appleby was a great lady. She will be truly missed."

Maybe by his party. I hadn't voted for him, and I was feeling pretty good about that decision now.

"Thank you."

"Mrs Appleby was your … aunt? Is that right?"

His eyes glinted with interest. Even the prime minister wasn't above a bit of gossip.

"That's right," I said, "though we haven't seen each other in years." I gave his hand an extra-hard squeeze before dropping it. "Excuse me, Prime Minister."

He tried not to wince, but didn't quite manage it. "Of course."

Ben gave him a wintry smile as we swept past. Guess he hadn't voted for him either. The noise grew as we approached the doors. When one of the ushers threw them open, the muffled shouting finally became plain.

"Monsters out! Monsters out!"

Luce met us at the doors. She took my arm as three trolls closed in around us and started herding us toward the waiting car. Mourners were packed shoulder to shoulder outside, but beyond the diamond-and-pearl-wearing set and carefully separated from them by a wall of scowling troll milled a crowd who definitely weren't here to mourn anyone.

A genuine demonstration, complete with waving placards. "Monsters out" was very popular. It looked like they'd had a number of these pre-printed. But there were also some hand-lettered variations on the theme, such as "Australia for Australians! No freaks allowed!" and one that showed a map of Australia, with "Monster-free Zone!" stamped in angry red capitals across it.

"Surely they don't know about Elizabeth?" Ben murmured as we worked our way through the crowd.

The media was full of suspicion that Valeria had been a dragon. That was a little hard to avoid when so many people had seen a dragon crash into Sydney Harbour, and hers was the body that floated to the surface. But there was nothing to connect her to Elizabeth. All the queen candidates had been set up with identities that were completely separate from our royal mother. All transactions between her and us had been routed through so many trusts and intermediaries it would take more investigation than the average journalist had in them to trace any connection.

"What else are they here for?" Luce muttered back, her face tight with anxiety.

They couldn't have found a bigger collection of shifters anywhere in the country if they'd tried. But how smart was it to bring placards to a fight with shifters? These people needed their heads read.

The crowd roared and surged forward against the line of trolls holding them back. Ben's hand crept inside his jacket and Luce and Garth closed in protectively, but the crowd wasn't looking at us. They'd caught sight of the prime minister leaving the chapel behind us.

I let out a relieved sigh. We weren't the target of all the placard-waving after all. Not that a bunch of protesters would have been much of a challenge for the shifters here, but a confrontation could raise a lot of awkward questions. And I certainly wasn't ready for a public showdown.

"Relax, guys. They're after him."

Half a dozen reporters had descended on the prime minister, shoving their microphones in his face. He was forced to stop on the front steps of the chapel, causing a bottleneck behind him of people trying to get out. Not that he seemed bothered. It wasn't in the man's nature to pass up any opportunity to play fearless leader for the cameras.

"Prime Minister! When will Parliament pass legislation to deal with the monster menace?"

"Prime Minister! Can you assure the people of Australia that they are safe from supernatural dangers?"

"Prime Minister, what is the government doing about the current situation?"

Okay, so maybe I'd been wrong about the reporters all being from staid financial publications. They'd obviously known the prime minister was attending, and somehow the protesters had found out too. Social media, probably.

"Monsters out! Monsters out!" the protesters chanted. They might have wanted to catch the prime minister's attention, but they clearly weren't interested in what he had to say. I could understand their fear. The world had suddenly become a much scarier place than they'd realised, and they were looking for reassurance that they weren't all about to be attacked in their beds by their childhood nightmares. Not that the prime minister could give it, but he made a brave attempt for the cameras.

"The government is doing all it can," he began.

Which meant what, exactly? His government couldn't seem to find its arse with both hands, even when dealing with regular economic issues. What could it possibly hope to do against supernatural creatures it knew nothing about? He had to say something, I guess, but being a politician, he kept it vague.

"Taskforce Jaeger is continuing its investigations." Big deal. A bunch of scientists weren't going to have much impact, if all they had to go on was Valeria's dead body. "And I'm flying to Canberra tonight for a special sitting of Parliament. We will be debating comprehensive legislation to ensure that police have all the powers they need to deal with any kind of threat to our great nation. The people of Australia can rest assured that we will work together to resolve this issue and contain any threats that might arise."

There was more, but I stopped listening and let Luce guide me to the car. How would he react if he knew that the woman whose funeral he'd just been to was one of the big bad dragons that had everyone so stirred up? That his party had been accepting money from "the monsters" for years? Amusing that he thought shifters were an "issue" to be "resolved". He might find that a little more challenging than he expected.

Still, I wasn't too worried. We'd had centuries of practice at hiding in plain sight from humans. Whatever legislation the mundane government passed wouldn't give them a magic tool for identifying shifters. They could run round squawking that the sky was falling all they liked, but they'd probably never see another dragon as long as they lived. So much for Dragageddon. The hatred in the faces of the chanting crowd was a little chilling, sure, and that could be a problem if it got a good foothold. But if we kept our heads down, the police wouldn't find anything to do with their new special powers, and the fuss would all die down eventually.

We drove away, the sound of chanting fading away behind us.

CHAPTER EIGHT

I kicked off my shoes and curled my feet under me on the lounge. Damn stilettos. Even shifters couldn't wear them without pain. They were one of the greatest instruments of torture ever invented.

At least shifter healing came in handy for more than just deadly wounds. I massaged the soles of my feet and sighed happily as the pain seeped away.

Ben flopped down in the armchair opposite and loosened his tie. Elizabeth's grand drawing room had probably never seen anything so casual. "Well, that was fun."

I quirked an eyebrow at him. "You were expecting to enjoy a funeral?"

He grunted. "I spent the whole time trying to see every direction at once, waiting for some idiot to take a potshot at you."

"It's not as if bullets are going to do much damage." Oops. His face closed up. Shouldn't have reminded him of my new dragon powers. I forged on, trying to keep my tone light. "You could have left the worrying to Luce. She does it so well."

Luce gave me an unimpressed look, but said nothing. She was perched on the edge of a brocade-covered chair that had probably cost more than the average Australian earned in a year. It looked truly uncomfortable, like most of the furniture in this formal, high-ceilinged room. I would have swapped it all for the torn and faded lounge in the tiny suburban house I'd shared with Lachie. We'd spent every Friday night curled up on that lounge together with a bowl of popcorn and a favourite movie. I missed him so much it hurt.

"True." He ran a hand through his curls, leaving them attractively messy. "But you're not exactly short of enemies. I was surprised Thorne didn't show up."

"He's probably planning something for the ball," Luce said. She moved to the window, hands shoved in the pockets of the black jeans she'd changed into when we got back. "The funeral was too public, and there was too much security. He'll pick a better time, when he's on his own turf."

She was such a little ray of sunshine. And now Ben would start with the arguments all over again. I braced myself but, though his jaw tightened, he said nothing.

We were sitting in what I thought of as the parlour. It was too formal to be something as cosy as a lounge room, but not as public as the throne room. It had the same high ceilings as the rest of the house, carved with ornate ceiling roses. The heavy velvet drapes at the window behind Luce were twice her height. Everything seemed larger than life and not meant for actual living. It was hard to imagine Elizabeth relaxing here with her feet up. Hard to imagine her with her feet up at all, actually. Though for most of her long life she'd looked as young as I did now, old was a state of mind, and Elizabeth had been old for a long time.

Dave came in carrying a tea service on a big silver tray, his usual cheery grin in place. That was one guy who was enjoying our move to bigger premises, despite the antiquity of the kitchen. He loved fussing around with beautiful china, and kept producing more and more elaborate cakes to display on them. Me, I liked my tea in a mug, made from a tea bag. It saved on washing up. And who had the time to sit around "taking tea" and eating cake?

Us, apparently, or at least Dave thought so.

"Mmm, chocolate cake." Ben sat forward, an eager look on his face.

"You're going to make me fat if you keep this up, Dave," I said. Chocolate was Lachie's favourite too. If only he were here I'd let him scoff as much as he liked.

Dave ran a critical eye over me. "You need to keep up your strength. Can't fight on an empty stomach."

"I couldn't *move* if I ate all the food you keep shoving at me. You should have been a chef."

"Almost was. Started an apprenticeship, but the hours were crap." He set the tray down and began to pour. The cups were such a delicate white china they were translucent. I could see the level of the tea rising through their glowing white sides. Nothing but the best for Elizabeth.

And now it was all mine. I felt uncomfortably like I was housesitting for someone with much more money and better taste than me, and any minute now they'd be back, demanding to know why I had my feet on their antique Louis XIV furniture. If I was going to make this my home, I'd have to redecorate. Make it *feel* like a home instead of Buckingham bloody Palace.

Not that anywhere could feel like home without Lachie. Jason had better be taking good care of him. My stomach clenched in a familiar anxious knot. What was he doing now? Probably not drinking tea out of cups so delicate I could barely fit my finger through the handle. I hoped Kasumi was looking out for him. Jason would probably be too busy trying to worm his way into Daiyu's good graces to have much time for his son.

And what was my loving ex up to now that his first assassination attempt had failed? Nothing that would be good news for me, that was for sure. More problems.

I sighed, and Dave glanced keenly at me as he offered the cake. "I hate to be the bearer of bad tidings, but there was a news report while you were gone that you should probably see."

"What now? Another Muslim woman attacked because they thought she was a werewolf underneath her veil?"

"Worse. Someone's been killed."

Like a dog that's just had bacon waved under its nose, Luce went from relaxed to instant alertness, though she didn't move. "A shifter?"

"I don't know. Probably not. But he was attacked in The Rocks."

Oh, joy. I knew already where this was going.

"Any footage?"

"Steve has it ready on his laptop."

Trust Steve. "Send him in, would you?"

He nodded and went off to find Steve, leaving the tea tray behind. Ben stole another piece of chocolate cake and munched absently, a frown on his face.

"Leandra's place at The Rocks?"

"Bound to be."

Mac came in, carrying a half-open laptop, her bright pink hair shocking against the tasteful muted colours of Elizabeth's parlour. Maybe I needed some hot pink furniture in here.

She plopped herself on the lounge next to me and put her booted feet up on the coffee table. Elizabeth's ghost would be having conniptions. I shifted over to give her more room, and Luce and Ben came to crane over her shoulder at the screen.

"Steve's on duty," she said, "but he left it all set up for you. He knew you'd want to see it."

Smart boy, that Steve. If we all survived the next few days I'd have to give him a pay rise.

She had a news site open. A video sat in the middle of the screen, big Play button ready to go. She clicked it and a serious-faced reporter began to speak. Behind her was a very familiar streetscape.

"Just a few hours ago a man was killed here by an angry mob."

Police tape marked off a section of the footpath that had only lately seen an even bigger crime. The road was still impassable, blocked with traffic barricades, the concrete broken and tilted at crazy angles, as if an extremely localised earthquake had burst the road open. In a way that was exactly what had happened, only the earthquake had been caused by leshies. The leshies had also destroyed the front steps of my house, and the door to my former residence hung bizarrely a metre off the ground in the left of the shot. Two good men had died in the attack. The anxious knot in my stomach clenched a little tighter at the memories of that night.

"The man is believed to be homeless and has not yet been identified by police. Eyewitnesses say a group of youths got into an altercation with the man around ten o'clock this morning. He then claimed to be a dragon and said he would burn them if they didn't leave."

The shot cut to a middle-aged man in a business suit, evidently one of the eyewitnesses.

"I was just coming out of the office and I heard all this shouting outside. I thought someone was drunk. But then a woman started screaming, and I saw this guy was on the ground and about a dozen people were kicking him. It was crazy. Everyone was shouting about dragons."

"Police and ambulance services were called," the reporter continued, "but the man died of his injuries in hospital. Police are appealing for anyone with information about the attack to come forward.

"It was only last week that this street was the scene of a dragon attack."

Blurred footage of the same streetscape began to play, and I saw myself in dragon form light up the night with fire. I'd seen this footage before, as had probably every person on the planet with a TV or Internet connection. Opinion was fairly evenly divided as to whether or not it was genuine. Some bloke in England had proved conclusively that no real dragon would be able to project fire in such a thin and focused stream, and therefore it must be a hoax. That suited me fine; I was more than happy to be a hoax. Others had dissected the footage practically frame by frame, demonstrating how it had been faked. The poor quality of the video was in my favour. Filmed by a terrified onlooker from some distance away in the dark, the footage lasted barely twenty seconds and shook like crazy. Except for when the flames lit my face, it was hard to make out anything except blurred shapes in the darkness.

"Is it possible that there is a connection between the man killed here today and the previous attack?" Not that I knew of. He was probably just some poor homeless guy trying to scare off a gang of teenage thugs by telling them he was a dragon. "Police say there is still no trace of the owner of this house behind me, damaged in the attack last week. She has been identified as Leandra Brooks, and police are anxious to speak to her in connection with their investigations."

A picture of Leandra filled the screen, in all her cool blonde beauty. Her blue eyes were like chips of ice.

"It's possible that she is the victim of foul play, but there is another possibility too—that she is one of these supernatural creatures. Anyone who has knowledge of her whereabouts is asked to contact Crime Stoppers."

The clip finished and Mac closed the laptop. She looked me over with those big puppy dog eyes of hers and smiled. "At least no one can dob you in to the cops looking like that. If they said you were Leandra they'd just get themselves sent to the funny farm."

True. With messy auburn hair and green eyes, I looked nothing like the blue-eyed blonde they were hunting.

"No shifter is going to involve the police anyway," said Luce.

Ben didn't look convinced. "I wouldn't put it past Gideon Thorne and his lot."

"No." Luce shook her head. "What need does he have of human laws and courts? Police would just be an annoyance, getting underfoot and asking awkward questions. Anonymity has always been a shifter's best friend."

Well, until I came along and revealed dragons to the world. And managed to get caught on camera doing it. Twice. I was determined there wasn't going to be a third time.

"Luce is right," I said. "Thorne's got his hopes pinned on this party of his. We just need to make sure that at the end of the night he's the one getting the nasty surprise, not us."

CHAPTER NINE

Gideon Thorne's property near Bowral in the Southern Highlands was lit up like a Christmas tree for the Presentation Ball. He must have had a team dedicated to doing nothing but stringing up fairy lights for days. The sweet sounds of a string quartet drifted on the warm night air as we got out of the car, along with the clink of glasses and the hum of conversation. Security was respectful but thorough. We'd brought no obvious weapons, but they would have been found if we had. No one looked twice at the ring I wore, or the packet of cigarettes in Blue's top pocket. They even made us walk through a metal detector as we entered the house. I had no doubt there were other less mundane precautions in place too.

"Check out the guys on the door," Blue muttered as we crossed the foyer. The large double doors ahead stood open; through them we could see a colourful crowd of shifters milling in the ballroom. A guard stood on either side of the doorway, both goblins, and both wearing glasses. Precautions like that.

"Are they mages?"

Blue snorted. "Not bloody likely. No clan chief in his right mind lets a mage out of his sight. They're too valuable. No, they're just sniffers."

"Sniffers?"

"Probably apprentice mages, or maybe just related to a mage, and got a little more talent than the average grunt. Checking for the presence of goblin magic."

Fortunately Blue's cigarettes were little more than trickery, and didn't carry enough magic to raise an alarm. They were only meant to create a small diversion.

I glanced at Yarrow, glad that we hadn't gone through with Garth's idea of disguising him as Bear, since a full-on seeming would certainly have been a powerful enough spell to register with the sniffers. Blue had carried on as if making a seeming was the world's most gruelling task, and insisted he couldn't do it without returning to his cave. I hadn't been willing to release him from his unofficial house arrest, even under guard. And in the end I hadn't been able to come up with anything clever enough that Yarrow could do with his borrowed face to justify the effort.

I was certain we wouldn't need Yarrow to get close enough to Thorne anyway. He'd brought me here to gloat, if nothing else, and I was bound to see plenty of him tonight. He'd want to enjoy my reactions when he paraded his queenlings in front of me. I only needed him distracted for a moment to give me the opportunity I needed to use the ring, and I was counting on Blue's fireworks to provide that.

We were nearly at the head of the short line of people waiting to be announced. Luce stood very close on my other side, her gaze darting around, trying to watch everything at once. We reached the door and I handed my invitation to the herald there, as protocol required. As if he didn't know exactly who I was. Already heads were turning in the ballroom.

A short flight of steps, no more than five or six, led down to the main floor, and we stood on the small landing at the top, Blue on my right and Luce on my left. Blue had actually scrubbed up all right for the occasion. He looked a different man in a tuxedo, with clean hair brushed neatly back from his forehead. Luce also wore a tux. Ball gowns were no good for fighting, and Luce always came prepared.

Behind me Yarrow escorted Corinne, the selkie woman. A distraction for Thorne, I hoped. Let him wonder what she was doing here, and whose side she was really on. Garth brought up the rear, looking even more delectable than usual in a suit, and that was the sum of our little party. Not much to bring down one of the domain's most powerful dragons, but this was one case where numbers made no difference. If I'd brought every supporter I had I still couldn't have matched the enemies ranged against me in this room.

"Leandra Elizabeth and her guests," the herald announced in a booming voice, and an instant hush fell over the crowd. I paused for a moment, then strode down the steps as if I owned them.

A small round man rose from his chair at the far end of the long room. Not quite a throne, but his intent was clear. Like the ballroom at my own palace, this one opened onto a terrace, and many of the guests were outside, enjoying what little breeze there was. A swimming pool glittered behind them, its waters lit from below.

The quiet continued as I walked the length of the room under the eyes of the gathered shifters. The dancing hadn't started yet: waiters were circulating with trays of canapes, and champagne in tall flutes. People opened a path for me, melting out of my way so that I felt like Moses parting the Red Sea. Like the sea, waves of whispers rose and fell as I passed. Thorne waited by his chair and let me come to him. If he thought that gave him any advantage in his power games, he was barking up the wrong tree. I didn't play games. I was here to win.

There were streaks of grey in his dark hair, which was oiled and swept back from his forehead in a style that had gone out of fashion before the invention of electricity. Now that Elizabeth was dead, he was the oldest dragon in the domain, and certainly one of the most powerful. I'd been glad not to face him in trueshape last time we'd met. Kasumi had saved me then; I wished she were here now.

"Leandra," he said, with an insultingly slight inclination of his head. His dark eyes glittered with malice. "So glad you could join us."

"Actually I go by Kate these days," I said. "How could I resist the opportunity to meet these so-called sisters of mine?"

He refused to rise to the bait, and looked past me at the others. "And I see you've brought some old friends. Good to see you again, Lucinda. You too, Corinne."

Luce's bow was as shallow as his had been. She'd been insulting shifters since before he'd been an egg, and had made it an art form. Corinne smiled but said nothing, her huge dark eyes downcast. She looked nervous, and her grip on Yarrow's arm seemed tighter than necessary. Fair enough. I'd be nervous too in her place, surrounded by enemies, with no resources to call on. Selkies were sweet, but the ability to turn into a seal wasn't something that came in handy too often.

I was pretty nervous myself, though the sight of Thorne's smug face brought anger boiling to the surface, washing away the nerves. I'd never liked him, even before he'd turned traitor. Now he was standing between me and my hopes for a happily ever after with Ben and Lachie at my side. The ordeal of the proving had gone on long enough. It would be my pleasure to rid the world of him and his hopes for a second one.

His eyes rested on Corinne for a long, thoughtful moment, then he turned back to me.

"I thought you might like to meet your sisters in private before the official ceremony."

"That's a little unorthodox of you."

He smiled. "This whole occasion is a little unorthodox, wouldn't you say? Of course, if you'd like to proceed with the ceremony instead …"

"Not at all." My smile was as insincere as his. "I'd love to meet them."

He waved us forward, and led the way through an unobtrusive door guarded by two goblins. These ones wore no glasses. We followed him down a short hallway and up a flight of stairs into a large sitting room that overlooked the pool. Two merfolk splashed in the shallows, performing tricks for the other guests, and the party looked to be in full swing.

Thorne closed the door behind us, and all outside noise instantly cut off. Interesting. A soundproof room. My heart began to beat a little faster.

Though the room was large, there were so many people in it that it felt crowded. A log fire crackled in a massive hearth on the wall opposite the door. Even in summer, evenings in the southern highlands could be cool. The room was furnished in a "country manor" style, with large leather lounges planted on a scattering of deep blue rugs. The wall opposite the windows was filled with glass-fronted bookcases in a dark-coloured wood. There was even a stag's head mounted on one wall.

Every head turned our way as we entered, and conversation died. Most of the people were standing, despite the number of empty seats. In fact, only seven were sitting, all women, and it didn't take a genius to figure out why. Six of them had blonde hair, piled high on their heads in a way that reminded me so much of Valeria I had to grit my teeth. The seventh had hair almost the same colour as mine, a rich deep auburn. Which was ironic, really, since my physical body was absolutely no relation to any of these women. Each had an identical hostile expression on her face and an aura that blazed dragon-red.

My new sisters.

The rest of the people in the room must be their various entourages, and the different auras of many kinds of shifters glowed among them. Now I looked more closely I could see they were clumped in separate untrusting groups, each hovering close to their own mistress. Just one big happy dragon family.

Thorne raised his voice, though there wasn't a sound in the room. "Ladies, if I could have your attention."

The guy obviously liked the sound of his own voice. Perhaps this was his big moment. This would be a good time to spring his trap, whatever it was. Behind me Luce and Garth fanned out in a not-so-subtle attempt to give themselves room. Best to be prepared. I caught Blue's eye, and he gave me the barest nod. *Ready when you are.* He slipped from the room, closing the door quietly behind him.

The laser-like focus in the room shifted from me to Thorne, though I noticed the auburn-haired one kept sneaking little looks my way. Maybe she was excited to finally have a sister that wasn't blonde.

"May I introduce Leandra Elizabeth." He spread his arms wide as if producing a rabbit out of a hat.

"It's Kate, actually," I said.

"Of course. And these are Elizabeth's other daughters: Faith, Hope, Charity, Virginia, Justine, Prudence and Valiant."

Each stood as he named them. Valiant was the auburn-haired one.

"Nice names," I said. "Mother must have been feeling very virtuous when you were born."

No one laughed. Tough crowd. Guess they'd heard it too many times before. Belatedly I recalled I was supposed to be wooing these women to my side, not pissing them off with stupid puns. My sense of humour often got the better of me when I was nervous.

"Please, don't stand on my account." I threw myself into the nearest armchair and crossed my legs. Rather a lot of leg showed through the slit in the dark green silk gown I wore, but I sat back, trying to project an air of relaxed confidence.

Gideon Thorne wasn't running this show any more, I was. I considered Valiant. I suppose "Valerie" would have been too close to "Valeria". Elizabeth did seem to go for names that made a statement. Thought what "Leandra" was supposed to mean I had no idea. "I bet you go by Val. Are you the youngest?"

Valiant sat down in a rustle of ivory silk, which looked amazing against her creamy skin and auburn hair.

"Only by two months," she said, cocking her head as if daring me to make something of it. "There's not such a big spread between us as there was in your clutch. And only my *friends* call me Val."

And I wasn't one of them, said her sneering expression.

Valeria's egg had hatched almost a full year before mine, which wasn't unusual in a queen clutch. Though the eggs were laid over a period of weeks, they matured at different rates, and a large gap between first and last to hatch was common. Usually this was bad news for the younger daughters. It certainly had been for Leandra, though it wasn't Valeria's bigger size that had killed her but the automatic bias that favoured the firstborn. More supporters flocked to the firstborn daughter, since her odds were better than most, and it became a self-fulfilling prophecy.

I wondered which one was the oldest here. Faith, probably, since Thorne had most likely introduced them in birth order. She was the one in the figure-hugging black dress. The others had already blended together into an indistinguishable lump of blonde hostility.

"And how old are you?"

Now the defiance was even clearer. "Eighteen."

Bloody hell. They were children. Only seven years older than Lachie. They must be old enough to take trueshape, or even Thorne wouldn't have risked this farce, but only just. They had at least another five years before they would be considered more than babies, by dragon standards. Leandra had been twenty-five when the proving started, and even that had been young. At twenty-nine, I felt like an old woman by comparison.

Thorne beckoned forward one of the servants standing around the walls and ordered champagne. "The Bollinger, I think."

The man bowed, and a Hermes charm swung forward as he did so. I checked the other servants. They all wore charms prominently displayed. Heralds. Not a bad idea. Their charms would neutralise any offensive magic in the immediate vicinity. Thorne wasn't taking any chances.

The herald returned and presented a bottle of champagne to Thorne as if he were ordering in a restaurant. The older dragons were such wine snobs.

And he was looking old. His jaw had sagged into jowls and there were bags under his eyes. He looked like a man on the brink of retirement, though clearly he had no thought of retiring. No doubt he meant to install one of these children on the throne and rule through her. He had the experience of being Elizabeth's right-hand man behind him, and if the lucky candidate didn't have too much spine he could probably manage it for a few years until she learned the ropes and kicked him out. But how many did he have left anyway? Dragons stayed young-looking right up until the end of their lives, when they suddenly aged enormously. To be looking nearly sixty was a bad sign.

Not that I was going to shed any tears over Gideon Thorne's life expectancy. In fact, I was going to do my damnedest to cut it short. He watched the herald pour the champagne with a predatory smile that made me wonder.

I turned my attention to the fizzing champagne. The herald had opened it in front of us, so it was unlikely to be poisoned. Why the smile, then? I watched the man's hands closely, but he merely picked each glass up, then set it down on the tray once it was filled. No odd furtive movements, no slipping anything into one particular glass that I could see.

"We should drink a toast," Thorne said as the bubbles subsided in the last glass.

"To what? The death of seven out of the eight sisters in this room?"

"To tradition." He ignored my dig, though several of the blondes scowled at me. Valiant shifted uncomfortably, as well she might, considering her odds. "To a successful proving."

He took a glass from the tray. The herald moved around the room, offering the tray to each sister. I was last. I took the remaining glass.

Thorne raised his. "May the best candidate win."

We all raised our glasses. If not the champagne, something about the glass itself? Mine looked identical to the others but, unlike my sisters, I hadn't been given a choice. Thorne took a sip, watching me over the rim of his glass like a kid waiting for Santa on Christmas Eve.

Definitely something about the glass, then.

I caught movement in the corner of my eye: Luce, shaking her head at me. I rose, and Thorne rose too, mere steps away. If I reached out my hand I could almost touch him.

Funny, I would never have called myself a gambler before. But Leandra's recklessness was part of me now, and besides, the odds were good. More than good. I knew Thorne had taken the bane leaf from Elizabeth's safe. The chance of the glass having been treated with du instead was vanishingly small. Thorne had no connection with the Chinese queen or her sister.

And he didn't know that bane leaf was no longer fatal to me.

I tipped back my head and drained the glass, setting it back on the herald's tray with a clink that echoed like a death knell in the suddenly silent room. Thorne's face was a picture of anticipation. Valiant let out a long slow breath, as if she'd been holding it, and took a sip from her own glass.

"About the winning," I began, stepping forward as if to address the room, but really positioning myself closer to Thorne. I wasn't going to need Blue's diversion after all. "I hate to spoil your party, but that's already been done. The official proving, begun by Elizabeth, is over, and I now hold the throne. I can see these girls are dragons"—I waved an airy hand at the blondes, their red dragon auras shimmering around them—"but I only have your word for it that they're Elizabeth's queen daughters. Far more likely that they're neuters. You'll forgive me if I'm not inclined to believe you."

Several of the blondes huffed in outrage, but it seemed to me that it was more for show than authentic. Their hungry eyes watched me like vultures circling a dying animal.

"I have documents drawn up and signed by your mother supporting the claims of her daughters," said Thorne. "*All* her daughters. There's even a proclamation explaining her reasons for the unorthodox nature of her actions to the domain."

"How thoughtful of her."

"Would you like to see the documents?"

"Of course." I didn't doubt such documents existed. They might even be genuine. Thorne sent a herald to fetch them and we settled in to wait. Everyone else was waiting for something else, though. The tension in the room had rocketed up the instant I swallowed that champagne.

It shouldn't take long. It had only been a couple of minutes for Leandra, before the cramps and the dizziness had taken hold. In my own case the poison had been delivered with a side order of knife through the heart, so I hadn't been paying as much attention to the symptoms, though I remembered the chucking. That part was hard to forget. Maybe I shouldn't have gone for quite such a melodramatic gesture in downing the whole damn glass, but I'd needed to keep Thorne feeling he had the upper hand. Right up until the minute he realised he didn't.

I perched on the arm of a chair, which took me a little closer still to Thorne. Sure enough, before the herald returned, an uneasy sensation began to churn in my gut. Luce had drifted a little closer, though not close enough to be perceived as a threat by the old dragon. I frowned, letting one hand creep to my stomach, and Thorne's eyes lit up.

"I feel …" I stood up and wobbled forward a step. My acting wouldn't have won me any Oscars, but Thorne was in the mood to be convinced.

"Yes?" he asked, his voice oozing fake solicitousness. He could hardly keep the smile from his face, the bastard. "You feel unwell?"

I grunted and doubled over, clutching one arm across my gut. The other I held out toward Thorne.

"Mistress?" said Luce. "What's wrong?"

But she stayed out of my way as I pitched forward in a sudden motion and let myself fall against Thorne. He held his arms out to receive me, staggering a little as my weight dragged him down. He must have felt the prick as the tiny needle in my ring stabbed into the fleshy part of his thumb, but his mind was so focused on his own apparently triumphant deception that he didn't notice mine.

At least, not until the effect of the du hit him. His body went stiff under my hands, and I pushed him down. To the others it must have looked as though my own collapse had pulled him off balance. But as I rose and his body began to thrash in spastic movements, the anticipation in the room turned to horror.

The blondes leapt to their feet, pretty faces aghast. Valiant's creamy skin had gone ashen, and she stared at me as if I were a ghost. My team closed in around me, menacing despite their lack of weapons. It was as if time stopped as we watched Thorne's struggles. His heels drummed on the carpet and his head jerked from side to side, though his eyes had rolled back in his head and he saw nothing.

"Somebody help him," said one of the blondes. It might have been Faith.

But they all knew there was no helping him. Abruptly his movements ceased. His head flopped to one side, and pink-tinged foam slid down his cheek from his open mouth.

I stepped forward, one hand pressed to my own rebellious stomach. Every eye in the room turned to me, some fearful, some filled with hate, all shocked by the sudden turn of events.

Naturally that was the moment my stomach chose to give up the fight, and I hurled all over Thorne's shiny leather shoes.

CHAPTER TEN

Luce whipped a napkin off the empty drinks tray and passed it to me without comment. I wiped my mouth and drew a deep breath, fighting to get myself under control. If this was anything like the time Kasumi had poisoned me, the nausea would last a good half hour.

"Excuse me." There was disgust on some of my new sisters' faces, but also a respect that hadn't been there before. Clearly they all knew what had been in that champagne glass—probably smeared all over the inside of it, enough to kill any dragon three times over—and the fact that I was still standing had them almost as spooked as the sudden death of their mentor. If they were a little older and wiser, one of them might have seized the opportunity to attack me while I was unwell. All I could say was thank God for teenagers.

I pressed the napkin to my lips again. "Just give me a minute. I'll be fine." No need to tell them about the half hour of chucking. If they thought I had superpowers, all the better. "I'm pretty hard to kill, as you'll find out if you try."

Hope came forward—I think it was Hope—and knelt by Thorne's side in a rustle of ruby silk. She pressed her fingers against the pulse point in his neck.

"Is he dead?" Valiant asked.

"Yes." Hope drew back, putting some more distance between herself and me, though whether through fear of me or worry that I'd throw up on her wine-coloured dress, I couldn't tell. If it was the latter, it was a pretty smart move. My stomach heaved, and I had to concentrate everything I had on resisting the urge to decorate the carpet again. Garth rested a warm hand on my bare shoulder. His worried eyes whirled with yellow. No doubt this brought back bad memories. He'd held me in his arms all too recently, thinking he was watching me die of poisoning.

"And a good thing, too," I said. "He had you believing you had no choice but to kill me and each other, didn't he?"

"That's because we don't," said Valiant. "And you needn't think we're defenceless just because you managed to knock off Thorne."

She held her chin high, but there was more bravado than conviction in her words. They were too young. Oh, I was sure they'd been raised, just as I had, in the knowledge that they must kill all their sisters if they hoped to win the prize of the throne. And dragons were a greedy lot: wanting the throne and the life of privilege that went with it wasn't difficult. Nor was the capacity for backstabbing—it was practically a birthright. But no other dragons grew up knowing how very small their chances of surviving were. It messed with your mind, having that hanging over you all your life. Not many were strong enough when push came to shove.

I looked around the room, meeting the eyes of each sister in turn. Most showed as much fear as defiance, and I certainly couldn't blame them. Leandra had been one of the most pragmatic of her clutch, but even she had found the proving tough going, and these girls were far too young. Only Faith in her stark black gown showed no fear as she glared back at me.

But even Faith might prefer a sure thing to the risk of the proving. As Leandra had discovered, anything could happen, no matter how well prepared you were.

"Of course you're not defenceless." I gestured at the tight knot of supporters clustering behind each girl, just as my team gathered protectively around me. "We all have our resources— but look around this room and ask yourself: *how many of these people will still be alive a year from now?*"

I let them take a moment for that to sink in. It was a sobering thought. Eight sisters, and only one of them could live to take the throne. All of the others would die, and many of their supporters with them.

The smell of vomit was strong, mixed with blood and a pungent odour that meant Thorne must have voided his bowels as he died. The mingled aromas were hard to take, but they made a vicious point: this was what awaited almost everyone in the room. Nothing but blood and death and ruin waited down the traditional path.

"How confident do you feel that you will be the lucky one, that lucky one out of eight, to make it through?" I glanced at

Faith, but her face was a mask. "I can tell you Valeria was plenty confident, but look where she ended up."

Floating in Sydney Harbour with an almighty hole punched through her heart, that's where. And I'd put her there. It certainly didn't hurt to remind my sisters of that. Their odds of coming through a proving alive had gone down considerably since I'd entered the game.

Faith glared at me, doing her best to project an icy calm. Shame the trembling of her aura gave her away. "And I suppose you have some other option? Apart from boring us to death?"

"I certainly do. Fighting is a loser's game. Seven of us will die so that one can win everything. Why not agree instead to split the prize?"

"What?" Angry tears sparkled in Valiant's eyes, and she clenched the ivory satin of her gown tight enough to wrinkle it. "I thought you had some sensible alternative. What kind of garbage is that?"

There was a murmur of agreement among the blondes.

"Are you suggesting we divide the domain between us?" Faith asked, an incredulous note in her voice. "Just agree to share the cake instead of fighting over it?"

It sounded perfectly reasonable to me. "Why not? Just because it's never been done before? This is the twenty-first century. Time to update a little."

"And I suppose you get the biggest slice?" Her eyes, green as my own, glittered with challenge. "You're out of your mind if you think I'm going to settle for some speck of dirt in the middle of the Pacific Ocean while you get Australia. I'd rather fight."

A couple of the others muttered their agreement, but several more seemed less sure. It was easier to feel that way when you were the eldest sister, I guess, brought up from birth to expect success in everything you did.

"Really? You'd really rather take almost certain death? Australia's a big place. And don't forget about New Zealand and Indonesia. I'm sure we could manage to stay out of each other's way and still keep everyone happy."

"Are you saying you'd be prepared to split Australia?" Hope joined the conversation, her big blue eyes alight with the possibilities. "I'd heard you were … different … but that seems positively undragonish."

"Sure. Why not? I'd keep New South Wales. I've always lived in Sydney, and I'm not interested in moving. The rest we can sort out later, if you're interested."

I could tell that some of them were for sure. Faith and a couple of others had a different sort of gleam in their eye, though. Stupid teenagers. They thought I was offering because I was too scared to fight.

They thought I was weak.

I sighed, and was about to set them straight when I noticed search lights swinging crazily in the dark beyond the pool. In our soundproof room we could hear nothing from outside, but heads were turning among the partygoers.

Luce noticed it too. At a nod from me she moved to the window and opened it. Noise rushed in from outside: cries of alarm and the tread of heavy booted feet on the paving around the pool.

"What's going on?" I asked.

The distinctive thumping of a helicopter's blades somewhere close nearly drowned out my words, then it set down on the grass beyond the pool, its lights raking the scene.

"Who else did Thorne invite?" I asked, but before anyone could answer, the door behind me burst open, and suddenly the room filled with men in black riot gear. Men who waved serious assault rifles around and yelled at everyone to get down.

I snatched at Garth's sleeve just in time. "Garth, no!"

He glared at me, his eyes fading back to grey from violent yellow. No one else had moved, but the sisters looked as shocked as if this was a surprise to them too, and the men wore badges on their arms proclaiming they were Australian Federal Police. I didn't want to turn dragon and toast a whole bunch of policemen just for doing their job, so I waited—and kept a firm hand on Garth's arm to encourage him to be patient too. His muscles were tense in my grip.

In a moment I was very glad I had. The police fanned out around the room, and a new figure strode in, an older man with a military bearing, though he wore civilian clothes.

"Ladies and gentlemen, these guns are loaded with silver bullets, so I'd advise you not to do anything rash."

Surely he was the one being rash, bursting into a dragon's home and waving firearms around. Though the fact they were loaded with silver meant he at least knew what he was facing. I stepped closer to Garth, still fighting nausea, but worried about those silver bullets. Getting shot was no walk in the park for any shifter, but for werewolves it was invariably fatal. Even the tiniest amount of silver in their system was enough to kill them, in the most gruesome way, too. Thorne's death was nothing to it.

"Who are you?" I pushed into his mind as I spoke, meaning to compel him, but he blocked me so well he could have been a dragon. That was weird: according to his aura he was nothing but human. "This is a private residence. What are you doing here? I hope you have a search warrant."

He tapped the breast pocket of his grey business suit. His clothes made him look more like a banker than a policeman. "I am Commander Wilson of Taskforce Jaeger. I have a warrant right here. I'll be only too happy to show it to the owner of this house, Mr Gideon Thorne. Where is he?"

I felt my face flush with heat. Oh, God, I was such an idiot. I'd completely forgotten Thorne's corpse stretched so incriminatingly on the floor behind me.

"He's right here," said Faith, a vicious smile curving her red lips.

If Commander Wilson was shocked to find a dead body on the floor, he didn't show it. He stepped closer and gazed down at Thorne's contorted face dispassionately. His men began to fan out through the room, and I felt Garth tense under my hand. I squeezed his bicep hard. It was like squeezing rock. A policeman with a gun trained on us stood just out of reach, and I was terrified one of those bullets might end up in my hot-headed werewolf. He had many fine qualities, but impulse control wasn't one of them. I'd already seen one werewolf die of silver poisoning, and I never wanted to repeat the experience. And the thought of losing Garth opened a pit of horror in my stomach that I couldn't examine too closely, for fear of what I might discover. I pressed closer to his warmth, ready to shield him with my body if I had to.

Wilson looked up from his examination of Thorne's body. "Would I be right in assuming Mr Thorne didn't die of natural causes?"

What a comedian. Said it with a straight face, too.

Faith flung a triumphant hand in my direction. "*She* killed him."

"Is that so?" He turned that unblinking gaze on me, then nodded to someone behind me.

Pain exploded through my head, and the world went black.

CHAPTER ELEVEN

I woke with a lingering headache and a peculiar taste in my mouth. My tongue felt like it was covered in peach fuzz, and about three times bigger than normal. I spent a moment trying to process that taste. Was it the after-effects of the bane leaf? I didn't remember that from last time.

My eyelids were crusted together, and I opened them with some difficulty. The room was unfamiliar, small and white. The glare of the fluorescent tubes in the ceiling hurt my eyes, and I rolled my head forward, feeling a strange resistance in my neck.

A figure swam into view. A face loomed over me, dark hair swinging forward to brush my skin. Luce? I blinked, trying to focus, and saw it was Corinne, the selkie woman.

"Mistress? Don't try to move. Keep still."

Naturally as soon as she told me to keep still, moving became the only thing I wanted to do. I tried to move my arms, but something prevented me. I was having trouble even turning my head. A red light blinked somewhere in the bottom of my peripheral vision, but I couldn't see properly.

She laid a hand on my arm. "Please! Don't move."

The fear in her voice jolted me fully awake, and I managed to focus on her face, so near I could smell the scent of the shampoo she used. Something with apples. There was no furniture in the room except the chair I sat in. I wriggled my hands, and realised I was tied to it.

"What the hell's going on?" I jerked my hands harder, adrenalin surging through my veins, and she grabbed my shoulder.

"Keep still! There's a bomb around your neck."

I stared into her terror-filled eyes for a long moment, then tried to see what she was talking about, but my head was held firmly in some kind of neck brace. I strained to get a good look at the little red light, but trying to see something that's around your neck is like trying to lick your own elbow. No matter how hard you try, it's never going to happen. That's why they invented mirrors.

"Someone put a collar bomb on me?" It certainly wasn't the craziest thing that had happened to me lately, but it hadn't been high on my list of possibilities of how the night at Thorne's might end either. Who would dare? "Was it that Wilson guy?"

Last thing I remembered was getting knocked out, just after the cops had burst in. Or were they really cops? Wilson had said something about a taskforce, and they'd looked like cops, but their whole *modus operandi* smelled more of *Mission Impossible* than the staid old Australian police force. And now I was wearing a collar bomb? Something was very wrong here—and not just the fact that I might be about to get my head blown off.

"I don't know who they were, mistress." The selkie's face was white with fear. She raised a shaking hand to brush her hair out of her face, and I saw both hands were shackled in silver handcuffs. There were angry red welts around her wrists already from the poisonous metal. "They caught us with silver nets, then they brought us here and separated us. I was left in this room on my own until two men in white coats wheeled you in a few minutes ago."

"In a wheelchair?"

"No, on a hospital bed. You were unconscious. Drugged, I think. Then they strapped you to this chair and fitted the bomb around your neck. They said I would be a familiar face when you woke up to stop you doing anything stupid, and I was to tell you that if you tried taking trueshape they'd detonate the bomb."

Well, that was a smart move. Whoever was running this show—and I seriously doubted it was Wilson—knew quite a bit about me. They'd used silver nets to capture a roomful of shifters without casualties, and had Corinne bound in silver, so they obviously knew that shifters couldn't take trueshape or access their other powers while constrained in silver. And somehow they'd discovered that silver no longer had that effect on me, alone of all the shifters. Since Leandra's consciousness had transferred to my human body through that damn channel stone that had started the whole ball game, I'd been immune to silver. And bane leaf, of course, which was a side effect that had saved my life twice already.

So, how to stop a dragon taking trueshape when you couldn't use the dampening effects of silver? The collar bomb was quite a neat solution. I would have been all admiration if it hadn't been my head in the firing line.

"How would they know? Have they got some way of measuring magic flow or something?"

"I don't think it's anything that sophisticated." She pointed to the camera mounted in the corner of the room. "They're watching us."

I glared at the camera. Its blank eye stared back, unconcerned. "Are we still at Thorne's place?"

"No. They took us somewhere in a helicopter. I was blindfolded, so I didn't see where we landed, but it wasn't a short trip. We could be back in Sydney. Or even Canberra, I suppose."

The nation's capital, where Parliament House proudly flew the Australian flag from atop its green hill. I suppose secret detention facilities for shifters weren't out of the question, though they'd never come up on any of the tourist guides I'd seen. They'd have to be pretty recent, too.

Or perhaps we were in a hospital. Corinne had mentioned a hospital bed. What had they been doing to me? The back of my head ached where I'd been knocked out, but only mildly. My dragon healing powers had mended that while I slept. Nothing else seemed sore. I had visions of being opened up in some kind of mad scientist's lab while people poked and prodded at my supernatural insides, but I would be hurting now if I'd been in surgery, so clearly that hadn't happened. What, then?

I strained my enhanced hearing to its limits, searching for any clues. I heard someone walking down the corridor outside, in high heels from the tapping sound of it. Each step echoed in a way that suggested lots of concrete. Further away I heard the boom of a heavy door closing. Again, concrete and echoes. We could be underground.

"Are there any windows?" The harsh fluorescent light in the room suggested not, but I couldn't see the wall behind me.

"No, but there's something like a TV screen back there."

"Turn me around so I can see it."

"I don't think we should move you."

"Corinne, they don't want their star prisoner blowing up by accident. I'm sure this thing will only go off if they deliberately detonate it." "Sure" might have been a little too strong, but I was fairly confident. "They're just trying to scare you."

"Well, it worked," she grumbled, but she tipped my chair and swivelled it carefully on its back legs till I was facing the far wall. Not an easy thing to do when she was wearing handcuffs, and she hissed as they bit into her skin.

The screen was set into the wall, not sitting on top of it, and if it was a TV there were no buttons to work it. It looked more like one of those one-way glass windows you see in interrogation rooms in movies, but since movies were my only experience of such things I couldn't be sure.

"What do you think's going on?" Corinne sat down on the floor and leaned against the wall, her silk ball gown puddling around her. She looked exhausted, with dark rings under her big brown eyes, and horribly overdressed for our current situation. Was it the middle of the night? How long had I been out?

"God knows. People have been getting pretty jumpy about shifters lately."

She nodded. "They're about to pass that new bill in Parliament, like the anti-terrorist one. Arrest without charge, detainment for seven days. Just on suspicion of being a shifter."

It was true. The government had responded to public hysteria with a show of force. Parliament had been recalled early from its summer recess. They had to look like they were doing something to combat the new menace, even if what they did was basically useless. It hadn't bothered me because I didn't see how they were going to arrest anyone when they couldn't tell who was a shifter and who wasn't. Besides, most dragons had politicians on the payroll. We were the last people who should have needed to worry. The new laws were more likely to be used against poor homeless guys as an excuse to get them off the streets.

I closed my eyes, wishing I had a wall to lean against too. "But why target Thorne's party?"

Someone had told them who'd be there—basically the cream of Sydney's shifter society. When they'd even known about my immunity to silver, it was obvious they had very specific inside information. Betrayal was nothing new for dragons, of course, but it seemed a dangerous game for a shifter to play. How could they be sure they wouldn't be caught in the trap themselves?

Perhaps it was Daiyu's latest move against me. She certainly had the most to gain from the sudden disappearance of the domain's queen and the seven women with the only other claim to it. But the new laws would only allow our captors to hold us for seven days without charge. What could she accomplish in seven days?

But then, it seemed pretty damned unlikely that the new laws allowed for strapping collar bombs around suspects' necks. If this taskforce was legit, they were certainly playing fast and loose with the rules. Could they even be in league with Daiyu?

God, things were always so complicated when you were dealing with dragons. My brain felt too woozy from the drugs to attempt to work it all out. It didn't seem likely that Daiyu would have that sort of pull away from Japan, but who knew?

A crackling noise from the camera made us both jump.

"Ms O'Connor, we would like to ask you a few questions."

I couldn't see the speaker, but the sound was so distorted I couldn't even tell if it was a man or a woman.

"Sure. Come in for a chat. You might have to bring your own chair, though."

"That won't be necessary. I can see you perfectly well from where I am."

I glared at the dark glass in front of me, but I could see nothing, not even the suspicion of a movement. "But I can't see you. I don't care for talking to disembodied voices."

"No need to take that attitude. Your associates are depending on you to be co-operative."

The black glass flickered, and a picture appeared, of a familiar glowering face. Garth stood, arms folded across his bulky chest, inside a cage whose bars shone with the familiar glint of silver. Two guards stood opposite his cage, guns levelled at him. Geez, Louise. Garth was good, but not *that* good. They didn't need the guns with that much silver surrounding him. There was no way he'd even be able to touch those bars, much less break through them. I suppose they might get scowled to death, but otherwise those guards were completely safe.

"Those guns you see are loaded with silver," the voice continued. Well, *der*. Of course they were. "If you do not co-operate fully, Mr Maclaren will be shot."

Now, at last, fear cut through the fog of drugs in my brain.

"Just like that? No charges, no trial, nothing? I thought you people worked for the government. You can't just go around murdering people."

"Yes, Ms O'Connor, just like that. Why, did you think dragons were the only people who got to kill whomever they please with impunity? I'm sure Mr Thorne would be interested in your opinion."

Fear sank its icy claws into my heart. How could I deal with this person? Whoever it was seemed to know everything, and I knew nothing, not even their identity. And Garth just stood there, so vulnerable. All his strength meant nothing against the threat of silver. The memory of Jerry's face, horribly contorted in death, sent a shiver down my spine.

"What proof do I even have that he's still alive?"

"Are your eyes not proof enough?"

"You could have recorded this hours ago. He might already be dead."

There was a crackling sound, then an amplified tap, like someone testing a microphone.

"Mr Maclaren, Ms O'Connor wishes to confirm your wellbeing."

Garth obviously heard the voice too, for on the screen he lifted his head, searching for the source of the sound.

"Oh, yeah? Let me talk to her then."

"Garth!" Oh, God, please let him be safe until I could get to him. My panicked heart pounded in my throat, and I had to swallow hard before I could speak. "Can you hear me?"

Garth's grey eyes softened as he turned to face the camera. "Loud and clear."

"Are you okay?"

His mouth twitched into a hard line. "I reckon you could call this a glass-half-empty moment. What about you?"

"Don't worry about me. Just don't do anything stupid, okay?"

"When have you ever known me to do anything stupid?"

Only about three times a day, you daft bastard. The picture disappeared from the screen before I could say anything else. *Just this once, let him make the smart decision.*

"Satisfied?" said the voice.

"What do you want from me?"

"Don't be so quick to assume I want something from you— other than information, of course. It's possible I might be able to offer you something very dear to your heart."

He meant Lachie. My stomach lurched. Oh, shit, he must be working for Daiyu. Was it Jason? My fists clenched at the thought. I'd kill him.

"Don't you want to know what it is?"

Corinne was watching me, wide-eyed and scared. I swallowed my fear and put on a brave face.

"Not particularly, but it sounds like you want to tell me, so knock yourself out."

There was a pause, as if the speaker were hoping I'd cave and ask him. Probably spoiled his big moment. Pretentious jerk. My heart hammered as I waited for his response.

"Your humanity, Ms O'Connor."

"My—what?" Not what I was expecting. I let out a relieved breath. He didn't have Lachie after all. "What are you talking about?"

"You know what I'm talking about. You started life as plain Kate O'Connor, then became entangled with Leandra Elizabeth, and now—now you are unique among dragons. A human with the strengths of a dragon. A dragon with some unusual human advantages. I want to know how you did it."

"Why? I thought you only cared about hunting down shifters. What does it matter how I became one?"

"Because if you tell me, I might be able to *un*do it. And I think that might interest you very much."

CHAPTER TWELVE

As the speaker fell silent, the door opened, catching us both by surprise. Corinne scrambled to her feet as three men entered the little room. They each carried a baton tipped with a silver-plated spike. One took Corinne by the arm and hustled her out the door. She looked back over her shoulder as she left, her eyes wide and desperate.

"Where are you taking her?" I didn't really expect a reply, but it was worth trying.

"She can rejoin the others now you're awake," the taller man said. "We weren't going to risk a human in here until you knew the situation." He jerked his head at the collar bomb.

Presumably it would have been fine with him if I'd accidentally blown Corinne up, since she was a shifter.

I studied them as they unbound me from the chair and hauled me to my feet. They were both human. The one who'd spoken wore a pair of glasses like something out of the fifties, with thick black rims. Real glass or goblin glass? I was suspicious of everything now. The other man had grey hair and the beginnings of a pot belly sagging over his belt. Both wore dark blue uniforms. They looked like policemen, but I was past believing everything I saw.

"Move," Glasses Guy said. "Don't do anything stupid, and the commander won't have to press the button."

My captors prodded me out into a concrete corridor that echoed to the sound of their booted feet. It was grey and poorly lit, and looked like something out of a B-grade spy movie.

"What is this place?" I asked.

"Somewhere that knows what to do with freaks like you." Pot Belly shoved me in the back with his baton, so I started walking.

"And where's that?"

"Wouldn't you like to know."

Excellent. My prison came complete with schoolyard taunts.

We arrived at a door painted with a large number three. Glasses Guy opened it to reveal a stairwell, and we clattered down, passing door number four and stopping at number five. Definitely underground, then. And everywhere I turned there were more cameras, so I gave up any idea of compelling these guys. Big Brother was watching.

Level five had blue lino on the floor and more effective lighting. But the long corridor that stretched out from the stairwell was just as deserted as the one on level three, which I'd now begun to think of as the prison level. There was an antiseptic smell here that gave me the uneasy feeling that this was the medical level.

The uneasiness increased as my escorts took me into a room that looked like a doctor's surgery, complete with an examination table and a selection of medical instruments. A scalpel gleamed invitingly, but the ever-present cameras were watching. Besides, I wanted to know what the hell was going on, so I let them shove me into the chair by the desk.

There was another door opposite the one I'd come through, and in a moment this opened and two men walked in, at which point my escorts left the way we'd come.

One of the men was Commander Wilson, still dapper in his grey suit, and he took the chair on the other side of the desk. The other was a small Indian man wearing a white lab coat over his scrubs. I'd never seen him before, but his aura gave him away.

"You're a goblin!"

Commander Wilson didn't blink an eyelid, so it obviously wasn't news to him.

"That's right," said the goblin.

"What are you doing working for these people?"

The goblin shrugged. "A man has to eat."

"But they're attacking shifters. Don't you care? What if they turn on you next?"

"Dr Patel is in no danger," Wilson said. "My organisation is charged with protecting the general public from dangerous shifters like yourself. A doctor is a benefit to the community, not a danger."

"But he's a goblin."

"And therefore not inherently powerful."

"Then why are you holding Corinne?" I demanded. "She's a selkie. What's she going to do? Turn into a seal and bark at you?"

"Your selkie friend will be released as soon as we have finished questioning her on recent events. Now, if we could move on, please. I believe you know that we're interested in how you became a shifter in the first place." He opened a folder that lay on the desk in front of him and read from the first page. "Up until recently you were fully human, correct?"

"That's right." There was no point lying when they obviously already knew. I couldn't risk anything happening to Garth or one of the others. For all his apparent businesslike manner, I didn't trust Wilson. Anyone who collared a prisoner with a bomb and threatened to blow their head off was not a man who operated by the book.

"And that changed the day Leandra Elizabeth died?"

For people who claimed to hate shifters, I found it quaint that they persisted in referring to Leandra as "Leandra Elizabeth" in that old-fashioned dragon way, with her matronymic instead of her regular surname.

"That's right," I said again.

Dr Patel gave me an encouraging smile. "Please tell us how this change was achieved."

This part I could lie about, since it wasn't public knowledge. I was tempted to say she gave me a magic potion or something stupid. But there was that damned bomb to consider. And also I liked my favourite werewolf without silver poisoning. Really, that was more of an issue than the bomb. If I'd been the only one in captivity I could have been out of this collar faster than you could say "dragon on the loose!", but Garth was here, and Luce and Yarrow and Corinne. Blue, too. I'd almost forgotten about him. Probably my new sisters as well. I hadn't actually thought to ask Corinne, but presumably the raid hadn't been aimed solely at me. They would have rounded up everyone at the ball. And if I didn't exactly owe them anything, it didn't seem right to leave them to the commander's tender mercies if I could help it.

"Think carefully before you lie to us," Wilson said, as if he'd been reading my mind. "We know it has to do with that stone in your chest."

I blinked, and barely managed to stop myself asking how they knew about that.

Dr Patel leaned over and removed an x-ray film from my file. He stuck it to the light box on the wall and turned it on.

"We took the opportunity to run a few scans while you were asleep."

Asleep. Yeah, right. Drugged to the eyeballs, more like. He sounded quite cheerful, as if he saw nothing untoward in his behaviour. I bet the new anti-shifter laws didn't give them the right to drug people and run medical tests without permission. He was just as much of a maverick as Wilson, despite the white coat and chatty bedside manner.

"Your x-ray showed up this odd mass here." He pointed to a lump on one of my ribs. "We can't be sure without opening you up, of course, but it looks remarkably similar to the strange stone found on Valeria's ribcage post mortem."

The coroner's report, which I'd seen courtesy of Kasumi's impersonation of the lead detective on the case, had mentioned it. That hadn't bothered me since the human coroner had no way of knowing what he was looking at. But the report had also mentioned Taskforce Jaeger, which had hardly even registered at the time. I'd been up to my armpits in bounty hunters trying to kill me, and some nebulous taskforce hadn't seemed much of a threat by comparison.

I might have been more concerned if I'd realised they had shifter traitors on the payroll.

"What do you get out of this?" I asked the goblin doctor. "What have they promised you to betray your people?"

His cheery mask slipped, and the hatred that peeked out in its place chilled me. "Dragons are not my people. Dragons are the scourge of the shifter world—and the human one too. The humans just didn't realise it until now."

Maybe that was how the taskforce had managed to move against people so highly placed in society. The politicians had found out just who was pulling their strings, and it had given them a nasty scare.

Wilson stirred restlessly in his chair. "Please confine yourself to answering the questions, Ms O'Connor. We're on a timetable here."

"Really? What's the rush?"

He scowled. "The stone, please. Or should we shoot the werewolf?"

The hairs on the back of my neck rose at his matter-of-fact tone.

"Where do dragons get these stones from?" Patel asked.

"They don't *get* them anywhere. They're born with them, same as their ribs and hearts and lungs. It's just a part of dragon anatomy."

He looked disappointed, as if he'd been expecting a less prosaic explanation.

"Tell us how this one got into your body, then. *You* were not born a dragon."

"I put it there."

God, the pain. I put a hand on my chest as I relived the moment. Flat on my back, bleeding out. Jason had just laid me open from shoulder to hip with his wicked claws. Knowing I was dying, that there was no way left to save Lachie from Valeria's clutches, yet still struggling for a way, any way. And Leandra in my head like a broken record, nagging me to use the stone, to let her take control.

"I was wounded in the fight at Valeria's house. There was a deep cut in my chest, and I pushed the stone in."

I'd felt it burrowing through my torn flesh like a hideous tick, munching its way to its current home on the rib above my heart. The pain was so fierce I'd blacked out, and when I'd woken Kate was gone, replaced by a Leandra exulting in her new body.

It should have been the end of me, but my love for Lachie was stronger than both of us. A new person had emerged in the struggle to save him. Not quite Leandra, but more than Kate, I was a world first—a messed-up kind of human/dragon hybrid.

"And that allowed Leandra to take over your body?"

"Yes."

But there was one crucial point I wasn't telling these guys. As she lay dying Leandra had poured her essence into that stone. That was what it was for. It was called a channel stone because it allowed a dragon to channel her mass between her human form and her trueshape. Leandra had merely found a new use for it. Enough of her was in the stone when I swallowed it originally to allow her to colonise my body, and that little piece had been enough to re-establish the connection with the rest of her essence once the stone found its rightful place nestled next to my heart.

"But how did you take the stone from her in the first place?"

"She wanted me to. She was dying, and thought it might give her a chance to live on in my body."

And that wild gamble had paid off, though not exactly as she'd hoped. Under a compulsion, she'd forced me to cut the stone from her dying body and swallow it. Sadly for her, I wasn't ready to let some damned lizard steal my body, and she wasn't strong enough to take it outright. And once I'd thrown up the stone she had even more trouble. Not until I surrendered to her and shoved the stupid stone into the gaping hole in my chest did she gain full control.

"Have you considered," said the goblin doctor, "that taking it out again could transform you to your fully human state?"

"No." That was a lie, of course. If I was human again, all my problems with Ben would disappear, and we could have that life I'd been dreaming of—the little house in the suburbs, the family of three. If I was human again, this whole dragon mess would be someone else's problem, and I wouldn't have to worry any more that my every decision was dooming the people I loved. Naturally I'd had the odd daydream of being able to turn back time. Who wouldn't?

The doctor watched me, his dark Indian eyes full of fake concern. "I'm sure it bothers you, knowing that you will outlive your son by hundreds of years."

Ouch. Touché, doctor. To watch my baby grow old and die, while I lived on through the lonely centuries without him, was the stuff of nightmares. I'd wept over his dead body once already; I didn't think I could do it again.

"Wouldn't you like to go back to a nice uncomplicated life with your boy and forget all this supernatural drama? Just think of it, Ms O'Connor. You could be human again."

Human again. True, it had a certain ring to it. No more living with the constant threat of death, no more watching my friends die. Friday nights on that battered old couch, curled up with Lachie and a bowl of popcorn, our biggest decision which movie to watch. And maybe Ben at my side? It was a delicious dream, but it could never be more than a dream, surely.

Leandra had been present since the minute I swallowed the damned stone. Even after I'd chucked it up again—even when it had been stolen and was physically miles away from me— Leandra had still been there inside me, fighting for control. If removing the stone hadn't been enough to unseat her then, when her hold on me was so tenuous, how could it help now that we'd melded into one personality?

"What's in it for you? What do you gain from helping me?" If helping me was really what it was. It seemed more likely that removing the channel stone now might simply take away my ability to take trueshape, and leave me stuck somewhere between dragon and human, but with the benefits of neither.

But oh! if it worked …

"We could set you up in a nice little house somewhere safe," Wilson said, as if he sensed the turn of my thoughts.

I folded my arms. He hadn't answered my question. "And what would you expect in return?"

"Your co-operation. That's all, Kate." Patel leaned in, almost friendly. "If it works on you, we will have a humane way of removing the threat that the dragons pose to all humanity."

My eyebrows shot up. "You mean you'd do this to other dragons?"

I couldn't see that being a popular option among dragonkind. The good doctor might find it a little more challenging than he expected.

Although, the taskforce had managed to round us up with little trouble. Maybe they really could do it. Why did that send a chill through me? I had no love for dragonkind.

"That seems the best option for everyone."

The best option? He had no idea what cutting a dragon's channel stone out might do. It could kill them. And all my teenaged sisters would never make it to adulthood.

"And if I co-operate, you'll let the other prisoners go?"

"Well, not the other dragons, obviously." He chuckled as if I'd made a joke. "But the selkie, your werewolf friend and the other shifters can leave."

My werewolf friend, who made no secret of his admiration of the dragon inside me. Did I even want that small life with Ben any more? Every time I tried to picture his dark brown eyes, a pair of grey ones kept interfering. And in my heart I knew the suburban life was lost to me. I'd made too many enemies as a dragon. Lachie and I wouldn't last a week if I were human.

Besides, how could I trust this smiling traitor to keep his word about anything? What if they didn't let Garth go, but turned their silver bullets on him instead? Without my dragon powers, I'd be helpless to save him.

And right now, saving that stubborn, irritating, gorgeous werewolf seemed to have made it to the top of my to-do list.

CHAPTER THIRTEEN

"This way," said Patel.

He and the two guards had marched me a short way down the corridor. I'd thought we were heading for the stairs and the little white room on level three, but we stopped just short of the stairwell at a pair of double doors with windows inset in them.

He held the right-hand door open and waved me through. Inside was a fully equipped operating theatre. A cold frisson of fear ran down my spine. No way was he cutting me open, bomb or no bomb. But before I could do more than take a short, panicked breath, I realised that they already had a patient.

A woman in a long black evening dress lay unconscious on a gurney. Faith.

An orderly moved her gurney closer to the operating table, and gloved hands reached out to help move her across.

"What are you going to do to her?"

Patel smiled. "Remove her stone, of course."

"You can't turn her into a human; she's never been one. You have no idea what removing her stone will do."

At best, she'd be a crippled dragon. At worst …

"We need to find out where the power resides. Is it in the stone, or in the person? Your own experience would suggest it is in the stone, but how can we be sure without running some tests? It's our job to keep the people of Australia safe from the shifter menace, and to do it we have to know as much as we can about shifters and their magic."

"The shifter menace? How can you say that with a straight face? You're a friggin goblin!"

"Exactly. And a less menacing shifter would be hard to find. Dragons, on the other hand …"

"You can't just take out her channel stone." A few tendrils of blonde hair had escaped Faith's formal hairstyle, and now curled sweetly around her pale face. She looked about twelve years old. "What if it kills her?"

"If it kills her, there'll be one less dragon for the world to worry about. I should think you'd be pleased. Isn't she a rival of yours?" He watched with satisfaction as Faith was hooked up to various machines. Someone—an anaesthetist, presumably—placed a mask over her face while the others waited. I could hear the soft hiss of her breathing through the plastic. "But I doubt she's in any danger. Leandra died from other causes, not because you removed her stone. Why should the removal of such a small body part be a problem? It's not an essential organ. Nobody dies if you cut off their little finger, do they?"

That depended, didn't it? A werewolf would, if you used a silver knife. That was the point—they were mucking around with things they didn't understand. But he clearly wasn't in the mood to be persuaded.

Which left me to decide—did I let them go ahead or not? The collar bomb was no deterrent. Their human reflexes were no match for my dragon ones. I could be out of it before they'd even finished thinking about pressing their damned detonator.

No, the real deterrent was the threat to Garth. The minute silver broke his skin, he was a dead man walking. Would they really give the order to shoot if I broke free? How long would it take someone to give that order? How quickly would Garth's guards respond? Maybe they'd hesitate. Maybe Garth could dodge the first bullet. Was I fast enough to find him in time?

If only I could somehow cut the power, or at least fry the camera system. If it was dark when I slipped my collar, they might suspect it was more than a blackout, but they couldn't be sure. I could find Garth and break him out while his guards were still wondering what happened to the lights.

If I found the power board, I could easily cut the power and kill the lights. Then I could lose the collar with no one the wiser. But to kill the lights I first had to get out of the collar and escape this room. It was a Catch-22.

I swallowed hard, looking at Faith's face so pale against the clinical white operating table. The surgeon made a clean slice with the scalpel in line with her armpit, just above her left breast. It wasn't very long, perhaps five centimetres. I had only moments left to reach a decision.

Who was I kidding? It was no choice. Any stunt I pulled to save her meant almost certain death for Garth. So I gritted my teeth and watched as the surgeon slid a tiny electric cutting blade into the incision in her chest. The whine of the little saw sounded like a dentist's drill. The beep of the machine monitoring her heart rate was the only other sound in the room.

The whining cut off abruptly and the surgeon reached for something that looked like a long pair of tweezers, sliding them into the wound.

Patel leaned forward, his face alight with excitement, as the surgeon withdrew the tweezers and held them up, showing off the prize clenched in their grip: a black stone, smeared with blood. There was so much blood I couldn't see the delicate silver tracery, almost like veins, that I knew lay underneath, covering the black surface in pretty patterns. The only one of these I'd ever seen before was the one now lodged in my chest.

"Blood pressure's spiking," said one of the nurses.

The beeping picked up the pace.

"Heart rate's climbing too," said the anaesthetist.

Patel strode forward and took the bloody stone. "What's happening?"

Relieved of the stone, the surgeon began to stitch her up. I glanced at the monitor's screen, where coloured lines were swooping up and down in great jagged spikes. The beeping became even more frenzied.

Her head moved, and the anaesthetist grabbed at it before she could dislodge the tube he had in her throat.

"Christ, she's waking up." The surgeon sewed faster. "Keep her under, can't you?"

"I'm trying!" The anaesthetist turned to adjust the flow of drugs, and Faith's head began to thrash from side to side.

"Hold her!" the surgeon demanded, as her arms began to twitch.

"Put it back!" I said. "You're killing her."

"Nonsense," said Patel. He slid the bloody stone into the pocket of his lab coat and left the room without a backward glance at the drama he'd caused.

A nurse grabbed each arm, and it soon became obvious they were working hard to keep her still. The muscles of her arms strained against them, and her body bucked. The surgeon stepped back in shock, then hurriedly placed the last few stitches. Alarms now blared from the monitor, but no one was looking at it any more. All eyes were focused on the body thrashing wildly on the operating table.

"What the hell are you doing?" The surgeon glared at the anaesthetist. "She's going to break the stitches." He hadn't had a chance yet to dress the wound; he was too busy, like everyone else, trying to hold her still.

The anaesthetist reached for a syringe, but before he could get it into her she threw off the two nurses, sat bolt upright on the table and screamed.

Okay, that was my cue. No one was watching me any more. I was betting even the guys monitoring the camera feed were glued to the spectacle on the operating table.

Faith shoved the anaesthetist so hard he slammed into the trolley of surgical instruments and they both went down in a metallic crash. One nurse screamed, but the other was made of sterner stuff; she scrabbled on the floor for the syringe, now rolling under the table. But it was too late. Things were about to go from bad to very much worse.

I reached for my essence and felt a familiar warmth in my chest as the link opened through my channel stone. The two parts of myself yearned to join together in trueshape and I fought the urge to take my rightful dragon form. Instead I focused on pushing mass away as I held the feel of trueshape in my mind, as I'd done the night I'd fought the ala to free Luce from the warehouse. Then I'd struggled with the unnatural feeling, but now it came more easily. Practice makes perfect, as they say.

Between one heartbeat and the next I shrank to the size of a mouse, every scale and claw a perfect miniature. The collar clanked as it hit the floor, but no one noticed in the pandemonium that raged around the operating table. I scurried away from it and threw the link wide open, and the rest of my self came roaring through. In the blink of an eye the ceiling was brushing against my back, and a momentary panic surged in my veins. The room was too small; I was trapped.

Deep breath. Dragons aren't afraid of anything. This could work in my favour.

The nurse who'd gone for the syringe stood up, the needle clenched in a triumphant fist. Her mouth fell open.

"Dragon!" The syringe clattered to the floor from her boneless hand.

Heads had barely begun to turn as I slammed into the ceiling. Dragon scales are better than any armour, and a line of spikes ran down my spine from head to tail. Belatedly the collar bomb exploded, as someone realised what was happening, but the charge was too small to damage me in my present form. In a moment the point was moot anyway: the ceiling groaned, then collapsed. All the lights went out, and broken concrete tumbled down with a noise like thunder. The operating theatre disappeared in a cloud of concrete dust. I was pretty sure Faith could survive that, even in her weakened state, but I wasn't so certain about the others. I couldn't find it in myself to care.

I battered my shoulders against the ceiling, making the hole bigger, being careful to keep my wings folded safely out of the way. It was the work of seconds to make it big enough to climb through. Pieces of furniture rained down on me but I flicked them away. There was no one in the room, which was too small to fit me properly, so I lashed my tail at the wall to make space, exposing the corridor. Alarms began to shrill, but I ignored them and attacked the ceiling and tore another hole. I was counting on Garth being held captive on level three, same as I'd been. I only had seconds left to find him.

Someone screamed as I half-leapt, half-clambered my way into the new room. It was Corinne, cowering in the corner.

"Where's Garth?" I growled.

Her aura flared bright with fear. My dragon sight was enhanced even further in trueshape, and she blazed like a green fire as I opened a gaping hole in the wall to the corridor with my tail.

"That way." She pointed left. "Two doors along."

It might already be too late. I could only hope confusion was on my side. I leapt into the corridor and blasted the camera there to melted slag with dragonfire. Perhaps that would give me a few more seconds. A new alarm added itself to the noise and the sprinkler system burst into life.

Corinne followed me into the corridor, but hung well back as I slammed the door she'd pointed out back against the wall. There were two guards in the room. One turned toward the noise. Him I sent flying with a swipe of my clawed foot as I heaved my shoulders through the concrete and into the room. The door, which had swung crazily from one hinge, gave up the fight and subsided onto a heap of concrete rubble.

The other, after a terrified glance at me, turned and fired at Garth, still trapped in his silver-barred cage. His aim was wild, and Garth was diving to the floor even as he squeezed the trigger, but the bullet whizzed through his hair and shaved a red line across his scalp.

"No!" I screamed.

CHAPTER FOURTEEN

The bottom fell out of my world. All I could see was that thin red line. I incinerated the poor guard, lashing out in a frenzy of agony. He was only doing his job, but there was no compassion left in my dragon heart when I saw the look on Garth's face. He met my eyes, and the knowledge of the terrible death that was coming for him was there in the bleakness of his gaze.

I sprang forward and slashed through the bars of his cage like slicing through butter. Without even thinking I lashed out at his head. Not even a second had passed since the bullet grazed him; he still lay where he'd fallen, hands gathered beneath him ready to spring up again. My claw took a deep chunk out of his head, and his eyes, which had already turned the wild yellow of the wolf in his terror, rolled back in his head as blood began to spurt.

Next thing I was crouched naked at his side. I grabbed his suit jacket from the floor and crumpled it into a ball. I had nothing else to staunch the bleeding.

"Is he dead?" Corinne asked from the doorway. Her eyes darted nervously from Garth to the blazing body of the gunman on the floor between us.

"No." There was a lot of blood, but his chest still rose and fell. Head wounds were always messy. I pressed down hard. Had I cut too deep? He might bleed to death.

Not that I'd had much choice. He'd have been dead in a minute anyway. I'd had a fraction of a second to act, and no time for finesse. If I'd managed it right—*please, God, let it have worked!*—I'd cut away the affected flesh in time to stop the silver spreading its deadly poison through his body. I watched anxiously for the telltale spread of blackening veins under his skin, though there was so much blood on his face it was hard to tell.

"Come on, Garth," I muttered, willing him to live. He was the most ornery bastard I'd ever met, and I loved him beyond all reason.

My timing sucked. *Now* I realised this? When I was about to lose him?

Water from the sprinklers above pattered down on us and my wet hair straggled across my face. I sniffed and scrubbed at my eyes with the back of my bloodied hand. Not all of the water there was from the sprinklers. As I leaned over him droplets fell from the ends of my hair onto his face, and his eyes flickered open.

"Kate." His voice was hoarse. One hand rose to wipe gently at the tears on my cheeks. "Don't cry, beautiful."

"I'm sorry. I tried … I just couldn't get here fast enough. This is all my fault."

"Don't give me that bullshit. It's all these Jaeger arseholes' fault. Don't blame yourself." Blood ran out from under my makeshift bandage and mingled with the water trickling across his face. He grimaced. "My head's on fire."

His irises were huge and golden, not a speck of grey left. The wolf was terrified, though the man was trying to stay strong. He'd been there when Jerry died; he knew how terrible the silver death was.

"What a shitty way to go." Those golden eyes were mesmerising. I couldn't look away. He stared at me as if he was trying to memorise every line of my face. "I don't want to leave you."

Cold water rained down on my naked back as I crouched over him. Dragonfire crackled in my ear as it consumed the guard's body, the bright flames writhing in my peripheral vision. Rain and fire; blood and death: I shivered as I leaned closer. This couldn't be the end. Our breath mingled, our lips almost close enough to touch.

"Kiss me," he whispered.

I closed the distance between us and tasted blood, and then his mouth opened under mine and I was lost in a desperate, frantic passion. Too late, too late. Why had it taken so long to see what was right before me? The one man who could match me for ferocity, who understood what it was to be human and then irrevocably changed. The man who'd saved my life, as I'd saved his, who'd watched over me and worried for me and who'd always, always, been there when I needed him.

His strong arms crushed me against him and heat roared through me, even as tears slid from my closed eyes. I tasted their salt, mingled with the salt of his blood, and then his arms, so tight around me, loosened suddenly and fear came roaring back, sweeping passion away in an icy gust.

"Garth?" I reared back and watched his eyelids sag closed. I trembled, terror clawing at my gut. "Garth!"

I pressed shaking fingers against the pulse point in his neck. His heart beat strongly; he'd only passed out. Dizzy with relief, I checked his wound, probing gently. It wasn't long, but deep, gouged right into the bone of his skull. I couldn't see any brain matter, so that was something.

Had I done enough?

"Corinne." I beckoned her closer. She came, bedraggled in her soggy ball gown, her hair plastered to her head. Still, at least she had clothes. I was so cold I couldn't stop shaking.

I tapped the link within me, and let a dragon claw spring from my index finger. She jumped, then looked down as if embarrassed.

"Hold out your hands."

She held her cuffed hands steady, and I sliced the handcuffs away. They clanged to the wet floor and she shook her hands with relief.

"Keep pressing here."

I guided her hands to the spot, then stood. Garth's face was deathly pale under the blood, but there were no black lines. It had been quick when Jerry was shot. She'd swelled up in seconds, her veins turning black as the poison spread its agonising death through her body. Did that mean Garth was safe? But she'd had a silver bullet lodged inside her. Perhaps this would be slower. I hardly dared to hope, but how could I keep going without hope? I had to get him out of here.

I stripped the first guard of his bloodstained shirt and trousers and dressed quickly. Everything was wet, and the pants were too loose, but I cinched my borrowed belt tight. It would do. I'd probably have to take trueshape again before this was over, but in the meantime I felt better not walking around in my birthday suit. The other guard's body was already falling into ashes, the dragonfire dwindling away. Just as well there was nothing else in the bare concrete cell to burn, or the whole place might go up.

"Stay here with him," I told Corinne. "I won't be far. Call out if there's any change."

She nodded, her face almost as pale as Garth's, but determined.

I took the guard's gun and slipped out into the corridor. Shouts rose through the hole in the floor, but no one was stirring yet on this floor. Garth had probably been the only one to rate an actual live guard because of his use as leverage against me. A locked door would be enough to contain the others.

I chose a door at random and extended my claws. Leandra might have shot the lock, but she'd been comfortable with guns and I wasn't. They made it look simple in the movies, but where exactly were you supposed to aim? Claws were more reliable. I knew what I was doing with them.

Which was peeling the metal door like an apple, a strip bending back like skin. Luce's face appeared in the gap.

"Good. I was hoping it was you." I handed her the gun. "Do your thing."

She immediately took aim and blasted the lock. The noise reverberated in the concrete corridor. Luce could always be relied upon for violence in any flavour. The door swung open at a touch.

Wordlessly she held out her cuffed hands, and I freed her as I'd freed Corinne.

"Find the others."

She nodded and turned to the next door. I headed back to Garth, hope warring with terror inside me. Would I find the dreaded black lines creeping across his tortured body?

Corinne looked up as I entered. "The bleeding's stopped."

"Let me see."

Heart in my mouth, I dropped to the floor next to the still-unconscious werewolf and peeled away the blood-soaked jacket with shaking hands. It was still a nasty wound … but that was all. No black twisting veins, no hideous swelling.

I sat back on my heels and breathed a silent prayer of thanks, feeling warmth flood my heart like sunshine after a storm. The knot of dread in my gut began to unwind. In this new light his unconsciousness looked like a good sign—he'd fallen into the healing sleep his body needed to repair itself.

Now all I had to do was get him to safety. I could hear voices in the corridor, but it sounded like shifters calling to each other, voices raised in fear and anger. I thought I recognised Hope's brittle tones. For a police headquarters, or whatever this place was, there seemed to be a remarkable shortage of policemen.

Luce appeared in the doorway. "Shit, what happened to Garth?"

"Silver bullet. But it's okay," I added as she drew in a horrified breath. "He's fine."

Well, not fine exactly. He still had a hole in his head. But the fact that he'd stopped bleeding meant that his shifter healing had kicked in. Within twenty-four hours there'd be little to show how close he'd come to a gruesome death.

"How the hell—? Never mind, you can tell me later. We need to get moving."

I dragged Garth out of the cage, being careful not to let the broken silver bars brush against his skin.

"Did you find everyone?"

"Nearly. Don't know where Faith is. Her people said she was taken away a few hours ago. No sign of Blue, either."

I sighed. "Keep looking, we need to find Blue. But I don't think Faith will be coming with us."

An angry young man pushed his way past Luce. "Why not? Do you know where she is?"

He was built like a New Zealand rugby player, dark-skinned and massive. I didn't even need to see his aura to know that he was a troll. Luce looked like a child standing next to him.

"You're one of Faith's people?"

He folded arms that were thicker round than my thigh and scowled as if I were personally responsible for her disappearance. "That's right. Where is she?"

I pointed at the gaping hole in the corridor floor just beyond them. "Two floors down. They were doing some kind of experiments on her."

No need to mention the channel stone. A low-level shifter like him wouldn't know what it was anyway.

His dark face paled. "Is she alive?"

"Last I saw she was. Giving them hell, too."

He turned without a word and strode into the corridor, bellowing for his friends. Luce helped me carry Garth out of the room in time to see the troll and three equally massive friends leap into the hole.

"Where are they going?" Hope asked. Her wine-red gown was almost black now it was wet, and clung to her legs in a way that looked very uncomfortable. She and my other sisters were milling in the corridor with their followers like a herd of sheep. Yarrow waited by the door. Everyone looked at me, some with suspicion, others with hope. Valiant seemed more friendly towards me, but Hope looked as if she hadn't made up her mind yet.

"Looking for Faith. I saw her down there." She didn't need to know more than that. She had no more love for Faith than she did for me.

"What now?" Luce asked.

"The lifts are that way." Hope pointed. "Let's go."

"Seen any Jaeger men?" I asked Luce, ignoring Hope.

"None. Looks bad."

I nodded.

"What do you mean?" Hope asked, glaring at each of us in turn.

Bloody teenagers. The girl didn't have two brain cells to rub together. "It means that if they're not here shooting at us, they must be setting up to shoot us somewhere else. Somewhere they think gives them a better chance of bringing us down."

"Like when we get out of the lift," Luce said pointedly.

That stopped her for a minute. But only for a minute.

"Then we'll take the stairs."

Luce rolled her eyes.

"Look after Garth," I told her, and she nodded, slinging him over her shoulder as if he weighed nothing. She was so short his long legs nearly reached the ground.

"Better to take them by surprise," I said to Hope, and opened myself to my essence.

She stepped back abruptly, suspicion turning to fear, and took trueshape herself, but I had no intention of attacking her. I turned my attention to the ceiling as the corridor filled with dragons, no one wanting to be the last one left in vulnerable human form. Hope was gold, like most of the others. Valiant was a reddish shade I'd never seen before, a beautiful coppery bronze.

Together we battered through the ceiling. I hurled blocks of concrete and pieces of twisted steel away, sheltering my friends with my body. The boom of exploding concrete shook the building, and I wondered if we might bring the whole thing down on our heads. Yarrow and Luce manhandled Garth up in our wake, though Yarrow could have done it on his own. He'd taken a form that looked like a walking tree, tall and strong.

I spared a glance to make sure Corinne was following too, then turned back to the task at hand. One or more of my sisters had used dragonfire to make the job easier, and bits of flaming debris fell past. The lights flickered and went out as we smashed our way higher, but there was plenty of light for dragon eyes.

Flame glowered below us in the pit we'd made, like a scene from Dante's Inferno. Minus the naked writhing bodies, of course. Concrete dust hung in the air, adding to the otherworldly feel. Somewhere water gushed from a broken pipe, and I bared my teeth in a dragon smile. That would teach them to take on the shifters. Their little hidey-hole was destroyed. But where had the insects scurried to?

We smashed through into a bigger space with high ceilings. The roar of assault rifles greeted us, but their bullets glanced harmlessly off dragon scales. We were in the foyer of a large building, all massive pillars and high ceilings. Outside it was night, and I caught a glimpse of green through the glass walls, but the only interest I had in my surroundings now was to find and destroy the insects that buzzed at us. Their bullets could not be permitted to hurt the one I loved again. I roared, and the building shook with my displeasure. My body thrummed with power, and the joy of the hunt thrilled in my veins.

The insects were using the pillars as cover. I leapt forward and blasted the nearest group with dragonfire, burning out their little nest. The smell of scorched flesh filled my mouth with saliva and my heart with satisfaction. Around me my sisters were doing the same, and the roar of flame and the screams of terrified humans made sweet music together. The fools had chosen a bad place to make their stand. Here we had enough room to move. Perhaps they had thought our size would make us slow, but their lack of knowledge proved fatal.

The chatter of gunfire died away as we hunted through the flames and smoke. We were in our element, fast and unstoppable. Silver bullets meant nothing to us. Even grenades had little effect. This was joy; this was living. There was nothing like the taking of another life, the slash of claws and the spray of blood, to make one feel truly alive. We were death incarnate, sinuous, beautiful. None could stand before us.

One of my sisters took a blast at close quarters. Her scales still sparkled, stronger than steel, as she flowed forward to claim the life of the one who had opposed her. I watched with satisfaction as she tore off the man's head, his blood running red from her jaws. There was a reason dragons were the most feared of all the shifters. In trueshape, the only thing that could damage us was another dragon. It was time the humans remembered us. Remembered us and feared us.

Gradually I became aware that the crackle of flame was the only sound I could hear. No more gunfire. Not even any screams or groans. I looked around the devastated foyer, eyeing the other dragons hulking through the smoke. My sisters gazed back, gold or silver bodies shining, their reptilian eyes unblinking. No one wanted to be first to resume human form.

I certainly wasn't ready to die yet, so I kept trueshape as I padded over broken concrete and shattered floor tiles toward the massive hole I'd come through. Dead bodies lay all around and the smell of roasting flesh made my mouth water. I peered through the smoke into the dark depths of the hole.

An improbable sight met my eyes: a grizzly bear holding an unconscious man, cradling him like a baby. Luce was at his side, still in human form. Other familiar faces crept into view, including Blue, thank God.

"It's safe to come up now," I said, my voice rumbling deep in my chest. Smoke huffed from my nostrils as I spoke. I hoped it was true—I didn't think my sisters would attack my friends, with their own supporters equally vulnerable.

Luce nodded and leapt for the edge of the hole, spraying concrete dust and bits of debris on the people below as she hauled herself up. Then she turned and gestured to the grizzly, who passed Garth up to her. Despite her small size, she took his weight and laid him gently down.

Yarrow was next, still in grizzly form. A much more sensible choice than his previous treelike incarnation, given the fire all around. Trees and flames were not a good combination.

The pillar nearest the hole creaked ominously. Luce's gaze flicked around the smoke-filled foyer, assessing the damage.

"Hurry up," she called into the hole. "We'll be lucky if the ceiling doesn't come down on us."

My sisters had been a little overeager with the dragonfire. Everything that could have burned, had. At one point during the battle I'd felt a few drops of water as the sprinkler system tried to come on, but someone had blasted that too and melted all the sprinkler heads out of existence. Water was cascading down the far wall from a broken—or more likely melted—pipe in the ceiling.

Now, as my temper cooled, I began to regret all the charred corpses. But I hadn't been prepared to risk Garth anywhere near their silver bullets, and they'd shown no desire to stop firing until we'd made them. Had they known what they were signing on for when they joined Taskforce Jaeger? I didn't want a war with the humans, but pacifism isn't an option when your enemy is trying to take you down. Not unless your name's

Gandhi, and I would be first to admit that I wasn't in his league.

Outside I could hear sirens wailing in the distance. Fire engines or police—probably both. It was still dark beyond the glass walls of the foyer, many of them shattered by gunfire or dragon tails, and there was no one on the street. Not that I could see, anyway. It would be just my luck if there was someone hidden, filming the whole thing on their damned mobile phone. I was getting mighty tired of starring in Internet videos.

"Let's go," I said when my team was all gathered around me. Corinne and Blue huddled close together. The selkie woman's face was white beneath the heavy fall of her dark hair, and her evening gown certainly wasn't improved by scrambling over broken concrete. It had been a rough night for everyone. Blue was swaying on his feet. Even Yarrow looked tired as he shimmered back into human form and started stripping the clothes from a dead body.

When he was dressed he hoisted Garth into his arms again. The werewolf was still unconscious, which worried me, but he was breathing and I saw no sign of silver poisoning. That would have to do until we could get him somewhere safer.

My sisters were all reunited with their followers. Faith's people were still missing. I had no idea if they'd managed to free her, or what condition she was in, but I wasn't waiting around to find out.

A golden dragon moved to intercept us as we headed for the nearest door. Hope, as imperious-looking in trueshape as she was in human form.

"Where are you going?"

It wasn't quite a challenge. I was bigger than her, I was pleased to note, and I lashed my tail as I glared at her.

"Wherever I damn well please," I growled. "Are you going to stop me?"

She glanced over her shoulder at her sisters, but none of them moved. Welcome to the proving, sweetheart. It was every dragon for herself. Together they might have been able to take me down, but none of them trusted the others enough to join forces.

The sirens were growing louder. "I suggest you follow my lead and get out of here before reinforcements arrive." And cameras.

Hope didn't appear to like the idea of following anyone's lead, but the suggestion made such good sense she'd be a fool to ignore it. Valiant nodded her beautiful coppery head to me and shepherded her people out into the warm night without another word. Hope stepped aside, glowering, as we followed, but those sirens were close now, and she didn't waste too much time glaring. The others began to disperse behind us as we headed off down a side street.

"Where the hell are we?" Yarrow asked.

"Canberra," said Luce, who had a sense of direction like a homing pigeon. "That's Black Mountain over there. We'll need to find some wheels pronto if we're going to get back to Sydney by dawn."

We were in some kind of business park. Nothing but neat streets of office buildings surrounded us, with not a car in sight.

Taxis were out of the question, even if there'd been any around, with Garth in his current condition. Too many questions.

I looked at Garth, his face a pale blur in the dark. He was stirring, trying to wriggle his way out of Yarrow's arms. "Give him to me."

Yarrow stopped and gave me an uncertain look. I reared up on my hind legs and took the groggy werewolf gently in my front claws.

"Put me down," he muttered. "I can walk."

"Bullcrap. A newborn puppy could beat you in a fight."

"I just need a bit of food and I'll be fine."

He was well enough to argue. Definitely not dying, then. My heart swelled with joy.

"Keep still," I hissed. Stupid werewolf needed someone to take care of him.

"What are you doing?" Luce's voice was sharp.

"I'm not wandering around out here with my homicidal sisters on the loose and half the police force as well." A blue light flashed past the end of the street as a police car headed for the building we'd just left. A plume of smoke spiralled into the dark sky above it, visible over the tops of the buildings between us. "I need to get Garth to safety."

I spread my wings. Luce gave me a shocked look.

"You're going to *fly* home?"

"Why not? It's a three-hour drive. I can fly it in two."

"But someone might *see* you."

She'd had centuries of living with the queens' edicts. The oldest taboo of all was showing yourself in trueshape anywhere humans might see you. And for centuries that taboo had kept the shifter world safely hidden.

"Luce. I'm so popular on YouTube already I've got channels dedicated to me. I think we've gone beyond the point of observing the old rules."

Commander Wilson had been conspicuously absent from the battle in the foyer, as had that goblin traitor Patel. Taskforce Jaeger had known enough about us already to turn up at Gideon Thorne's house and take us all in, easy as rounding up sheep. Hiding didn't seem to be an option any more.

And I was sick of being a sheep. I spread my wings and leapt skyward.

CHAPTER FIFTEEN

I kept an eye on the horizon as I flew. I'd headed due east to get myself over the sea as quickly as possible. No point starting a new shifter panic if I could avoid it. Canberra had glittered below me as I passed, its neat circles and grids of streetlights showing the care with which the city had been laid out. It was still a hole, and cold as a dragon's heart in winter, but at least it was easy to navigate around.

There was no sign of the grey before dawn yet, but I knew it couldn't be far away. Elizabeth's home—now mine—was on the very eastern edge of Sydney. With a bit of luck I could drop down out of the night sky with no one the wiser. Just as well I'd had Blue adjust the security spells already to attune them to me instead of Elizabeth, otherwise World War III would erupt when a strange dragon touched down in her garden.

I flew as high as I could without causing trouble for Garth. He was too precious to me to risk any further. Werewolves were sturdy creatures, but they weren't completely impervious to cold, and at the speed I was travelling the wind tore at us.

Damn Wilson and his pet goblin. The evening had been going so well—Thorne dead and my sisters, if not enthusiastic about the idea of sharing the domain, at least not outright rejecting it.

Instead of which, here I was, flying home with an injured werewolf clutched in my claws, the rest of my team reduced to car theft. Not the triumphant end to the evening I'd hoped for. I reckon I could have talked my sisters round given a little more time. Perhaps I still could. And there was probably one less of them to split with now.

Poor Faith. Was she even still alive? And if she was, what kind of state was she in? What Patel had done to her was sickening. She'd had no chance to prepare as Leandra had. Leandra had been a willing participant in the removal of her channel stone, forcing her essence into the stone so that she could colonise my body once I'd swallowed it. Poor Faith had been unconscious when hers was ripped from her chest, and I was very much afraid that that meant the stone was now nothing more than a pretty trinket, and Faith's connection to her essence had been severed forever. She could never take trueshape again. What did that make her now? Not a dragon, that's for sure. Certainly not a queen in the making any more. It might have been kinder to kill her than condemn her to such a half-life.

Garth stirred as the glow of Sydney came into view, and I finally faced the subject I'd been avoiding all this way: Garth and my new feelings for him. Everything had seemed so clear, so sharp, as I stared into his golden eyes amid the wreckage of the silver-barred cell. Now doubts were starting to creep in. I stared grimly at the horizon and that glowing city, my wing muscles burning with the labour of the long flight. I'd only known him a short time—could I really be so sure he was my soulmate? Plus he was my employee. That could make for some awkward situations.

And then there was Ben.

I headed even further out to sea, till the glow of the city was just a smudge on the horizon. I might show up on the radar at Sydney airport, but I didn't want them getting a look at me.

What should I do about Ben? I still loved him too, didn't I? It didn't feel the same as what I felt for Garth, but it was still love. I wouldn't even be here if it wasn't for Ben. He'd saved my life, taking the blow Jason had meant for me. How could I cast him aside so soon? He'd think it was just dragon libido hankering after a new conquest. And maybe he'd be right, in a way. There was no doubt I'd changed. I experienced new heights of emotion every day—lust, hate, and a white-hot rage that terrified me. Dragon emotions were as powerful as were dragons themselves. And there was no doubt that dragons didn't view sex and relationships in the same way that humans did.

The two sides of my personality struggled to find a compromise that I could live with, but Ben didn't seem prepared to live with any kind of compromise. Ben had been a rock to cling to as my whole life was torn apart and put back together in a different shape, the only familiar face in a world gone crazy. For that I would be forever grateful. But he couldn't seem to accept that I'd been changed by what I'd gone through. He still wanted the old Kate, and rejected any signs of the new one. No matter how much I tried, I couldn't give him what he wanted. I simply wasn't the person Ben had fallen in love with any more. I was both more and less than that woman, and she was gone forever.

I turned homeward as the horizon behind me began to lighten with the first faint hint of dawn approaching. Talk about cutting it fine. Not that a big city like Sydney ever truly slept, but there'd be people up and about already, shift workers heading for work, maybe even fitness freaks out jogging in the cool pre-dawn. It couldn't be helped. I'd just have to take my chances of being spotted.

Arrowing down out of the east, I scanned the shoreline for Elizabeth's palatial home. It stood proud on the edge of its cliff, looking out over the ocean. The grounds were well lit. That was a good thing when you were trying to fend off intruders, but not so great when you were trying to sneak in. Hopefully the neighbours were all good sleepers.

I settled on the grass by the fountain, letting Garth down gently. He groaned and rolled into a sitting position. I released trueshape and knelt beside him. Wordlessly he reached for my hands as two figures raced from the house.

"Took you long enough," I said to Steve. "What if I'd been Gideon Thorne invading?"

"I can tell the difference between a black dragon and a gold one," he said, but he wasn't looking at me. "God, what happened to him?"

Garth did look pretty scary, his face a mask of dried blood.

"Where's everyone else?" asked Dave, helping Garth to his feet. The big werewolf staggered and Dave wedged a shoulder into his armpit, helping to prop him up.

Steve and Dave both had the tight expressions of professional men expecting bad news and trying not to show their anxiety. They kept their gazes firmly on Garth, avoiding my naked body. Such gentlemen. It was something you had to get used to when you worked with shifters. Kasumi was the only shifter I'd ever met who could take clothes with her when she changed forms. Garth had no such compunction about staring at me.

"I've always had a thing for redheads," he said, in that chatty way common in the truly drunk. Guess a blow to the head could have the same effect. He seemed to be having trouble focusing.

Steve and Dave exchanged a startled glance.

"It's the head wound." *Please shut up, you idiot.* They'd already seen us holding hands. "He's not quite himself. And the others are on their way home from Canberra." *I hope.*

"Canberra?"

"We had an unexpected detour. Taskforce Jaeger crashed the party at Thorne's house. They had silver ammo, so it was a little hard to resist their invitation to visit."

"Shit." Steve rocked back on his heels, meeting my gaze for the first time.

"We didn't lose anyone," I assured him. "But Garth got shot, and I had to rip a chunk out of his head to save him."

"You *saved* him?" Both of them stared at me now, never mind manners, wearing identical shocked expressions.

"Well, I know he's annoying," I said, deliberately misunderstanding, "but I've got kind of used to having him around."

"You said they were using silver bullets. Werewolves always die of silver." Steve looked back at Garth as if to assure himself that the big werewolf really was alive.

"Sorry to disappoint you." That sounded more like the Garth we knew. He explored his bloodstained head with tentative fingers.

"How do you feel?" I asked.

He didn't answer for a long moment, and I had to look away from the intensity of his gaze. That look spoke of things that couldn't be addressed in front of Steve and Dave. Things that maybe I wasn't ready to face at all.

"I owe you my life. Again." Then he broke the solemn moment with a lopsided grin. "And I feel like shit. But at least I'm alive to feel like shit."

"Get some rest." Werewolves were exceptional healers, as long as they were given enough rest and protein to work with. A good feed and a decent sleep would work wonders for him. And maybe for me too. I needed time to think.

I motioned for them to lead the way into the house. They might be gentlemen, but I knew where their eyes would be if my naked butt was walking in front of them. Especially Garth's.

Ben met us just inside the door, a dressing gown draped over his arm.

"I thought I heard voices." He held it while I shrugged into it. "Saw you out here."

"Thanks." He held out his arms and I stepped into his embrace a little stiffly, conscious of Garth watching.

It was uncanny: I could *feel* where he was, as if an invisible cord connected us. Dave helped him up the stairs, and he didn't look back, but I could see the tension in his thick neck and the way he carried his broad shoulders high.

Ben saw me watching Garth and raised a questioning eyebrow.

I sighed. "I need coffee. Come into the kitchen."

Steve came too, since he was next in command with both Luce and Garth out of action temporarily. By the time I'd filled them in on the events of the night, sunlight lay warm across the kitchen tiles and I'd drunk three cups of coffee. Dave cooked breakfast and sent a tray of bacon the size of the great outdoors up to Garth's room. I made a fairly decent dent in the world supply of bacon myself. Flying sure worked up an appetite.

At last I pushed my plate away, the bacon and the story all finished. "So what's been happening here? Anything?" *Has there been any news about Lachie?* But I didn't ask that. I knew there wouldn't be any good news until I created it myself.

Ben shook his head. "All quiet. Wonder what the official line is on your demolition job in Canberra?"

"See if there's anything on the news," I said to Steve, and he turned on the TV that hung on the far wall. Dave liked to watch it while he cooked. Steve flicked between the various morning shows till he found one giving the news.

"—has died in a house fire in Sydney's west overnight," the newsreader was saying. "Neighbours alerted the fire brigade at two o'clock this morning after hearing the sound of glass shattering, but by the time they arrived the house was well alight. Our reporter has more on this story."

They crossed to the scene, where the reporter stood in front of a blackened shell that had probably once been a neat brick bungalow like the houses on either side.

"I'm here in Church Street outside the home of fifty-one-year-old mother of two Elise Woods. Mrs Woods was home alone last night when someone threw what police believe to have been a Molotov cocktail through her front window. Neighbours heard the sound of breaking glass and a car leaving the scene at high speed. Next-door neighbour Geoff Burrows was first on the scene. Geoff, can you tell me what happened last night?"

Geoff looked like he hadn't slept. His stubbly face held the expression of a man who's seen things he would rather forget.

"Yeah, I was in bed with the wife when a noise woke me up. Sounded like glass breaking. And then I heard the squeal of tyres." He gestured vaguely behind him. "Our bedroom's at the front of the house, so I looked out but I couldn't see nothing, and then I smelled the smoke. So I come outside and Elise's house is alight. I tried to get in, to see if anyone was there, but the flames were too much, you know?"

He rubbed a hand across his bald head, his face anxious, and it was then that I noticed the bandages on his hands. "I was yelling at the missus to call the fire brigade, and screaming out to Elise. Her bedroom was at the front too, same as ours. I tried, I really did. Burnt me hands." He shook his head. "That poor woman. She was a lovely lady, much nicer than the last one. I can't understand why anyone would do this to her."

Ben made a strangled sound, and I turned away from the poor man on the TV trying to convince himself that he'd done everything he could to try to save his neighbour.

"What?"

He was staring at the screen, a look of horror on his face.

"Did you know her?" I racked my brain. Should I have heard of Elise Woods? Or Geoff whatever-his-name-was?

"No."

The TV news moved on to the now-familiar story of the demonstrators picketing Parliament House. Some thought the new anti-shifter laws were the first steps on the slippery slope to dictatorship; others thought they weren't harsh enough and were agitating for the death penalty. There were a lot of angry faces on the TV.

"I didn't know her," said Ben, "but I know that house. I'm betting she hadn't lived there very long."

"Why?"

"Because it used to belong to a rusalka named Melina."

"How do you know?"

"I was a herald for ten years. I've delivered to just about every shifter in Sydney."

Right. It was hard sometimes to remember there'd ever been anything before our current bizarre existence, always running and fighting. I'd been an ordinary person myself, living in a house not much different from the one we'd just seen smouldering on the TV.

"Melina was one of Valeria's people. I bet she did a runner when Valeria went down, and this poor woman moved in instead."

"What are you saying? You think the attackers meant to kill Melina?"

"It makes more sense, doesn't it? Why firebomb the house of some suburban mum? You heard the guy—she was *much nicer* than the last woman who lived there. Rusalkas don't make the best neighbours."

"But why would anyone be trying to kill Melina?" Steve objected. "No one's going after Valeria's supporters. She's out of the game."

"No *shifters* would be trying to kill her." He gestured at the scene on the TV now, where people chanted and waved their hate-filled signs. "But what about them? There's some nutjob frothing under every rock you turn over these days. I bet someone remembered the scary lady in Church Street and decided she was a witch or something."

I sighed. "A werewolf, probably. They all seem to be obsessing over werewolves."

Weren't we all?

"Right. So they lob a Molotov cocktail through her window and go off congratulating themselves on a job well done. No more werewolf. Except they didn't bother to check first if she still lived there."

God. I closed my eyes. That poor woman. If he was right, she'd died for nothing. And I thought shifters were bad. Humans could be just as violent and hateful.

"Turn it off."

Steve clicked off the TV, and we sat in silence for a moment. If people could do this on a mere suspicion, what might they do if they ever found proof? The old queens had been right to keep the shifter world hidden. Shifters were powerful, but there were so many more humans. They might be ants in comparison, but enough ants could pick clean even the corpse of an elephant.

And these ants came with pitchforks and torches. Welcome back to the Middle Ages. What next? Witch trials? Parliament seemed to be heading that way with their new laws. I'd say they were draconian but that wasn't even funny.

"Well, there's nothing we can do about it," I said, "except warn everyone to lay low."

"Says the woman who just flew into Sydney in trueshape." Ben gave me an exasperated look. "What the hell were you thinking?"

Déjà vu. Ben was mad with me again for taking trueshape. The way he was looking at me right now, you'd think he didn't even like me. It was a slap in the face every time, reminding me how much he hated something that was a part of me.

"Maybe I was thinking that I needed to get Garth to safety."

"That bonehead is indestructible. By tomorrow he'll be bouncing around like nothing ever happened." Back to that again. Shifter strength—particularly werewolf strength—was a bitter demon that gnawed at Ben's soul.

"What is your problem? Are you *jealous* of Garth?" This was treading on dangerous ground. What was the matter with me? Was I *trying* to provoke him? The dragon side of me was tired of all this pussyfooting around.

"Of course I'm jealous of Garth! He's a friggin *werewolf*." He threw his arms up in frustration. "He goes everywhere with you. He protects you. He's *useful.*"

And he doesn't look at me as if he'd tasted something nasty every time I take trueshape.

"You should be worrying more about yourself," he continued. "Don't we have enough to deal with without you leading the foaming nutcases straight to our door?"

I shoved my chair back, swallowing an angry reply. I couldn't deal with this now.

"I'm going to get some sleep. Wake me when Luce and the others get back."

CHAPTER SIXTEEN

I jolted awake as Ben laid a hand on my shoulder.

"Sorry, I didn't mean to startle you."

"What time is it?" I'd pulled the blinds, but a thin streak of bright white light glared through the gap at the bottom. Still daytime, then. For a moment I'd been afraid I'd slept the day away.

"Just after eleven. Luce is back."

"She's just got back now? That was a long trip."

"No, she's been back a while, but I thought you needed the sleep."

I frowned. I'd left orders to be woken as soon as she arrived. It wasn't his place to decide something different. I shut my eyes again and drew a deep breath. Sometimes the rage caught me by surprise. It seemed to be always simmering just below the surface. Did all dragons feel this way, or was it just me, with my screwed-up head?

Take a chill pill, Kate. He's not your thrall. But there was so much to do. Had everyone but me forgotten about Lachie, still in the claws of that bitch Daiyu? I bet no one was fussing over how much sleep *he* needed. I didn't have time to lie around.

"Everyone okay?" Firmly I shoved the rage back down into the dark recesses of Leandra's dragon sense of entitlement.

"They're fine. Luce stomped off to check on Garth, and pronounced herself satisfied with his condition. She's off making Steve's life miserable in the comms room now, trying to work out how she can beef up security."

That would be my fault, I guess. She too was worried about what I might have led to our door with my flight home. Bet the radar operators at Sydney airport were still scratching their heads.

"A herald came while you were asleep, too. Kasumi—"

"Kasumi?" I bounced off the bed as if it were a trampoline, my fury returning. Kasumi had been here and he hadn't thought to wake me? "She came again?"

"No, no. It wasn't Kasumi. A real human herald with a *message* from Kasumi."

That was almost as bad. "Where is it?"

He handed me an envelope. Already open. I glared at him. Not even another dragon would dare open the queen's mail. Who did he think he was?

Geez, what was wrong with me? I must be more tired than I'd thought. Usually I had better control. I drew a shaky breath, struggling for calm, and lifted the flap of the envelope.

"Be careful," he said. "There's some hair in there."

Hair? Gently I withdrew the paper. Three dark hairs lay within its fold. Kasumi's? Why was she sending me her hairs? Quickly I scanned the note.

Daiyu's pilots on standby at the Airport Hilton. Thralls. No contact until there are orders for them.

That was it. No mention of the hairs. The writing scrawled across the page, as if she'd been in a hurry. No signature. I frowned, chewing over the possibilities. Did she mean me to abduct them? But what good would that do if they were thralls? They'd only take orders from Daiyu, or someone she'd deputised.

"Why do we need Daiyu's pilots anyway? And what's with the hair?" Ben said. "I assume she means for us to steal Daiyu's plane, but why would we risk that when we could catch a commercial flight, or take our own private jet?"

I sat down on the edge of the bed and read the note again. She certainly wasn't big on detail. But if Kasumi had the authority to pass orders on to these pilots …

"The commercial flights are probably always monitored. If not, they certainly would be now, with Daiyu up to her traitorous neck in plots. That goes double for private jets. Probably the only way to get into Japan without being picked up is in Daiyu's own plane, disguised as someone they would expect to be using it."

"But what if Daiyu discovers it's gone? All it would take would be one phone call and you'd be walking into a death trap the minute you landed."

"True." *No contact until there are orders for them.* "But the note basically says Daiyu only bothers with the plane and its pilots when she wants to use it. As long as she has things to amuse herself with in Sydney, she won't even know it's gone. You can stay here and cover for me. Ramp up the preparations for the coronation. She won't be going anywhere while there's still a chance she can get to me before I get that crown on my head."

"Stay here?" You'd think I'd asked him to eat raw sewage. "While you go off to assault the Japanese queen's stronghold singlehanded? I'm not letting you go alone."

He wasn't *letting* me? Rage boiled in my chest. "As if you have any choice."

"*What* did you say?"

A terrible silence filled the room. Each of us stared at the other as if we were strangers. I had a sense of teetering on the brink of something momentous, something there was no going back from.

"I said you have no choice. I am the queen and I decide." My words were clipped; there was no disguising the anger simmering inside me.

"Spoken like a true dragon." The way he said "dragon" made it sound like a swear word.

I took the step into the abyss.

"If you hate dragons so much, what are you doing here?"

He laughed, a brittle sound. "I've been wondering that myself. I thought I was here for Kate." His mouth twisted. "But I don't know where she's gone."

Falling, falling. I'd never seen that look in his dark eyes before.

"Every time you take trueshape, you change a little more. It's like a drug, an addiction, isn't it? You just can't stop, whatever the consequences. You won't be happy until you bring down the world on our heads. Go be a dragon, then. Play with your shifter friends. I've seen how you look at that werewolf."

A shaft of guilt pierced my anger. "This is not about Garth. This is about us."

"What us? There's only you, running off, saving the world or damning it, while I wait here and wonder if you're coming back. Do you even care about us?"

"I do care. I care about you." But not enough. Not in the way he meant. I took a deep breath. "But I don't think this is working."

His shoulders sagged, and he turned away abruptly.

"I don't think it is either." His voice was so quiet I barely caught the words.

I stared at his rigid back, contemplating might-have-beens. If we'd found each other sooner, when I'd still been fully human. If I'd never gone on that courier job to Leandra's house.

But then I would never have gotten Lachie back, and whatever this change meant for me personally, I couldn't regret the circumstances that had brought Lachie back to me. After believing him dead for seven months, to hold him in my arms again had been one of the greatest moments of my life.

This relationship with Ben had been doomed before it even began. Once Leandra had forced me to swallow that channel stone, I'd been on a one-way ride that there was no getting off. The old Kate had been gradually slipping away even before we'd had our first kiss.

"I'll get out of your hair," he said at last. "I'll go to ground somewhere so no one can use me against you." When he turned around his face was a mask. "I hope you get Lachie back safely."

"I hope so too." I stared helplessly at him. What now? Did I kiss him goodbye? That closed-in face said no. But it didn't seem right to just walk away.

He solved the problem by stalking into the walk-in wardrobe. I stood for a moment, listening to him rustling around taking clothes off hangers and out of drawers, then looked down at the note I still held.

Yes. Getting Lachie back was my first priority. What sort of mother thought about her stupid, messed-up love life when her son needed her? That one curly-headed little boy meant more to me than anyone else in the world.

I strode from the room, Kasumi's letter and her hairs clutched in a tight fist, and went to find Blue.

He was in the comms room with Luce and Steve and the two thralls on duty. He had a mutinous look on his face and brightened when he saw me come in.

"Tell this stupid wyvern I can't sow the whole property with dragon's teeth," he demanded. "Does she have any idea how much work that would be? And it would be a complete waste of time given the bindings we've done already."

"He can't sow the whole property with dragon's teeth." Blue flashed a triumphant grin at Luce. "Because I have another job that's more important."

The grin slipped a little, and Luce's tight expression relaxed into the hint of a smile.

"What job is that?"

"You will make a seeming for me."

Luce's smile faded at my expressionless tone, but I ignored her. *Focus on what needs to be done. Lachie first.*

Blue took the envelope suspiciously. "Whose hairs are they?"

"Kasumi's."

"The kitsune?" He peeked into the envelope with more interest. "Only three. It won't make much potion. Enough for maybe ten hours. What are you planning? Will that be long enough?"

The potion had to last me from the moment I arrived in Japan until I'd managed to free the kitsune hostages and steal their hoshi no tama back from wherever Daiyu had hidden them. Ten days might be enough. Ten hours was impossible.

"It will have to be."

CHAPTER SEVENTEEN

We got out of the car on the side of a dirt four-wheel-drive track high in the Blue Mountains. Gum trees crowded close to the road, and there was nothing to show that this spot was any different to anywhere else we'd passed on the long drive. This far from hot and muggy Sydney, the air had a chill to it; even in summer the mountains were high enough to stay relatively cool.

That didn't mean things never heated up around here, of course. I eyed the undergrowth, taller than my head, with misgiving. We were only about half an hour from where Alicia's old place had stood before Valeria burned her out, and the memory of that fire was still strong.

Fortunately there was no hint of smoke in the air today as we plunged off the track and into the bush, following Blue. Luce had stayed behind today, working on all the protocols for the coronation. Unlike the rest of us, she'd lived long enough to have actually been to one before. Steve was here in her place, and Garth, barely recovered from his brush with silver but refusing to be left behind, brought up the rear.

Having him here was my one concession to weakness. Ben was gone. Everyone knew it, though no one mentioned it. As if he'd died, people tiptoed around me, carefully avoiding any mention of his name.

If I'd had any sense I would have insisted Garth stay behind. His presence was distracting, when I needed to stay focused, but I also needed the comfort of knowing he had my back.

We followed a path of sorts, but it was so faint and winding I couldn't have kept to it without Blue to lead the way. It looked like it had been made by a drunken chicken, meandering over sandstone outcrops, climbing up and down. One minute it was bare dirt, the next it would disappear under drifts of leaves, or dive into the bracken. Leaves and sticks crunched under my feet as we walked; the bush was dry, everything crying out for water.

I glanced over my shoulder at Garth as we descended a steep slope and felt an instant lift in my spirits as he gazed steadily back, warmth in those grey-blue eyes. A slash of shiny new pink skin where no hair grew was the only sign of how close to death he'd come.

"How the hell did Ben find this place?" I wasn't going to pretend that he'd never existed, even if everyone else did.

I'd be hard-pressed already to find my way back to the road. The tree trunks all looked the same, the unrelenting grey-green of the Australian bush pressing in on us, suffocatingly close. Yet somehow Ben had unearthed Blue from this little hidey-hole, without any shifter skills to help him.

"I gave him directions," said Garth evenly.

"Really?" I stumbled on a rock and had to face front again. Carrying on a conversation was tricky. Blue was setting a punishing pace, as if he was keen to get there and get this over with. "Was Blue here when you got him to come and take the traps off my old house?"

The goblin was so far ahead that for a moment I wondered if he was trying to give us the slip. But Steve was on his tail, and of course hiding from a werewolf's nose was an exercise in futility anyway. Nevertheless I stepped up the pace, my leg muscles protesting at the workout.

"No. But he's been up here a lot since he's been hiding out from his clan. Jason winkled him out originally. He sent me up here after him."

This was news to me, though clearly Leandra hadn't known everything Jason was up to, or she wouldn't have wound up dying and looking for a new body to colonise. The fact that he'd had dealings with a goblin mage and kept it from her was the kind of information that could have saved her life.

"When was this? Recently?"

"Months ago. Before Leandra and Jason split up."

Something in the werewolf's tone made me stop and turn around. He nearly walked into me, so close I could smell his sweat. I fought the urge to touch him.

"And what happened once you found him?"

"Nothing. I gave him a message."

No, there was more to the story than that. Garth was too honest to make a good liar.

"About what?"

"I don't know. I wasn't going to read Jason's messages, was I?"

"But you must have some idea. Why was he keeping it from Leandra?"

"I didn't know he was. The two of them were so tight … It wasn't like me and Leandra were best buddies or anything. We didn't talk unless she was giving orders."

Garth never said "you" when he talked about Leandra. Luce was much more likely to act as if I were just a continuation of her dragon mistress in a convenient new body, but Garth was different. There was a clear delineation between the two of us in his head. I should be so lucky.

"And that was it? That was the only contact he had with Blue?" There was more to this and I wasn't moving from this spot until I'd gotten to the bottom of it.

He sighed. "We're getting left behind."

"So? You know the way." I folded my arms.

"God. Has anyone ever told you you're a nagger?"

"Jason. All the time. Now tell me what it is that's so obviously under your skin and get it over with."

He glared at me, but I'd been glared at by experts and I wasn't cowed by a grumpy werewolf.

"Fine. Blue gave me a parcel to take back to Jason." He looked down at the rock-strewn trail. "I think I delivered the bane leaf that killed Leandra."

Ouch. No wonder he looked so hangdog. For a loyal guy like Garth, that would be a hard thing to live with. He looked up, and his grey eyes were clouded with pain.

"I'm the reason your life is so screwed up." His deep voice was gruff. "I'm sorry, Kate."

Poor bastard. He looked so guilty I couldn't stop myself. I closed the gap between us and wrapped my arms around him. He froze for a startled moment, then he crushed me against him and buried his face in my hair.

"Garth, you idiot," I mumbled into his chest, "how is it your fault that Jason's a backstabbing bastard?"

"I should have known. It smelt funny. If I'd said something …"

He was still crushing me. His arms were like steel bands. I pushed on his chest till he loosened his hold and let me breathe again. His lips were so close. If I just stood on tiptoe …

I stepped back abruptly. Lachie first. The mess I'd made of my love life could wait.

"A week later he sent me back up here with orders to kill Blue."

That sounded so like Jason. No loose ends.

"Why didn't you?"

"Blue and I go way back. He helped me once when no one else would. I told Jason he was gone. And then Jason planted that bomb and suddenly I wasn't taking orders from him any more."

Strange that Jason had resorted to the bombing if he'd had bane leaf already. The poison would have been much easier for someone living in Leandra's house, sharing her bed. Perhaps Valeria had demanded something that made more of a statement as a demonstration of his commitment. They'd nearly killed Luce as well in that debacle.

Suddenly I came out of my thoughts and realised how close Garth still stood. His wild wolf scent mixed with the clean fragrance of eucalyptus, creating a heady mixture.

"We'd better catch up with the others." But I didn't move. Couldn't move.

"Kate. You know how I feel about you. And the way you kissed me, I know you feel it too." His voice was husky with need. "I'll do anything for you, be anyone you need—"

"Hush." I put my fingers on his mouth to stop him. I couldn't deal with this now. Even that much contact sent a buzz of excitement arrowing straight to my groin. Damned dragon sex drives. I wanted nothing more than to tear his clothes off right there. But it was more than a purely physical longing. I couldn't bear to look too closely at my feelings for him, not so soon after Ben. "I can't—I have to focus on Lachie right now. Only Lachie. Do you understand what I'm saying?"

He nodded, grey eyes serious. Well, that was good, because I hardly knew what I was saying myself. The inside of my head was a serious mess, between fear for Lachie, regret over Ben, my sisters, the coronation, the problem with the kitsune … I just couldn't manage another relationship and all its complications right now. Even if I felt that if I didn't have this man soon I would die.

"I can wait," he growled, and the heat in that promise nearly melted my resolve.

I spun and headed off blindly in the direction Steve and Blue had taken. In the end Garth had to take the lead as the trail petered out. I felt a tingle as he brushed past me, and drew a long, shuddering breath. Enough. *Focus, dammit.*

We heard voices, and found Blue and Steve waiting by a low rocky outcrop.

"There you are," Steve said with relief. "I told Blue he was going too fast."

"It's fine," I said. "Let's keep moving."

Blue laughed. "But we're here."

Where? I couldn't see anything that looked like a cave, just blank rock walls. A couple of little crannies that might have made a cave for a small animal, but nothing goblin-sized.

Then Blue turned and walked straight into the rock and disappeared.

"Shit!" said Steve. "How did he do that?"

Garth stepped up to the rock face and calmly inserted his arm. It disappeared up to the elbow, as if it had been hacked off. Looking at it gave me the horrors.

"It's an illusion."

Blue's face suddenly thrust out of the rock. I squeaked and jumped back. He grinned at my reaction. "You going to stay out there all day, or are you coming inside?"

He disappeared again, and I looked at Garth. "If you can't see through the illusion, how did you ever find this place?"

"Don't need to see. The whole place stinks of goblin." He tapped his nose. "Gotta trust the nose."

I stepped forward, but couldn't help shutting my eyes at the last moment. With my eyes open, it was very hard to persuade my brain that I wasn't about to headbutt a rock wall. Now I knew how Harry Potter felt trying to get onto Platform 9¾.

Despite what my eyes told me, there was no physical sensation as I entered the cave. I looked back once I was inside. From this side the illusion was invisible. The cave mouth was completely open. I could see Steve still standing there as clear as day, not a thing between us. And then I had to scramble out of the way as he nearly trod on me, since he couldn't see me standing there gawking and blocking the entrance.

It wasn't a very wide opening, just big enough for two people to stand side by side. More of a fissure in the rocks than a cave. I could see a slice of blue sky above us. But that slice soon narrowed and disappeared as I followed Garth's broad back deeper in.

The light disappeared too as the floor fell away and we edged cautiously down a slope. Behind me Steve stumbled. His eyes weren't adapted for the dark as ours were, though even I was having trouble until a soft green glow sprang up.

By its light I saw the tunnel had widened into a cavern with a few dead stalactites hanging from the roof. Somewhere close I heard the faint trickle of water, but this cavern was dry. The green light came from small glass bowls lined up along a natural shelf in the cave wall, each flickering with what looked like candlelight but cast too much radiance for candles. Probably some kind of goblin magic. They'd been cave dwellers and miners long before they discovered the delights of housing estates with pools and tennis courts.

Arranged among the lights was a huge range of containers. Some were glass and looked old and dusty. Others were Tupperware, labelled in neat handwriting. The modern age had come to goblin mages as it had to the rest of the shifters. Some might have held food, but most were probably the tools of his trade, judging by the labels on the ones I could read.

I moved closer, scanning the line, but didn't see one in particular.

"Got any bane leaf here?" I asked.

Blue snorted. "Don't you know how rare that stuff is?"

"I hear you were selling it not so long ago."

"My last customer bought my whole stock."

"And that was Jason, right?"

He cast a quick glance at Garth. "Might have been."

A small camp bed was set up against one wall, and a couple of plastic crates held tinned food and basic camping supplies. It wasn't exactly palatial.

"How long have you been out here?"

"I come and go."

"But why here? You're a goblin mage."

Half his clan was living it up on the Gold Coast. As a mage he should be raking the money in, even without the support of his clan.

"I'm a wanted man. I refused to be the slave of my clan any more. Funnily enough, they didn't like the idea of their gravy train drying up. Some of them might have actually had to work." His mouth twisted into a bitter line. "They had me chained like a prisoner, constantly watched. I had one chance to break out, and I took it, but they'll never stop hunting me."

"Couldn't you use a seeming and hide somewhere better than this?" Garth's tone showed his opinion of the sad little refuge.

Blue's eyes glittered in the eerie green light. "Maybe I like the quiet, away from shifters and their ignorant questions."

And maybe there were too many pairs of goblin glasses like his out in the world for a seeming to hide him effectively.

"Shall we get on?" I said before they could erupt into a full-blown argument.

"Of course. Mustn't keep the queen waiting."

Garth growled, but Blue ignored him. He pulled the camp bed away from the wall, revealing a small dark hole.

"This way." He got down on his belly and wriggled into the hole.

My stomach lurched. I did *not* like confined spaces. Garth crouched down and assessed the gap as Blue's feet disappeared. He looked up at me doubtfully.

"I don't think I'll fit." He jerked his head at Steve. "You either."

Steve grabbed one of the glowing bowls from the shelf and shoved it into the gap. They were both big guys, built like rugby players. Garth was right. They'd never make it through an opening that size. Great. Looked like I was on my own for this one.

I dropped to the floor, glad of the little green light at least. By its dim glow I could see that the space seemed to open up into a larger area quite quickly. My visions of getting trapped in the tiny space faded somewhat.

"I don't like you going in there alone," said Garth, his face anxious.

Me neither. I shoved my head in and began to squirm forwards before I lost my nerve. "I won't be alone. I've got Blue."

Not that that was much comfort. Blue wasn't on my side. I'd given him no choice but to help me, and maybe he wouldn't have helped my enemies either given the option, but

Blue was on nobody's side but Blue's. I wouldn't have cared if I'd been able to lay my hands on a better mage as easily, but negotiating with a goblin clan for their mage's aid was a protracted and costly business, even for a queen. Always I could hear that clock ticking in my head, reminding me that every second wasted was another second Lachie had to spend with his father, under the nose of Daiyu.

I dusted myself off, relieved to be able to stand again. This cavern was much bigger than the first, and as more of the little green lights sprang to life, I gasped. The space was roughly bowl-shaped, and cupped in the centre of the bowl lay a pool of water, glittering darkly. All around it stalagmites reached for the ceiling like grasping fingers. Some had even managed to join with the stalactites that hung there, creating twisted pillars that sparkled in the dim light as if sprinkled with fairy dust, shining with a wet gleam.

Blue crouched by the black pool. I weaved through the gleaming pillars, past a shawl of rock so thin the light glowed softly through it, highlighting the different-coloured streaks that twisted through it like veins. Blue had removed his shirt and his pale skin glowed a sickly hue in the green goblin light. A fresh scar on his chest just above his left nipple looked nasty.

"Do you have the hairs?" he asked.

I withdrew the envelope from my pocket and passed the three dark hairs to him. His fingers were cold, his naked skin already beginning to sprout goosebumps. It was noticeably colder in here than in the first cavern.

"You all right in there?" Garth called, his voice echoing oddly through the crack.

"Fine," I called back.

"You may as well take a seat," said Blue. "This will take a while."

I perched myself on a rock and settled down to watch the goblin's preparations. He started a fire in a small circle of rocks that had obviously been used for the same purpose before, feeding it from a pile of sticks that must have taken a long time to drag in here through the little crawl space. If there was another way into this cavern I couldn't see it in the dim light. The fire did little for either the warmth or the light in the vast, cold space. I could feel the chill of the rock I sat on seeping through my jeans, sending my butt to sleep and numbing my legs.

Blue filled a large earthenware pot with water from the dark pool and set it over the fire to heat. He sat cross-legged beside the flames, feeding them the occasional twig, while he carved a little figure from a twisted piece of root. He muttered to himself in the sibilant goblin tongue as he worked, little offcuts flying from under his knife. His sharp features lit from beneath looked like some grotesque Halloween mask.

When the first wisps of steam began to curl from the pot, he wrapped Kasumi's hairs around the head of the finished mannikin. It didn't look like anyone in particular, but I guess that wasn't the point. He took trueshape, which made his human form look like a movie star. Goblins, with their knobbly blue skin, big ears and hairless heads, were not one of the better-looking types of shifter. Still muttering his chant, he turned the knife on himself and cut a long shallow slice down his forearm. Blue goblin blood welled, and he wiped it all over the little figure, until it was well and truly coated.

When the water was boiling he dropped the disgusting mannikin into the pot. The stench of superheated goblin blood made my nose twitch in distaste. He added leaves and powders from various containers to his mannikin soup, prodding at the foul-smelling mess with a stick every now and then until he seemed satisfied. I thought that was the end of it, but no, the ritual entered a whole new phase.

Still chanting, he began to carve short lines into his chest. Guess that was where the angry-looking scar above his nipple had come from. I'd never realised goblin magic required so much blood. The knife trembled as he cut. I could see his hand shaking even in the dim light. He never paused in his chant, though his voice rasped and his breath came in short pants. Gradually it dawned on me that the new cuts were not random, but were forming words cut into his flesh. Now I wished I'd learned to read goblin script.

He was swaying now as he chanted, eyes shut, his upper body swinging over the fire and the boiling pot, backwards and forwards like a demented, blood-soaked metronome. I shifted uneasily on my cold stone. Should I be ready to grab him in case he toppled into the fire?

The smell from the pot was enough to turn my stomach. Whatever those powders were, they hadn't done anything to improve the aroma of boiling blood. Blood sheeted down his chest, obscuring whatever words he'd carved there. Sweat stood out on his forehead, and one drop hung from the tip of his pointed nose, despite the cold.

The chanting rose to a shrieking crescendo, then a cloud of stinking green vapour rolled off the pot like a storm cloud, making my eyes water.

I leapt up, eyes streaming. Garth was calling me from the other cavern, his voice panicked, but I was more concerned with Blue, who'd keeled over like a puppet whose strings had been cut. Fortunately, not into the fire, but the rock floor wouldn't have done his head any favours either.

"Blue? Are you okay?"

Stupid bloody question. Of course he wasn't okay. He was back in his human form, but he had more blood on the outside than the inside, judging by the mess he was in. The fire had gone out, as suddenly as if it had been doused with water, and all the green goblin lights had faded almost to nothing. Probably connected to his essence, which wasn't in the best of shape at the moment. I grabbed his shirt, ready to make a bandage for his bleeding chest, but when I picked it up I saw the bleeding had stopped already. That was probably tied up with the ritual too.

I rolled him onto his side and draped the shirt over him for some warmth.

"Garth! Shove a couple of those blankets through."

"What's happening? Was that Blue screaming?"

I could see Garth's shape silhouetted against the brighter light behind him as I wriggled a little way into the tunnel that separated us to retrieve the blankets.

"It's okay," I said. "Blue just needs a little time to recover."

Not that I would know if something had gone wrong with Blue's ritual. The only goblin magic I'd seen performed before was the very minor spell Blue had cast to dispel the traps on my old house, and the scrying he'd done in the fountain—and frankly, I'd be perfectly happy if I never had to watch anything bigger than that again, thank you very much. There was way too much blood involved for my taste. No wonder Blue was a little ambivalent about his gifts. Sure, he would heal easily, but shifter healing didn't protect you from the pain in the first place. If I had to go through an ordeal like that to call on my magic I mightn't be too keen on using it either. No wonder goblin mages charged a king's ransom for their services.

I hurried back to Blue's side and wrapped the blankets securely around his skinny form. He was awake, but watched me without saying anything.

"Do you need anything?" I asked. "Something to eat, or drink?"

"Whiskey and soda might be nice," he said. "Don't suppose you've got one of those on you."

"Afraid not. I can give you a double when we get back, though. How are you feeling?"

"Fantastic." He levered himself up on one elbow, moving like a little old man. "Never better. Pass me that bottle, would you?"

I picked up the bottle lying by the dead fire, a tiny little pill bottle no longer than my thumb. I caught a whiff of the contents of the pot as I passed. Disgusting.

He sat up. "And you wonder why I hide out here? This is why. Look at me! I can barely move. People might notice if I lay on the floor of my hotel room for a few days. Magic strips my defences."

He picked up the pot, and for the first time I noticed it had a lip on one side. There was barely anything left in it, just a smear of darkness in the bottom. He tipped the pot carefully, his hands shaking so much I wondered if I should offer to do it for him, and let the evil liquid ooze into the tiny bottle.

It seemed like a lot of effort for such a small result, but he regarded the bottle with satisfaction.

"Damn, I'm good. At least ten hours right there."

He screwed the lid on and offered me the bottle. That was when it hit me—I was going to have to *drink* that shit.

"Thanks," I said, trying to conceal my revulsion as I took it. Yep, I could see definite downsides to goblin magic. I thrust it into my pocket and stood up. "We should probably get going, if you're up to it."

"Sure." He shifted the blanket so it covered more of his shoulders, his hand still shaking. "As long as you carry me."

Well, that could be a problem. I eyed him in the dim light, trying to figure if he was messing with me or not. Probably not. That shaking looked real. So how were we going to get him back through that tight little tunnel?

I got his arm over my shoulders and helped him to his feet, but he was right, he really couldn't walk. We reeled like a pair of drunkards as I basically dragged him across the uneven floor to the little crawl space. He was clammy with sweat and smelled atrocious. His greasy head lolled against my cheek and he moaned softly.

"Garth?"

"Here." The reply came immediately. Thank God for Garth. I could always rely on him.

"Blue's in bad shape. I'm going to have to push him partway through the gap. Can you grab him and pull him through the rest of the way?"

"Sure." A man of few words, but they were nearly always the right ones. As long as he wasn't arguing, of course.

I almost shoved Blue into the claustrophobic little gap headfirst, but thought better of it before I gave the poor bastard concussion along with his other ills. Much better to work his feet through to Garth, so I could support his head from this side.

It was still an awkward job, and I don't know if I could have managed it without my dragon strength. Forcing a limp, unresponsive body through a tight space is one thing; trying to do it without hurting the body adds a whole new level of difficulty, and I was breathing hard by the time Garth called out: "Got him!"

Then it went much easier. All I had to do was commando-crawl on my elbows while protecting Blue's head from bumping along the rough floor of the passage. Not exactly a picnic, but at least the tunnel was short, and the torture came to an end as I popped out of the crawl space at last. Garth dumped Blue on the bed and the three of us hovered over him like anxious parents.

He cracked an eyelid and demanded food. Steve hurried to open a tin of baked beans. Blue seemed to spill as many as he ate, but he looked a little better for it, so we found him another one, and he hoed into those too. We gave him water from the flasks we'd brought, and I even tried to clean him up a little, but he pushed me away with a snarl.

"What's the time?" I asked Garth. I had no idea how much time had passed in the inner cavern. It felt like an eternity, but it might have only been half an hour.

"After four," he said. "We'd better head off soon."

We still had nearly a three-hour drive ahead of us, and that was after we'd hiked back to the car. Clearly Blue wasn't going to make it there under his own steam, so that would slow us down too.

In the end Steve drew the short straw. Garth led the way, since neither Steve nor I could find the trail, which meant Steve had to carry Blue. He held him in his arms like a child, since I was worried about the pressure of a fireman's carry on all those wounds sliced into his chest. He was covered in dirt and blood and stank like three-day-old meat. Garth was probably thrilled to keep his sensitive nose as far away as possible.

We had to stop a few times for Steve to rest. My dragon muscles would have been up to the job, and I offered to take a turn carrying him, but Steve wouldn't hear of it, and I didn't argue as hard as I might have.

It was nearly five by the time we got back to the car and hit the road again, though, being daylight saving, there was plenty of sunshine. I relaxed into the passenger seat with a sigh when we made it back to the tarred road. Civilisation felt within reach again, and the sudden silence as we left the dirt surface was a relief.

Garth glanced across at me but didn't comment, and there was silence in the car for another ten minutes. Then we must have come into signal range again, because Steve's phone chirped at an incoming text. And then another. And another.

"You're a popular guy." I leaned back against the headrest and shut my eyes. I was yet again without a mobile phone. Garth and I had both had ours taken by Taskforce Jaeger.

The texts kept coming in. Steve's phone sounded like a party in a hen house. What was going on?

He looked up from his screen and met my curious gaze.

"Oh, shit," he said.

CHAPTER EIGHTEEN

"What's wrong?"

A million possibilities flashed through my mind. Lachie was hurt. Daiyu was threatening him to bring Jason to heel. Someone else was hurt. Luce? Ben? One of my sisters had done something stupid. *All* of my sisters had done something stupid. My heart sank. It was Faith. She was dead.

Why should I care so much? Okay, maybe someone else was dead. Taskforce Jaeger was at the gates. *Daiyu* was at the gates. Daiyu had found out Kasumi had told us about her pilots. How would I ever free the kitsune now and win Lachie back? Maybe Kasumi was dead.

"A document's been leaked. It's all over the Internet."

My racing heart slowed. Was that all? A document. No one had died. "What document?"

"A list of shifters. Luce says it's gone viral. Everybody knows."

"What? Give me that!"

I scanned the texts, horror blooming in my gut. There were texts from all over the place, from Luce, Mac, Dave, other shifters, people I didn't even know, but they all said the same thing.

I punched in Luce's number. She picked up straight away, as if she'd been sitting on top of the thing, willing it to ring.

"Lucinda Chan."

"Luce, it's me. What the hell is happening?"

"Hell is about right. It's hitting the fan good and hard. Where are you? Everything okay?"

"We're fine." I didn't waste time going into details on Blue's condition. If he wasn't quite "fine" now, he soon would be. He was sleeping like a baby in the back seat, drooling all over the headrest. "It just took a little longer than we expected. Tell me about this list. Who's on it?"

"You. Me. The sisters and all the overseas queens, plus a few other dragons, including Jason. Garth and Mac, but none of the Sydney pack except Trevor. It seems almost random. Corinne and Bear and Yarrow, but not the other leshies that joined us with Yarrow."

She named a few more familiar names, most of them well-known overseas identities. Considering how few dragons there were, dragons seemed over-represented on the list.

"And then there's a whole pile of goblins. Most of the Stromboli clan, all the Baders, the Everharts, a few others ... it makes no sense."

"But they're all really shifters? There's no humans on there?"

"No. This list is from someone who knows what they're doing. It's got to be a shifter."

"But why would a shifter leak a list like that? They've got to know it's going to come back to bite them in the arse. Once people start finding real shifters, they're not going to stop poking around until they've uncovered them all."

Could it have been that traitor, Patel? He was already working with Taskforce Jaeger. But how could it benefit the taskforce to have all these names out in the open? Their work was better done in private, without the glare of publicity this information would bring. Besides, he was a goblin himself. With that many goblin names on the list, one of them was bound to lead to him. It would be suicide to let this kind of information out.

"I don't know. If it was just dragons, I'd say it was someone who wasn't happy with the status quo—maybe one of the males who thinks he'd like to go it alone without a queen. I could see someone like Gideon Thorne pulling a stunt like this."

Except he was dead. Could he have released this list before he died? But he'd been perfectly happy with the rule of the queens. He just wanted to have one in his pocket.

"But who gains from putting the goblin clans out of business?"

"It's got to be someone local with so many from this domain."

God, what a mess. As if the shifter world needed any more attention focused on it at the moment. People had already been killed just on suspicion of being a shifter. What would happen now the haters had real targets? "What's the reaction been like so far?"

"As you'd expect. Some group calling themselves Christians Against Demons is whipping up a storm on the Internet. Talkback radio is running hot. The nutters are out in full force. I've lost count of the number of times I've seen the same clip of the prime minister calling for calm on TV—but the stations have also interviewed enough people frothing at the mouth about the threat to our children, our way of life, our whatever-you-care-to-name, to make sure that nobody's listening."

Not that calls for calm meant much from the man who'd rushed his divisive hate-filled legislation through Parliament. He'd make pious noises about national security and be first in line for a pitchfork when the burning started.

"Okay. Everything quiet at the house?"

"Yeah. I figure we've got a while before they trace any of the names on the list here."

"Hope so. Well, sit tight until we get there. We'll be a couple of hours yet."

I hung up and stared out the window, mind whirling. Nothing made sense.

Garth cocked an eyebrow at me. "So I'm a wanted man, am I?"

Baby, you have no idea how much.

"Probably not for the first time." I dragged my mind back from contemplating how his smile lit his whole face and handed the phone back to Steve. "See what you can find."

Steve had the list in no time flat. It wasn't hard; it was all over every social media and news site. He found the footage of the prime minister that Luce had mentioned, but I didn't want to see it.

"Here's something. Maria del Fuente's made a statement."

He passed the phone back to me and the familiar face of the Spanish queen filled the little screen. She was based in Argentina these days, since she held the whole of the South American continent, but was still known as "the Spanish queen" in the same way Celeste Rousseau was "the French queen", despite France being the smallest part of her extensive domain. She was the public face of a hugely successful fashion house in her current incarnation—the "designer", though I'd be surprised if she actually did the designing. More likely she had some dryads on staff. They were wizards with a needle. High fashion wouldn't be too much of a stretch.

It was an odd choice for a queen. Usually their lives were designed for maximum luxury with minimal publicity. Having such a well-known face made it harder when the time inevitably came to disappear and start a new life as someone else. Already the speculation had started on what work she'd had done to retain her youthful good looks so long. It wouldn't be too many more years before Maria del Fuente's brilliant career would have to be cut short by a tragic accident.

That is, unless someone decided to kill her now her name was out there. They might get a surprise when they discovered how difficult that was.

But the attempts, whether successful or not, would surely come. This list changed everything. It gave targets to those baying for our blood already, put faces to the names. No more hiding in our comfortable anonymity. The cracks that had started when Valeria took to the sky above Sydney Harbour had been blown wide open, and the world would never be the same again.

I started the video and she began speaking. Half a dozen reporters thrust their microphones at her face. She was on the steps of a ritzy hotel, her usual look of boredom twisted into a sneer.

"Ridiculous." She spoke English with a hint of British upper-class in her accent. "This is obviously some hoax by a rival fashion house. And no, I'm not going to name names. My new spring collection is going to be the talk of Fashion Week and they're looking for ways to cut me down."

"Ms del Fuente, do you know any of the other people on the list? What do you think the connection is between you?"

"I doubt there is one," she said. "They've named people at random to divert suspicion from their real aim. Excuse me."

She pushed her way through the reporters, ignoring their cries of "Ms del Fuente! Ms del Fuente!" and got into a black Merc waiting at the kerb. The video ended with two reporters chasing the car down the street.

No doubt the other queens on the list were getting the same treatment. They were all richer than Midas, though none were as well known as Maria del Fuente. They wouldn't be hard to track down, though.

I ran my eye down the other articles on the site. More than half were to do with the list in some way, either profiling people named on it or trying to find links between them. Conspiracy theories ranged from the bizarre—they were all terrorists and the list had been circulated by the FBI in an effort to get vigilantes to take them down—to the more credible: that someone with a grudge was trying to harm their enemies. No one knew where the list had come from. Someone "highly placed" in the Australian government, according to some reports, though the CIA and even the UN got a mention. The fact that Australians were over-represented in the list seemed a compelling argument for the Australian government connection to most. Some thought it was a hoax, but most seemed to think the list itself was genuine, though debate raged about whether the people it named were really "supernaturals" or not. The press hadn't adopted our name for ourselves yet. "Supernaturals" sounded so much more angels-and-demons than "shifters", and the press loved a good scare tactic.

Nowhere was Taskforce Jaeger mentioned, though ASIO got a lot more publicity than they probably preferred. The Australian Security and Intelligence Organisation wasn't part of the everyday vernacular the way the CIA and the FBI were for Americans. Nobody made thrillers featuring their operatives playing cloak-and-dagger with the Russians or al Qaeda. If Australians ever thought about them at all, they probably assumed they had glorified desk jobs listening in on tapped telephone calls.

I was every bit as ignorant as any other Australian, but I didn't believe that Taskforce Jaeger operated under an ASIO umbrella. Though well set up, they'd had a cavalier attitude to legalities that made them seem more of a cowboy operation. Patel's sick experiment seemed way out of line even in the current climate of fear. The anti-supernatural laws might allow for arrest without charge but I was pretty damned sure that medical experiments weren't mentioned anywhere. That was the problem with giving a lot of power to men with an agenda. Even my friend the prime minister would surely be horrified at how far his hounds had gone once they'd slipped their leash.

We'd killed a lot of them, but they were just grunts. Poor glorified police officers just doing their job. Wilson and Patel were still at large, and they could easily re-establish themselves somewhere else with new recruits. Maybe even without the thin veneer of government legitimacy they'd had before. They'd have plenty of work now. But how would they cope with the extra publicity the list had caused? Those guys really didn't want the government—or the media—poking into their affairs and finding out what atrocities had been committed on behalf of the people of Australia. Publicity would make it harder to attack people and spirit them away to an underground lab. Those people would be watched now, and it would be noticed if they went missing. That, more than anything else, convinced me that our friends at Taskforce Jaeger couldn't be responsible for the leak.

But then who was? And what did it mean for the people who'd been named?

Steve's phone buzzed in my hand, making me jump. I passed it back to him to answer, but a moment later he was offering it to me again.

"It's for you. Valiant."

"Valiant?" I took the phone. "How did you get this number?"

"I rang the queen's palace, and your wyvern gave it to me. She thought you'd want to hear from me."

"She was right. I suppose you've heard about the list?"

"Of course. That's why I'm ringing." A quiver in her voice told me she wasn't as confident as she was trying to sound. "It's all over the Internet, the TV, the radio. What are we going to do?"

By the end of that sentence, she sounded like the teenager she was. If she'd been human, she'd still be in high school. To have a disaster of this magnitude land in her lap must be stressing her out of her tree.

"First of all, we're not going to panic. We're going to beef up our security, keep our heads down, and deny, deny, deny."

"Some of the others thought you might have leaked this list."

"Me? Why would I do that? My name's on it too. So are half my staff's."

"Maybe as a way to set the humans on us, so you didn't have to share. You could have put your own name on it to divert suspicion."

She sounded like she couldn't decide whether to accuse me or beg me to deny it.

"Easier just to not offer to share in the first place, don't you think? Landing myself in the shit right next to you doesn't seem a great trade-off for keeping the domain to myself."

"No, I suppose not." There was definite relief in her tone. "Who do you think released it, then?"

"Obviously a shifter." Although it could have been a herald, come to think of it. They knew all the shifters. I wasn't going to put that idea in anyone's head, though. I didn't want to set anyone on Ben's tail. "Someone who wants to watch the world burn."

"What about Taskforce Jaeger? They attacked us—and they killed Faith."

"She's dead?" I hadn't heard that.

"Yeah. Her people got her out of the building before it burned down, but she was already dead when they found her."

I'd love to know how she died. Had removing her channel stone killed her? Or had its removal weakened her to the point where she could be killed by ordinary means? It didn't seem like the right time to press for details, though.

"This isn't going to go away, is it?" she said. "I mean, once it's on the Internet, it's out there forever. How are we going to deal with it?"

"In the long run? I think we'll have to come to some agreement with the humans." It felt odd to speak of "the humans" as something "other". "The world is changing, and we'll have to change with it. It makes it even more important for us to be able to work together. Do you think your sisters will agree to share the domain?"

"I think so. I've talked Charity, Justine and Prudence round already. I only have to persuade Hope and Virginia now, but I think this list will have scared them. They won't want to face this on their own."

"Good. Let's work on getting them on board and getting through the coronation first. That will get the foreign queens off our backs. Then we can work out how to handle this going forward."

"Maybe the queens will be too busy with their own problems now to bother us."

"Maybe." From what I knew of them, that didn't seem likely. "You keep your head down. We'll talk again soon. Take care of yourself."

"You too." She hung up.

"That's a good sign, that she wants to talk," Steve said when I handed his phone back.

"Yes."

I stared out the window, watching the world unfold beside the motorway. We passed a cheap motel, just like the one Garth and I had stayed at the night we went to the cemetery and dug up Lachie's grave. The night I discovered that he was still alive.

We had spent too much time apart. I needed to hold my boy in my arms again, to know he was safe, to make sure he was eating properly. He was such a picky little eater. I needed to know he was happy, and not lying awake at night worrying what his father might do next. The poor kid needed a life. He'd spent so much of the last year shunted around, abandoned, endangered.

"You're very quiet," Garth said.

"Just thinking. What will we do if Jason goes to ground and takes Lachie with him?"

What if I was in Japan and Jason just disappeared? All that risk and effort to free the kitsune, and Jason might do a runner and it would all be wasted. Lachie would be gone.

"Ain't gonna happen." Garth sounded very assured. "Daiyu isn't going to let him out of her sight, however many lists he gets his name on. Besides, we'll be watching. Just because you're away doesn't mean the rest of us will be sitting around on our arses."

Just as well. I couldn't bear it if the fallout from this stupid list put Lachie into more danger.

"God, I wish this was over." I couldn't wait to get on that plane. I felt so helpless. I needed to *do* something.

"Amen to that," said Garth.

CHAPTER NINETEEN

I was all set to ring Kasumi straight away. No time like the present, right? I'd waited long enough, and I was itching to set things in motion to free Lachie. Every moment that he spent with Daiyu was a moment he was at risk. Sure, Jason was allied with her now, but she knew he was my son. The thought of using him against me must be very tempting. I just prayed that Jason didn't offer her any reason to be dissatisfied with his alliance.

Mac met us at the door. She usually looked sad—it wasn't that long since Jerry had died—but now her face had that fake cheerfulness that meant she had bad news and was trying not to worry me. I'd seen it enough times to know.

"What's wrong?" My first thought was for the leaked list of shifters. "Are there more names?"

"No. Detective Hartley wants to see you."

"When?"

"Now."

"It's eight o'clock at night. Doesn't she have a home to go to?"

"I'll put Blue to bed," said Garth, who had carried the goblin in behind me. The orange head, damp with sweat and covered in the kind of muck you'd expect to gather crawling around a cave, lolled against the werewolf's shoulder. He was barely awake.

I smoothed my own hair, conscious that it probably didn't look much better. "Get someone to look at his chest."

"I'm on it."

Mac watched them disappear down the corridor towards the staff quarters. The cheerful mask slipped, showing the troubled look in her big puppy dog eyes. "What happened to him?"

"Goblin magic. It's brutal stuff. What did Hartley say?"

"She was very insistent. Said it was urgent, and that if you didn't show by nine o'clock she was sending a squad car round to arrest you."

"Geez. What's the rush?"

She shrugged. "I don't know."

I sighed, and scrubbed at my face with a weary hand. "All right, just give me a few minutes to get cleaned up. Where does she want to meet?"

"At the Park Hyatt. Room 330."

Oh, Lord, not that again. That was the room Jason had booby-trapped and blown up. I'd hoped my part in that investigation was over. No such luck, apparently. Just what I needed—more complications. Would I *never* get to Japan?

I cocked an eyebrow at Steve, still hovering at my elbow. "You up for another run tonight?"

"No problem."

In twenty minutes I was showered and changed, and feeling much better. Dinner would have been the icing on the cake, but Mac was so unnerved by Detective Hartley's threats that I didn't stay long enough for that, though the smells emanating from the kitchen were certainly tempting. Instead I grabbed a bread roll to snack on.

"You need to eat," Dave said, giving me a disapproving look. His apron had "Kiss the Cook" blazoned across it in big red letters. "You're getting too skinny."

"What are you, my mother?" I brandished the bread roll at him. "Besides, I *am* eating."

"Proper food. Man doesn't live on bread alone, you know."

"Lucky I'm a woman, then."

I headed for the car, Steve on my heels. Luce had offered to come too, but it was only a meeting. It would look weird if I turned up with a cast of thousands.

"Why are we meeting at the hotel?" Steve asked. "Did she say?"

Though she'd threatened me with arrest before, in the past Detective Hartley had always come to me. The change bothered me. So late at night, too. Something was different.

"No."

Steve drove, and one of the thralls took the passenger seat, at Luce's insistence. Evan, his name was. Unlike Leandra, I could tell my thralls apart. Naturally Garth had wanted to come, but his skills weren't exactly suited to diplomacy, and I didn't need shifter protection from the police force. Besides, I needed to focus on Detective Hartley and I was finding him more and more distracting.

Steve pulled up in front of the hotel's arched entry.

"Stay with the car," I told him. "Evan can come with me. This won't take long."

At least I hoped so. Did I need a lawyer? What reason could she have for asking for a meeting here?

Evan and I stepped into the lift, and I remembered to check. No camera. Well, that was one weight off my mind.

The lift pinged and the doors slid open on level three. No camera in the lift lobby either, or the corridor. So the only footage she had of me was from the hotel lobby. Nothing there that would contradict the story I'd given her. So why was I here?

We walked down the familiar brown-toned corridor, past the weird little phallic sculpture. Room 330 had a new door, its dark wood as sleek and undamaged as all its neighbours'. It was closed, so Evan knocked. Footsteps approached, then the door opened and a pair of familiar eyes squinted at us with suspicion.

"She's here," Detective Franks called over his shoulder, then he opened the door wide and stepped back to let us through.

The sour tang of smoke lingered on the air inside. The windows had been replaced, and the litter cleared away, but no effort had been made otherwise to repair or repaint. There were no lights on, which seemed odd.

I don't know what saved me. A hint of something, a smell? I sensed movement behind me as Franks stepped between me and Evan. He felt close, and I turned to see his arm upraised. My shocked brain took a fraction of a second to realise I was under attack, and then the fight-or-flight instinct kicked in, and I leapt back just in time to avoid the syringe slamming in a vicious arc toward my neck.

I caught my foot on something and went down. Guns barked in front and behind as Evan and someone silhouetted by the windows opened fire, but I only had eyes for Franks. He hurled himself on me and I caught his arm with both hands, straining against him. He was a big guy, and my arms quivered despite my dragon strength. The point of the syringe glistened a handsbreadth from my face.

Evan cried out, but my ears were ringing from the gunfire, and I couldn't make out his words. He lunged forward and caught at Franks's broad back in an effort to drag him off me, but the gun behind me barked again and Evan collapsed limply to the floor.

A bullet struck my shoulder, and the strength in that arm melted away in an instant. The needle hovered closer to my face, drawing inexorably nearer. I squirmed, trying to throw Franks off me, but his bulk pinned me down. Panic's claws dug into me, sharp as knives.

I panted for air, but I couldn't hear myself. Blood crept along my shoulder, spreading its wet warmth across my shoulder blades. Franks's breath was hot in my face, his squinty eyes bulging so close to mine. I glared into them. I'd almost forgotten I was a dragon in the terror of the moment. Gritting my teeth, I pushed into his mind, determined to put an end to this.

Only I found the way barred. Someone had been here before me, and Franks was enthralled to another. There was no way to command him.

Panic consumed me. Only another dragon could have enthralled him, and if a dragon had sent him against me like this, there was only one thing that could be in that syringe. Fear surged like bile in my throat and I struggled like an animal. My left arm collapsed, useless, at my side.

Instinctively I reached for my essence, but fear throttled the channel between the parts of my soul. Trueshape hovered just out of reach as my arm gave way and the syringe slammed down.

It shattered against the armour of my face.

Franks reared back in shock and I backhanded him across the face. He collapsed into the wall and I scrambled to my feet, one scaled arm dripping blood. The gunman by the window emptied his clip at me. I heard the click of the empty chamber. None of the bullets hurt me.

Well, this was new. I was covered in scales but still in human form. Just call me Lizard Woman.

The shadowy gunman turned out to be Detective Hartley. She still pointed her gun at me, though she was out of ammo, and her hands shook so much I could see the movement from across the room. I closed the gap between us in three quick strides and punched her hard enough to drop her to the singed carpet, out cold. Then I fell to my knees at Evan's side and fumbled his phone out of his pocket.

Steve answered straight away.

"Get up here," I said. "We've got a problem."

CHAPTER TWENTY

How long did we have before hotel security arrived? Someone would have reported the sound of gunshots. Steve brought the first aid kit with him from the car, and rigged a competent field dressing on Evan's bicep, where the bullet had torn completely through. Another had grazed his thigh, which meant he walked with a limp, but at least he could walk. All the while I stood in the dim alcove just outside the door, watching the corridor, Detective Franks's syringe in my hand.

My shoulder throbbed a song of agony in time with my heartbeat, but the wound had already closed. I was feeling kind of wobbly, but we were running out of time. Steve hoisted Evan to his feet, and I urged them to the door.

"What are we going to do with them?" Steve indicated the two detectives still unconscious on the floor.

"I don't know." If we left them, the first thing they would do when they woke would be go get a warrant for my arrest. But if we took them with us we'd have the whole police force on our trail baying for blood. "They've been enthralled. Franks tried to stick me with a syringe full of du. Whoever's pulling their strings isn't going to let this rest."

"Want me to …?" He made a gun with his hand and mimed a headshot.

I have to admit, I didn't say no straight away. The dragon part of me had grown impatient with the danger represented by these two. Dragons didn't put up with insects buzzing around being a nuisance. They swatted them.

I'd tried to play the game by their rules, and look where that had gotten me. Some other dragon had enthralled them instead and turned them from a nuisance to a deadly threat. Maybe it wouldn't be long before someone in the force noticed their erratic behaviour and started investigating, but in the meantime there was nothing they wouldn't do for their master or mistress, whoever it was. Jason or Daiyu, clearly, given the presence of that syringe. Proper police procedures, due process, logic: it was all out the window. These two wouldn't rest now until I was brought down.

I stared down at Detective Hartley for a long moment. She would be a thrall for the rest of her life unless the dragon who'd enthralled her died, unable to think for herself beyond the basic functions. If that dragon told her to, she'd kill without blinking. That went against everything she'd dedicated her life to. She was the victim here, even more than I was.

I shook my head. "Leave them. Let's go."

We took the elevator down and marched straight out the front door, under the apprehensive gaze of the woman at the front desk. Hotel security must have been waiting for police backup. We looked like extras from a zombie movie, spattered in blood, but the woman sensibly decided not to get involved.

Evan groaned as Steve eased him into the back seat.

"Hang in there," I said. "We'll get you some major-league painkillers when we get home. How are you doing?"

He blushed as he looked up at me, eyes adoring. "Don't worry about me, mistress. I'd take a hundred bullets for you."

I looked away, chastened. Was I any better than whoever had enthralled the detectives? I hated the unthinking adulation of the thralls, but what could I do? Evan was a middle-aged man. He must have been in Elizabeth's service twenty years or more. Like his fellow thralls, his mind had been so warped by his long enthralment to Elizabeth that he would have been reduced to drooling idiocy if I hadn't enthralled him as soon as she died. None of her thralls could have functioned any more without the bond. One of them had been too far gone to save, and he'd died within the hour. The others—I could enthral them, or leave them catatonic.

Wasn't a life of enthralled service to me better than no life at all? I didn't treat my thralls like slaves or cannon fodder, as so many other dragons did. He could have a long and happy life within the limits of the enchantment that bound him to me. Was life without freedom truly worse than death?

Then why did I have this bad taste in my mouth? I got into the front seat, letting him lie on the back seat. At least I'd been trying to save those men when I enthralled them. Whoever had enthralled Hartley and Franks hadn't been thinking of their welfare, just using them as a means to an end. Even though Hartley's cool intellect had been used against me in the past, I hated to see her reduced to virtual slavery in the service of some dragon's ambition.

And which dragon was it? The answer to that question mattered. If it was one of my sisters, my hopes for brokering a peace between us were at an end. But the syringe in my hand said Daiyu. Those girls all knew I was immune to bane leaf now, but where would they get their hands on the only other alternative? I didn't need to analyse a sample to know what must be in this syringe, and the only dragon around with guaranteed access to it was the Japanese queen. She probably wouldn't even give a syringe like this to Jason. I know I wouldn't, though the prospect of injecting *him* was pretty damn appealing. I stared out the window at the night city sliding by, neon lights ablaze, and decided it was time for a leap of faith.

"Give me your phone."

Steve took one hand off the wheel and passed it across with a curious glance. "Who are you ringing?"

I pulled her card out of my pocket and dialled the number. "Valiant."

"You going to ask her if she enthralled Hartley and Franks? She's not going to admit to it if she did."

I didn't answer, just listened to the phone ringing.

"Yes?" Her voice was crisp and firm.

"It's Kate."

Her voice was calm, if a little wary. "Good to hear from you. What can I do for you?"

"We need to meet. Now. Tonight."

"Where?"

"I'm in the city. Name somewhere."

"The Art Gallery steps. I can be there in ten minutes."

"See you then." I hung up and told Steve to head to the Art Gallery.

"What about Evan? I thought we were taking him home?"

Evan's face was so pale I felt guilty. He needed to be home, in bed, dosed up to the eyeballs with painkillers.

"This won't take long."

Home wasn't likely to be a very safe place for me now. Any time now the police would come knocking with a warrant for my arrest. I dialled another number and gave Luce a long list of instructions. She seemed unfazed by the change in plans, but then, it took a lot to faze Luce. By the time I'd finished the call we'd arrived at the Art Gallery.

At this time of night we were the only car around and Steve parked right next to a "No Standing" sign at the base of the wide flight of steps. The many-pillared front of the building looked a little like the Parthenon, and even boasted bas-relief sculptures like the famous temple, though here they were in special niches on each of the two wings that jutted from the sides of the central building. The money must have run out, though, because most of the niches were bare, and had been as long as I could remember. Floodlights lit the warm honey-gold sandstone façade and we waited in their soft glow.

I took the opportunity to make another call.

"Time to book that holiday," I said when Kasumi's voice answered.

"Immediately." In the background I heard a piping child's voice.

"Is that Lachie?" My heart leapt. "Can I talk to him?"

"Bad time. Did you get the—later."

She hung up. Obviously she wasn't free to talk. Did I get the hairs? Yes, indeed, thank you kindly. Now all I needed was for her to pass on the order for my "holiday", and I could finally do something about getting my boy back.

"You might want to do something with that." Steve nodded at the syringe in my hand. "I doubt she's going to feel like chatting if she sees you with that in your hand."

The minutes ticked over, and I'd just begun to wonder if I'd set myself up for another attack when a dark blue sedan pulled in behind us. Doors slammed as Valiant and a large man whose aura proclaimed him to be a troll got out. The car's windows were tinted, so I couldn't see if there was anyone else in the car.

What was I going to do with the damn syringe? Its contents were worth a fortune, and deadly dangerous. And yet I was really hoping not to have to kill any more dragons.

On impulse I squirted the stuff onto the floor of the car and watched it soak into the carpet.

Steve shook his head. "Luce isn't going to be happy with you."

"Then you'd better not tell her," I said, and got out of the car.

The big troll folded his arms, making sure I couldn't miss the size of his biceps, but I was more interested in the young woman standing next to him. She wore a T-shirt and cut-off denim shorts, quite a change from the beautiful ivory ball gown I'd last seen her in. Her long red-gold hair was loose, and she tossed her head to flick it out of her eyes.

"When you said we'd talk soon, I wasn't expecting quite this soon."

My dragon self bristled at her tone. Did she expect an apology? She'd be waiting a long time. My more rational self approved of her effort to control our meeting. She had guts, that was for sure.

"Have you spoken to your sisters since our chat?"

"Our sisters." Her gaze was cool. "They're your sisters too."

I shrugged, and gazed out across the road at the park-like grounds of the Domain opposite. "*Our* sisters, then."

"Hope and Virginia have decided to be realistic. They figure they can't beat you if it comes to a fight, so they may as well settle for what they can get. I seem to have become the unofficial spokeswoman."

"Maybe they figure you're the most expendable. Makes sense, I guess. If something goes wrong between us there's no sense all of you being in the firing line. And you are the youngest."

She stiffened. "Are you planning for something to go wrong?"

"No." I sighed, thinking of Detective Hartley. "But things do seem to keep going wrong, whatever my plans."

"Well, since we're being so frank, I don't trust most of them any more than I trust you. But I think that list of names being leaked has got them running scared. They're all looking for backup. No one wants to face the mobs alone." She cocked her head to one side and regarded me thoughtfully. "It makes me wonder if it really wasn't you that leaked it."

"It wasn't. I told you that." A bat flitted overhead, en route to the sheltering trees of the Domain. I could hear others squeaking and rustling among the dark branches of the great park. "I can see why you might think so, but I'm really not that Machiavellian. And I have no desire to drag the shifter world into the light of day."

Like those bats, parts of that world would never survive the glare.

"I can't imagine why any shifter would." Graciously she didn't mention that the initial exposure was partly my fault, though we both knew it. The Harbour Bridge, scene of my epic New Year's Eve battle with Valeria, was very close, just the other side of the Domain. "But someone obviously does. It can't be a dragon. When the world is arranged to favour you above everyone else, you don't mess with the status quo."

"Unless you're a dragon with only a one in eight chance of surviving to enjoy life at the top of the heap, perhaps," I pointed out gently.

She shook her head. "I really don't think they'd do it. The girls all seem happy to discuss your … ah … ideas about the future."

"Even Hope?"

"I'm not saying she's enthusiastic, but there's no harm in talking, is there? It's up to you to prove you're genuine."

I sat down on the broad step and patted the spot beside me. The rough sandstone still held the heat of the day. My shoulder was throbbing something fierce and I figured it was better to sit down than fall down.

"Well, I am genuine, and I hope you are too, because I need your help."

She sat next to me and hugged her knees. In the shorts and T-shirt she looked younger than her eighteen years. Suddenly I really, really wanted this to work. I couldn't bear the thought of killing this child.

"Really? I don't know how the others would feel about that." Her eyes held a wary look.

"The others do realise, don't they, that if we're going to share this domain between us, none of us individually will be strong enough to withstand the overseas queens? We won't be going our separate ways and never seeing each other again. We'll have to get used to working together and helping each other out or they'll pick us off one by one."

She frowned down at her feet, where summery pink toenails peeked out of her sandals. "What do you want me to do?"

"I have to leave town for a day or two. There's something important I have to do, and it can't wait." I took a deep breath. Time to roll the dice. I could almost hear the clatter of them in my head. How would they fall? "But tonight two police detectives attacked me. I've been dealing with them since New Year. They were assigned to investigate the mysterious body in the harbour."

Her eyebrows rose. "And how did they manage to connect you with that?"

"It's a long story. And there've been complications since." I waved my hand in a dismissive gesture. I didn't have time to go into it. "Anyway, tonight I discovered someone has enthralled them. They had a syringe full of du. They knew what they were doing. They could have killed me."

She stared out at the dark trees. I could almost hear her mind ticking over, putting it all together.

"You don't know who enthralled them?"

"The du points to Daiyu as most likely, but it could have been Jason. Either way, they're not going to stop."

She nodded. "They'll come after you for any excuse—or none at all."

"Exactly." I was pleased she saw the problem so quickly. "The men who were with me will be arrested on sight. And any of my people could be arrested on no charge at all, thanks to these new laws. The dragon controlling them can set them on anyone they please."

"And they're prepared to kill."

"Yes. You can see my problem. I don't want to go away and leave my people vulnerable."

"But if they're already enthralled we can't compel them. How are we going to protect your people?"

I glanced at her massive troll, still glowering at us from beside the car. "Sometimes muscle can work just as well as brains. They're only humans."

She gave me an uncertain look. "So you want us to, what? Hold them captive?"

"Sounds like a plan."

"Couldn't your own people do that? You've got dungeons in that mansion of yours."

"But that mansion will be the first place people look if they go missing. The police would be there with a search warrant faster than you can say dragonfire. Someone else needs to do this."

"And when you get back? What then? We can't hold them forever."

By then I hoped Daiyu would have run home, tail between her legs. Or better yet, suffered an unfortunate accident at the hands of a vengeful kitsune. Of course, if she wasn't the one responsible for enthralling the detectives, things could get interesting, but she'd already revealed she knew the secret of du when she sent Kasumi against me disguised as a herald. Usually the most obvious answer is the correct one. I had my fingers crossed, anyway.

"It won't be forever. A couple of days is all I need. We should be in a much stronger position when I get back. The seven of us can sit down and talk and we can have this coronation and get these damn overseas queens to mind their own bloody business for a while."

She stared at the sandstone beneath her feet for a while. I didn't rush her, though I longed for a hot shower and a cool pillow, not necessarily in that order.

"Okay," she said at last. "I can't promise anything for the others, but I'll help. Who are these detectives?"

Thank God. She seemed genuine, and that was all I could ask at this stage. It would take a while to build trust between us, but if she did this it would go a long way toward establishing a working relationship.

"Detective Ellen Hartley and her partner Detective Franks. They were both unconscious in Room 330 of the Park Hyatt hotel when I left them a few minutes ago. The place is probably overrun with cops by now, but if you're lucky they might still be there. If not—"

"If not, I'll figure something out." She stood up and brushed down the back of her shorts. "I'm on my way."

CHAPTER TWENTY-ONE

Garth pulled into the small car park in front of an unassuming building that backed onto the airport. High steel fences topped with coils of barbed wire surrounded the airport, and through them we could see half a dozen private planes on the tarmac behind the building, including one with a stylised red dragon on its side. I was betting that one was Daiyu's. Trust her to advertise.

We got out of the car, backpacks over our shoulders. Luce had only brought the essentials, which in her case was mainly firearms. There were probably a few knives weighing her pack down too. It certainly felt a lot heavier than mine, which held nothing but a change of clothes and a very small, very important glass bottle. What do you bring when you're invading another queen's domain? Either you bring an army, or you travel very light and rely on speed. We'd gone for Option B.

Garth got out too. The rumble of jets taking off and landing competed with the traffic roaring past the car park. The air smelled of jet fuel and sunbaked asphalt.

"I hate that you're going without me."

He stood very close, and I swayed toward him, feeling that invisible connection.

"You worry too much. Remember when I went to confront Valeria on New Year's Eve? You wanted to come then, too, and I managed all right without you."

"So? That was before—"

He broke off, but I knew what he meant. That was before this … feeling … had sprung up between us.

I opened my mouth to say something, but he growled in frustration and took my face in his hands.

"You'd better come back." Then his lips brushed mine in a kiss so tender it stole my breath away.

"Or what?"

"Or nothing. Just don't do anything stupid."

"Why? You don't like competition?" I pushed him away, trying to keep my tone light, though I ached to stay in the circle of those muscular arms.

He smiled, a softer look than I was used to seeing on his hard face. "That smart mouth's going to get you into trouble one day."

"So I'm told." I waited while he drove away, then turned to find Luce watching me with a raised eyebrow. "Don't you start."

"I'm not saying anything." But a half smile played around her lips.

We entered the building, which belonged to an aircraft management service that catered to the wealthy and their private jets. Strange to think that I was now in that category.

The smart young man behind the counter looked up as we entered. If he thought we didn't look quite like his normal class of customers, he was too well-trained to say so.

"Can I help you?"

"We don't need your help." I snared him in a light compulsion. "We'll just go straight through. You can forget we were ever here."

"Okay, then." He was still nodding as we stepped out onto the tarmac.

Daiyu's plane was a 737, and a set of air stairs waited in front of the open door. The stewardess appeared in the doorway as we approached and offered a deep bow.

We horrified her by carrying our own luggage aboard. She hurried down the stairs and tried to take it but Luce barked at her in Japanese, which produced a flurry of apologetic bowing. I was tense until we were aboard, half-expecting an ambush, but nothing happened. The interior of the plane was every bit as luxurious as I would have expected from the queen of Japan. We entered a lounge area that would have been at home in a high-class hotel, full of padded reclining seats for the comfort of Daiyu's guests. The seats were grey and the carpet a deep blood red. A corridor led away from the main area to other rooms, most likely bedrooms and bathrooms.

I chose a seat and Luce dropped into the one next to me. Kasumi had come through for us. The flight crew obviously expected us, and no questions had been asked. As far as they were concerned, they were following their mistress's orders to convey these guests to Tokyo. The stewardess offered refreshments but I sent her away. I felt uncomfortable with her hovering around.

We'd managed the first hurdle, but time was not on our side here. Would Kasumi's deception be discovered? Probably only if Daiyu decided she needed her plane after all, but I was reasonably confident she wouldn't. There was plenty to occupy her in Sydney.

Still, if she did discover her plane was missing, it wouldn't be too difficult to figure out who was responsible. There wouldn't be too many in her party with the authority to instruct the flight crew. Kasumi would be well and truly screwed in that case, so the faster I got this done the better.

A quick offensive was our best chance. The longer we stayed, the more chance of being caught out in our deception, and there were a million little things that could go wrong.

Blue's potion had a limited life. Once I drank it the clock started ticking. Ten hours, he said. Ten hours to get in and out without coming into contact with any other dragons—because goblin potions couldn't disguise the aura of the underlying shifter. If a single dragon saw Kasumi with a red dragon aura glowing around her, the game would be up. We'd be reduced to fighting our way out of hostile territory, the two of us against Daiyu's whole establishment. Not good odds.

Best not to think about it. We couldn't make a plan until we got there and saw what we were up against anyway. That was why I'd had to come myself. Dragon compulsions were likely to feature heavily in any plan, even with Blue's potion.

We were going in blind, and no matter how many times I reminded myself that "no plan survives contact with the enemy" I couldn't help feeling twitchy. Luce must be feeling even worse. I'd never met a more dedicated control freak.

I glanced across at her and she gave me a fierce grin. "Better strap in. I think we're getting ready to move."

The engine noise had changed to a louder rumble, and I could feel the vibrations of it through the carpeted floor. I felt a jolt and looked out the window. The view swung around as the plane began the slow trek to its designated runway.

The captain's voice came over the address system, a babble of Japanese. The stewardess must have told him we spoke the language after her encounter with Luce.

"What did he say?"

"Just the usual," Luce said. "Welcome aboard, flight time to Narita is eight hours, blah blah blah."

"I wish I spoke as many languages as you. This is really going to be a problem for us. What am I going to do? Pretend I've got laryngitis and let you do all the talking?"

"Just compel anyone who becomes a problem."

"That'll work for small groups, but compelling more than a handful of people at once is pretty tough to manage for any length of time. And if any of them are high-level shifters we're really up shit creek."

"Well ..." She tipped her head to one side and regarded me thoughtfully. "Maybe there's something else we could try. When I was still living in the Chinese Court, the Russian queen's consort visited us. He spoke no Chinese and my queen spoke no Russian, but she was too proud to admit she couldn't understand him."

"Couldn't she just use an interpreter?"

"Well, you'd think so, but she knew the language of every other domain and felt she would lose face by admitting her ignorance of this one."

"So what did she do?"

The engine's rumble rose to a higher-pitched shriek and we were pressed back into our seats as the plane accelerated down the runway.

"She found a thrall who could speak Russian and somehow used his knowledge to speak it herself."

"How?"

She shrugged. "I don't know. I only know what I saw. She carried on a conversation for half an hour with the Russian, and he never noticed anything odd. The thrall was in the room the whole time serving as a waiter."

"Wow."

The vibrations suddenly ceased as the plane surged off the ground. I looked out the window and watched Sydney dwindle away beneath us, the blue waters of Botany Bay sparkling in the sun.

How had the Chinese queen managed that trick? I'd never heard of such a thing before, though words and mind control went hand in hand with dragons. They were as much our weapons as fire—probably more these days, when so much of our lives was lived in human form rather than trueshape.

"Can you see into my mind?" Luce asked.

"I don't know. I've never tried just looking." Always before I'd been either enthralling someone or placing a temporary compulsion. I didn't go snooping around in people's minds just for kicks—particularly not the minds of my friends. "Maybe it only worked because he was enthralled to her."

"Maybe. Why don't you try it and see?"

"If you're sure …" The idea of poking around in Luce's mind was oddly repellent. What if I damaged her? Or saw something I didn't want to know?

"Go ahead."

I stared at her, and she stared back, trusting me not to harm her. Wyverns were an unusually loyal species among shifters. Backstabbing and betrayal were completely foreign to them, though they'd been on the receiving end often enough to learn a certain wariness in giving their trust. But once it was given, it was yours forever.

Okay. Deep breath. If I could kill people I could do this. I extended my will slowly, carefully, probing her mind with a feather-light touch. I found the joy of the open sky and a fierce protectiveness which was the core of Luce's personality. Tentatively I peeked around, being careful not to push too hard.

"Think at me," I said. "Try to communicate."

"I am. Can't you hear me?"

I shook my head and tried harder. Though I found plenty of things that felt like Luce, they were all images and feelings. There was no soundtrack to go with them.

At length I gave up. "I can't do it. There must be something more to it. Maybe you have to be a thrall for it to work."

"Maybe. Have you got a headache?"

I took my hand away from my forehead guiltily. "Just a little."

"Let's get some food into you and try again."

She went in search of the stewardess, who soon reappeared with a tray of exquisitely presented sushi. When we'd finished eating, Luce turned straight back to the subject with single-minded determination.

"I know you can't enthral me," she said, "and naturally I wouldn't want you to—but couldn't you try a compulsion?"

"Do you think it'll make a difference?"

"How should I know? But it's worth trying."

"Well, I guess we've got nothing else to do for the next"—I checked my watch—"six and a half hours." And Luce would nag me for every minute of them if I didn't try.

I pushed into her mind with my usual determination, and grasped a firm hold of her will. It certainly felt more comfortable, at least from my end, than my previous tentative attempt.

"Speak to me in your mind," I said.

She nodded dreamily. I waited, but heard nothing. "Are you speaking?"

"Yes."

Not a peep. Bummer. It would have been so useful.

Frustrated, I pushed deeper, past the surface layers of her mind. Her consciousness was a vast cavern boasting many doors, all closed. I began opening doors at random.

"You have to let me in," I said. "Speak to me again."

Yes, mistress.

Caught up in my explorations, it took a minute to realise I hadn't heard that with my ears.

"Again! Tell me something about yourself."

What would you like to know?

It was faint. If I hadn't been listening so hard, I might not have caught it.

Can you hear me? I sent to her, and she nodded. A thrill of excitement shot through me. We could do this! *Say something in Japanese.*

Ohayo gozaimasu. Good morning.

"*Ohayo gozaimasu*," I repeated aloud.

"Your accent needs work," she said. "We'll have to limit your conversations. Try again."

Obediently I set to work. We had a lot to do before we landed.

CHAPTER TWENTY-TWO

Our pilot arranged for a limo to meet us on arrival at Narita—not one of Daiyu's, just a hire car, since we didn't want to announce our arrival. It would be just our luck if one of Daiyu's household rang her to find out why she had sent these guests to Japan. The game would be up before we'd even begun.

"Are you going to take the potion now?" Luce asked once we'd left the plane.

"Think I'll wait. We only get ten hours—I don't want to waste any of them."

I had the official who came to greet us under a compulsion before he'd even straightened from his bow, and he wasted no time in seeing us through to our limo. A bitter wind blew, cutting right through my jacket, and I was glad I had warmer clothes in my pack. The driver got out to load our backpacks into the boot, but I waved him off and hurried into the car, glad to slam the door on the winter night. Sleet lashed the car as we sped off down the long freeway towards Tokyo.

Our destination wasn't the city itself, but a classier suburb further out from the smog and noise of the central district. Basically the Beverly Hills of Tokyo. Daiyu had a residence there—house wasn't a grand enough word to cover it—built in the traditional style and surrounded by gardens that Luce said were the envy of Tokyo.

When we were a couple of blocks away, she gave me the nod, and I pulled the small bottle from my pack, feeling the tremor of nerves in the pit of my stomach. I unscrewed the lid and raised the bottle to my lips. It smelled even worse than I remembered. Would it still work if I threw it back up?

I downed it in one quick gulp, before the stench unsettled my stomach any further. Heat flushed through my body, and in the rear-vision mirror I saw the driver's mouth fall open in amazement. I thrust myself into his mind at once and compelled him to forget what he'd just seen. He looked out the windscreen, bored, and I turned to Luce, only to find the same stunned look on her face.

"How do I look?"

Her throat worked as she swallowed hard. "Like … like Daiyu."

"*What?*"

"Holy *shit*," she breathed. "I thought that was Kasumi's hair in the potion."

"So did I." I shifted so I could see my own face in the rear-vision mirror. Kasumi had never actually said whose hairs they were; we'd all just assumed they were hers. I raised a hand to explore my new features. Daiyu's cold dark eyes stared back at me.

My mind raced. A lucky break at last. Now my aura would match my outward seeming, and as Daiyu I'd have unfettered access to everything. Flying under the radar would be harder, but that seemed a small price to pay. Our chances of making it out of here alive had just gone up by several factors, thanks to a certain devious fox lady.

On our left, a high wall was separated from the street by a canal—a moat, I guess. The car turned at a bridge that crossed the moat and stopped, the way barred by a pair of massive gates. Though they were covered by ornamental carving, they weren't just for show. Two uniformed men stood guard, one on either side. They must have been freezing, but their faces showed no sign of discomfort. Probably thralls. One approached the car, barking something stern in Japanese at the driver, who swivelled in his seat to look helplessly at Luce.

I looked at her too, long enough to establish a light compulsion, then lowered the window.

Open the gate, I said in my mind, and Luce obligingly gave me the Japanese translation. I glared at the guard and repeated the phrase.

He jumped as if shocked with an electric cattle prod and bowed so low I thought he was going to lose his balance and faceplant into the slush on the pavement.

A thousand apologies, mistress, Luce translated into my mind. *I did not know it was you.*

He shouted to his companion and together they hurried to heave open the gates, then bowed deeply in unison as the car swept past them up a long drive to a low, rambling house that stretched off into the darkness.

"Ready?" Luce asked as the car stopped in front of the doors.

"Ready."

I handed her my backpack. Kasumi might have carried her own, but Daiyu certainly wouldn't. We got out of the car, the twin thuds of the doors closing loud in the chill night air. As if summoned by the noise a servant appeared in the doorway, dressed in an ornate kimono. He squeaked at the sight of me and fell to his knees, pressing his forehead to the wet ground in full obeisance.

I glanced at Luce and she waved me forward, so I moved past the man as if he wasn't there and stepped up onto the verandah. The servant scurried after me and knelt to remove my shoes. Luce took hers off too.

"Shall I inform Hakawa of your arrival, mistress?" the servant asked, head bowed.

Luce silently translated and added that Hakawa was the steward, an ancient griffin who had served the Japanese throne for decades.

I'd learnt a few basic words and phrases on the flight. "Yes" was one of them.

"*Hai.*"

The man hurried away in search of Hakawa. We followed more slowly. The first room was large and almost completely empty. The floor was covered in the traditional tatami mats. Braziers in the four corners provided some heat, and a beautiful flower arrangement was displayed in a niche.

Daiyu's apartments are this way, if I remember correctly, Luce said into my mind. Safer than using English aloud. She slid aside a door painted with sprays of cherry blossom to reveal a corridor and I followed her along it. We passed several more sliding doors, all closed. A light shone through the thin paper screen of one door, but the other rooms were dark.

How long since you've been here?

Close on a hundred years. It was back before the wyverns were driven out of China, when I still served the Chinese queen. She came here to visit not long after Daiyu had taken the Japanese throne. It was cold then, too. I'd forgotten how much I hate northern hemisphere winters. She slid back another door and grinned with satisfaction. *Here we are.*

The room was dark and chilly. The braziers here weren't lit, since no one used the room when Daiyu was away. Goosebumps prickled into life on my arms under my jacket. What did she have against central heating? Traditions were all very well, but dragons liked to be warm. I was surprised Daiyu was prepared to live like this.

A man whose round face was twisted into an anguished expression hurried into the room, waving the servants who followed him toward the unlit lamps and braziers. He fell to his knees and touched his greying head to the matting. From his light blue aura I guessed that here was the griffin steward, Hakawa.

"Lady! Forgive me for such a poor welcome home. I did not expect you."

"No matter," I said, repeating the sounds from Luce's mind.

A servant hurried to place seating cushions for Luce and me. The room brightened as I knelt and sat back on my heels in the style of Japanese women. I added "chairs" to my wish list for Daiyu's home. I wasn't going to be able to sit like this for long.

Hakawa remained kneeling but lifted his head from the floor. "I regret that Lord Akira is out. I will have him summoned."

"No." Akira was Daiyu's current consort, a young red dragon who'd managed to hang on to her favour for the last decade, which was practically unheard of. Queens weren't usually the faithful type. The last thing I needed was trying to pull off my deception in front of someone who knew her so well. "I wish to be alone."

The necessary gaps in the conversation while Luce translated and then supplied my next words felt glaring and unnatural to me. If Hakawa thought so he gave no sign. Perhaps he was used to Daiyu giving him a long, slow death glare before she spoke.

"As you wish, mistress. Shall I bring a meal?"

"Yes."

He sat back, his eyes alight with a curiosity tradition dictated he could not express. "I am delighted to see you home safely. I trust everything is well?"

"Yes."

"Are we to expect the other members of your party too?"

"No, they remain in Sydney. I shall not stay long." That was the longest thing I'd had to say yet, and I stumbled a little over the words. He shot me a curious look.

"Forgive me, Lady, you are tired. I will bring food." He rose and bowed his way to the door.

"Bring the kitsune leader too." I waved him out before he could speak again. Reluctantly he left, taking the two serving girls with him, though one of them knelt just the other side of the closed door, ready to respond to any orders.

I rose and paced the room while we waited, partly to keep warm, and partly because my legs would go to sleep if I stayed in that unnatural position much longer. Japanese people were used to sitting on the floor, but my Western muscles were complaining already.

A commotion in the corridor announced Hakawa's return. Two guards came behind him, one either side of a slight Japanese man in a black turtleneck sweater and black pants. Like Hakawa, his hair was greying at the temples, which meant he must be considerably older than the forty-odd that he looked.

He bowed, as shallowly as he could without causing outright offence, and kept his dark eyes lowered, as if indifferent to the reason for my summons. His yellow kitsune aura was paler even than Kasumi's, as if he were sick. Perhaps he was just depressed from his long incarceration. Or maybe it was the weather. I'd be miserable too if I had to put up with the freezing conditions in this house. The braziers had barely made a difference to the temperature in here. I swear I could see my breath fogging when I spoke.

"You may go," I said to Hakawa and the guards. I could tell from the way he hesitated that he would have liked to argue, but he pressed his lips together and bowed instead, and they all left the room. He must have learnt from bitter experience the futility of arguing with Daiyu. "You too," I said to the serving girl who was sinking to her knees outside the door.

"Sit," I said to the kitsune once they were all gone, and that caused a flicker of surprise. He lowered himself to a cushion before resuming his contemplation of the floor.

I leaned forward and dropped my voice so that even Luce had to strain to hear. "Do you speak English?" I asked in that language.

For the first time he met my eyes, and his own held a wary look. He answered equally softly. "Yes."

I continued in English; it was easier than the mental back-and-forth between me and Luce.

"What is your name?"

His eyebrows shot up. He must be wondering what kind of trap Daiyu was laying for him now. At length he answered: "My lady knows it: I am Yamada Toko."

"What relation are you to Yamada Kasumi?"

His voice grew frosty with distrust. "I am her father."

I glanced at Luce. The next part would be tricky.

"You kitsune can take on the form of any other person."

"This is true."

"Are you aware that there are other ways of impersonating someone, through the use of goblin spells, for instance?"

He inclined his head, suspicion bright in his eyes. "I have heard it is so."

"Do you know your daughter's phone number?"

"Yes."

Luce pulled out her mobile and offered it to him. He glanced from one to the other of us, but made no move to take it.

"Ring her," I said.

"What am I to say to her?"

"Ask her where Daiyu is."

He took the phone as if afraid it might bite and dialled, pressing each number with a slow deliberation that made me want to scream. My mental clock was counting down: eight and a half hours remaining till Blue's potion wore off. We needed to move faster.

Someone answered and he burst into a stream of incomprehensible Japanese.

"Speak English," I hissed.

"And put it on loudspeaker," Luce added.

"– didn't tell you to do anything," Kasumi was saying.

"Kasumi," I broke in. "It's me."

"You made it," she breathed. "Father, I know what it looks like, but that isn't Daiyu. She's here in Sydney with me."

The phone trembled in his hand. He stared at me, eyes huge. "I don't understand."

"It's Kate, queen of Oceania, the one I told you about. She's wearing a seeming. She's come to help you."

"No …"

"*Yes*. Trust me, Father." There were noises in the background, and Kasumi dropped her voice. "I have to go. Listen to her. Do whatever she says."

The line went dead. Toko handed the phone back to Luce with a sigh.

"If this is a trap, it is too clever for me. I do not understand."

"It's no trap," Luce said. "Believe us. Believe your daughter. Daiyu already has you in her power. What would be the point of a trap?"

He shook his head. "It seems so strange. You look exactly like her."

"Goblin seemings are every bit as good as kitsune ones. They just don't last as long. In a few more hours this disguise will evaporate. We all need to be far away before that happens."

Hope dawned in his eyes. "You mean to free us?"

"I do. But first we need to restore your hoshi no tama to you. Do you know where they are?"

"Yes, but getting them back may prove difficult."

"Why?"

The slightest noise in the corridor was the only warning we had. The door slid open and a young man entered, his dragon aura bright red with strength and virility. I leapt to my feet.

Akira, Luce whispered into my mind. *Daiyu's consort.*

He stopped short on the threshold at the sight of the kitsune, but his eyebrows nearly disappeared into his hair when he saw Luce.

"Daiyu, my darling—back so soon? And what is the Chan woman doing here?"

CHAPTER TWENTY-THREE

We all froze. We must have looked guilty as hell—it was just as well he had no reason to suspect anything. Luckily for me Luce kept her wits, and she fed me my lines.

"Lucinda Chan has sworn allegiance to me."

He frowned, his gaze lingering on Luce for a long moment. She stared back at him, her face giving nothing away.

At length he turned back to me. "Why have you come back so soon? I thought you were to stay until the throne of Oceania was secured?"

Luce told me what he'd said. *Answer him in English.*

"Oceania is falling apart." Obediently I spoke in English, hoping that the real Daiyu was fluent in that tongue. But I trusted Luce not to give me a bum steer. She'd never let me down before. "There are a host of new pretenders to the throne. I fear I must delay my plans until they have killed each other off and the dust settles. It is easier than becoming directly involved."

"Why are you speaking English?" His English was good, without trace of a Japanese accent. He sounded like a BBC announcer.

"Our guest is not fluent in Japanese." Hopefully he didn't know Luce well enough to catch me in the lie.

How was I going to get rid of him? The more we spoke the more opportunities I had to shoot myself in the foot. I didn't know anything about him apart from his name. He might even be expecting a joyous physical reunion. I had to get him out of here.

Sure enough he crossed the room to my side and bent closer for a kiss. At the last moment I turned my face so his lips grazed my cheek and not my mouth, but even so my pulse started hammering in my throat. The dragon scent of him was hard to resist. For a moment I entertained a wild thought of distracting him with sex. At least then we wouldn't have to talk.

I swallowed hard and focused on a pair of golden werewolf eyes instead.

"Something wrong?" he murmured in tender Japanese.

In answer I stepped close, wrapping my arms about him. Trying not to be obvious about it, I pressed my lips against his collar, leaving a perfect lipstick kiss. He was dressed in Western style, in an expensive-looking grey suit and white shirt. My lipstick stood out sharply against its crisp whiteness.

"You smell of sake," I said, drawing back from him and folding my arms across my chest in the universal symbol for *now you're in deep shit, mate.*

He drew himself up, surprised at my hostile tone. "I've been at a business dinner. You know what those are like."

"But they were not all business*men*, were they? You have lipstick on your collar."

He glanced at Luce and Toko and switched to Japanese again. "Why do you bring this up in front of these unworthy ones? Send them away and let me make it up to you."

Clearly he didn't like having witnesses to our little domestic squabble, but I stuck resolutely to English, determined to rile him.

"How long did you wait before you sought out other women? Was my plane even in the air?"

"We have always had an open relationship," he began in Japanese.

"Speak English," I commanded him. "And now you come to me, fresh from another woman's bed, and expect to be welcomed."

He pressed his lips together and swallowed whatever heated answer was trying to force its way out. Arguing with one's queen was always a risky proposition, even if you were her lover.

"I was not expecting you back so soon."

"Obviously! You might have been here then, instead of drinking and sleeping your way around Tokyo."

"If my presence offends you I can always remove it," he ground out between clenched teeth.

He bowed, a sharp, jerky affair, and left the room in angry strides. If he could have, I'm sure he would have slammed the door. That was the trouble with sliding screens—no dramatic potential.

Luce crossed to the door and slid it shut, a gleam of amusement in her eyes. "Hopefully that's the last we'll be seeing of him for a while."

I nodded, feeling some of the tension in my shoulders ease. This was going to be hard enough to pull off without Akira poking his nose in.

"You were speaking of the hoshi no tama," I said to Kasumi's father. He hadn't moved from his cushion the whole time Akira was here. "Why will it be difficult to retrieve them? Where are they hidden?"

"There is a cave on the grounds of the estate," he said. "It is hidden behind a waterfall, and guarded by a jorogumo called Miyako."

"What's a jorogumo?" The Japanese had a thousand thousand monsters in their various mythologies, many of whom were real shifters, but Leandra hadn't heard of them all. Luce looked troubled, but she let Toko explain.

"A spider-woman. She is old and strong and more than a little crazy. She takes the form of a giant spider at night and lurks in her waterfall, waiting for a victim to happen by, to be dragged to their death in the lake. Daiyu occasionally sends her a prisoner, or someone who has displeased her. But not even Daiyu herself dares come too close during the hours of darkness."

Curious. Surely even the most fearsome spider was no match for a dragon.

"Isn't she Daiyu's servant? What does Daiyu have to fear from this Miyako?"

Toko shook his head. "Jorogumo are free spirits. They are no one's servants. She and Daiyu have an arrangement, that is all. She guards the hoshi no tama for Daiyu, and in return Daiyu provides her a place to live and the occasional snack. In spider form Miyako is fearsomely strong, and lightning fast. It is possible she could even dispatch a dragon in the right circumstances."

"Then how does Daiyu ever deal with her?"

"She is much weaker in the daylight hours. She takes her human form then, and spends most of the day sleeping in her cave. It is only safe to approach her at dawn before she goes to sleep, or in the evening when she wakes, before it is full dark and she takes her spider form."

A sick feeling began to bubble in my stomach. "So you're saying I can't try to get the hoshi no tama back until dawn?" Bloody hell, that would be cutting it fine. I'd only have half an hour or so before my disguise dissolved. I turned to Luce. "We can't wait that long. Is there anything else we can do?"

Luce shrugged. "You could try wearing Daiyu's perfume. Like most spiders, a jorogumo has very bad eyesight. She may not even realise who you are until after she has attacked. But if she can smell you …"

"No, no." Toko shook his head. "I beg you not to attempt it. It is not safe."

"It isn't safe to be caught here wearing my own face, either," I pointed out. "We could try burning her out, perhaps, but we don't know where she's hidden the hoshi no tama."

Toko drew back in horror. "If our hoshi no tama are destroyed, my people will die."

"Probably not worth risking, then," Luce said dryly. "It would be a shame to come all this way to free the kitsune and end up killing them instead."

"Not an ideal rescue," I agreed. "Where are your people held? Are they guarded?"

"We are housed in the west wing. Guards prevent us from entering the other parts of the house, and there are guards on the gates, of course, but they are more to keep track of our movements than to keep us in. Several of us leave the compound every day for work, and the older children go to school, though the little ones are not allowed to leave. As long as Daiyu holds our hoshi no tama we dare not step out of line. That threat controls us better than a hundred guards could."

"Then we'd better hurry up and get them back. Lead us to this waterfall."

Luce stood, and checked her knives in their sheaths. Toko rose too, a look of distress on his face.

"Please reconsider. There is nothing to be gained, and only death to be won, by meeting the jorogumo in the dark."

"We'll think of something," I said, with more confidence than the situation perhaps warranted. I'd been in some tough corners lately, but I'd never dealt with a rampaging spider-woman before, and no great ideas were presenting themselves. Better get it over with, though. Time was ticking away.

Luce moved to a chest tucked in the corner and began rummaging through the kimonos and other belongings folded inside.

"What are you doing?"

"Looking for Daiyu's perfume." She pulled out a small glass bottle and uncorked it. "This smells like it." She passed it to me and I dabbed it on sparingly. It had a pleasant jasmine scent, but it was very strong.

Toko pounced as Luce was repacking the chest.

"Take that." He indicated the shamisen inside, the Japanese three-stringed version of a guitar. "Perhaps we can soothe the jorogumo with music."

"Does she like music?" It wasn't much of a plan, but it was better than nothing.

Toko sighed. "Not as much as she likes killing people."

CHAPTER TWENTY-FOUR

Toko led the way down smooth paths, past austere rock gardens where the sand was raked into decorative swirls and nothing stirred. I was glad I'd packed my thick jacket; our breath fogged in the night air. He carried the shamisen, a resigned slump to his shoulders, clearly unhappy with the whole idea. A guard on the wide verandah had watched us slip on sandals without comment. We saw no one else as we meandered through the dark garden.

Luce and I hung back as we left the rock gardens and entered a section where mature rhododendrons towered overhead. We crossed an arched wooden bridge painted red and hung with lanterns, while beneath us fat carp slid lazily through the cool water of a small ornamental pond. The air was bitingly cold.

"You know," said Luce, "I've heard rumours about the secret component of du."

"Oh?"

Du was the only poison that killed dragons apart from bane leaf, and the secret of its manufacture was known only to the Chinese queens. I'd always supposed that bane leaf must be at least part of the lethal formula.

"Yes—that the recipe involved milking the fangs of a venomous shifter."

"Oh, great." I stopped and stared at her in the faint glow of the distant lanterns. Somewhere an owl hooted, while nearby something small rustled around beneath the rhododendrons, probably hoping not to become an owl's dinner. "You think it's from a jorogumo?"

"How many venomous shifters do you know?"

"Apart from wyverns, you mean?"

She smiled, her teeth white in the dark. "We don't have fangs. And I think I might have heard if our venom had such an … interesting … use. I know whatever it came from, the venom could only be gathered at night."

"And here we have a shifter who only takes her monstrous form at night." I sighed. Nothing was ever easy. "It certainly looks possible—assuming they have jorogumo in China?"

"Well, we don't call them that, but we do have something similar. This one could be related."

"I guess it would explain why Daiyu is so careful around her."

That had been bothering me. A dragon had little to fear from any shifter, however fast or crazed they were.

Toko noticed we'd stopped, and looked back hopefully. "You've changed your mind?"

"No." I waved him on. "Keep going."

The gardens were huge. Even at night they were lovely, filled with evergreens and artfully arranged shrubs. To our night-seeing eyes, a new vista opened up around every bend of the path. It must have been spectacular in the daylight. We passed through a less-manicured section, almost like a mini forest, and emerged on the top of a slight rise, with a beautiful lake laid out before us. A teahouse modelled after the famous Golden Pavilion of Kyoto jutted out over the water to our right, and on the other side of the lake a small waterfall emptied into the water below after splashing prettily over rocks. Each one looked carefully placed to give the most pleasing arrangement.

"That's it?" I asked.

Toko turned pleading eyes to me. "Wait until morning, great lady. A few more steps will take us into the jorogumo's domain. We would be fools to go any further."

The man's fear was infectious. I had to remind myself of the risk of delay before I could take another step.

"You can stay here if you like," I said gently. "But we're going on."

He accompanied us a little further down the path, then chose a boulder a safe distance from the water's edge.

"I will sit here and play, and hope that the jorogumo is soothed."

He set the instrument on his lap, and soon its atonal music floated across the still water. The night was calm, the only other sound the gentle splash and gurgle of the waterfall emptying into the lake. It was beautiful, but I wasn't fooled. Toko didn't seem the type to jump at shadows.

Luce drew two of her many blades and strode forward with one in each hand, her gaze constantly travelling over the quiet landscape, searching for danger. I watched the waterfall: its rippling movement seemed designed to mislead the eye. At any minute I expected a giant spider to leap out of it.

In fact, I almost wished she would. The waiting was the worst part. Luce and I slowed right down, trying to watch every direction at once. Whichever way I faced, I had the uncomfortable feeling that something terrible was sneaking up behind me. My nerves were wound so tight I cried out when the music cut off mid-note, followed by a thump as the shamisen hit the ground.

I whirled, and saw Toko straining against a rope wrapped around his leg. The other end of it disappeared into the water. I ran to him, but Luce was faster. She hacked through it with a few blows of her knife, and Toko scrambled away, his face a mask of horror.

Luce caught at the rope before it retracted and looped it around the boulder Toko had been sitting on. She had trouble pulling her hands away, and I realised it was sticky.

That was no rope—that was spider's web.

Holy shit, the spider that it came from must have been *enormous*. I backed away from the water, dragging a shaking Toko with me. Just as Luce managed to free herself from the sticky stuff the boulder twitched, then it flew into the lake, jerked on the end of the web as if it weighed nothing.

I stared, open-mouthed, at the ripples spreading across the dark water, making the dried reeds in the shallows shake and shiver, the only sign that the boulder had ever existed. Miyako would be disappointed to find rock was the only thing on the menu.

Luce hurried back to join us where we stood, a considerable distance from the water's edge. Clearly my original estimate of what constituted a safe distance had been off. The shamisen lay abandoned on the shore, but none of us felt inclined to go fetch it.

"Miyako!" I shouted. "Come out! It is I, Daiyu. I need to talk to you."

The boulder exploded out of the water, and we leapt out of the way as it crashed into the spot where we'd been standing.

I drew a shaky breath. "I guess we wait for sunrise after all."

"Good decision," said Luce.

"I will warn the other kitsune to be ready," said Toko, already beating a hasty retreat back up the path.

We followed him, not much slower. Luce still had her knives out. She looked as shaken as I felt. Okay, so maybe there were some things dragons should fear. I fretted over the delay, but I'd hate to come this far only to become a spider sandwich. I'd just have to wait a little longer. Lachie was counting on me.

CHAPTER TWENTY-FIVE

I passed what was left of the night chasing sleep on a mattress unrolled on the floor. Luce didn't seem to sleep at all: every time I woke, trying to find a more comfortable position, she was up, silhouetted against the soft light coming through the screens from the passageway.

"Is it morning yet?" I asked a couple of times, until she told me sternly to go to sleep and that she would wake me in plenty of time before dawn. But knowing you have to get up at a certain time always makes sleeping hard. I kept rousing, worried that I'd overslept.

When she finally did shake me awake, I was lost in a complicated dream involving hundreds of tiny spiders and a giant can of fly spray, and I felt groggy, as if I hadn't slept at all.

"Time to go," she whispered. "The sun is rising."

I don't know how she knew. When I staggered outside the cold slapped me in the face, but it was still dark. No stars peeked through the heavy cloud cover. Looked like Tokyo might be in for snow.

We trudged back down the path to the lake, our footsteps crunching on the frosty ground. Luce carried a sword that she hadn't had last night; she must have found it among Daiyu's things, or "borrowed" it from one of the displays we'd passed in the house.

By the time we crested the rise that looked over the lake, an orange glow had appeared in the sky to the east, in the small clear space between the horizon and the thick grey clouds. My breath made billowing clouds of my own in the cold air when I spoke.

"Let's hope she's in a more receptive mood this morning."

We entered the ornate teahouse that jutted over the lake. Its large windows were open to the elements, allowing an unobstructed view of the pretty waterfall across the lake, everything washed to grey in the dim light.

"Miyako," I called. "Show yourself."

Luce stood beside me, her sword drawn, watching the dark water below us. Nothing stirred except the hairs on the back of my neck, which were insisting we head back to the safety of the house *right now*, dammit.

What was wrong with me? I was too old to be afraid of the dark, and too powerful a shifter to be afraid of another. The temptation to take trueshape and be sure of my invincibility hovered, but I couldn't risk it. Miyako might be too blind to tell the difference between my trueshape and Daiyu's, but who knew if Blue's seeming would survive the transition to trueshape and back? I couldn't risk losing the protection of my disguise before I had to.

"Miyako! Come out. I need to talk to you."

A shivering among the reeds had Luce bracing for action, but no boulders appeared this time, only a woman's head, rising from the water like the birth of a Japanese Venus.

"Who calls?" She spoke English, as I had, and it only then occurred to me that I probably should have used Japanese. Oh, well, I could use Luce's supposed inability to understand as an excuse, as I had with Akira.

"Daiyu," I said.

She glided closer, more of her body rising from the lake as she did. She wore a soft pink kimono, and looked the picture of Japanese beauty—until she heaved herself up onto the bank, and I saw that her bottom half was still in spider form. She reared over us, even though the teahouse was raised above the lake, and I stepped back.

The spider body was huge, coated in thick dark hair that dripped water. Each leg ended in a vicious claw the length of my hand. It seemed all the more hideous for coming out of the bottom of that pretty pink kimono with the lovely dark-eyed face on top. If Shelob ever played dress-ups, this is what she would look like.

"Your voice sounds different." Her eyes looked in our direction, but there was a vagueness to her gaze, as if we were unclear to her in the shadows of the teahouse. No one else had noticed my voice was wrong for Daiyu, too taken in by the evidence of their eyes. But the jorogumo didn't rely on her eyes.

"I have a sore throat." Okay, it was lame, but it was the best excuse I could come up with at short notice. Out of the corner of my eye I saw Luce wince, but the jorogumo didn't pursue it.

She sniffed at the air—probably checking out my perfume—and seemed satisfied.

She settled her bulk on the lake shore, and I was glad she didn't want to share the teahouse with us. At least, with the spider head gone, I didn't have to worry about poisonous fangs, but those hideous claw-tipped legs were enough to give me a whole new set of nightmares, and I didn't want to get any closer to them than I had to.

"Who is your companion?"

"This is Lucinda Chan. She is helping me with the Australian situation."

"Ah. I was hoping you had brought me a snack."

I shuddered. The light was growing, though the sun hadn't yet topped the horizon, but better illumination wasn't doing Miyako any favours. The sooner she could take full human form, the happier I would be.

"No. No snack."

"Another time, perhaps. It has been too long since I have felt live prey squirming in my grasp."

She sounded wistful. Clearly here was a shifter who had never adapted to modern life. I wondered how old she was. Her human face had the unlined beauty of youth, but that told me nothing. Toko had called her "old and crazed". She could be centuries old, if jorogumo were one of the more long-lived types of shifter.

Not that I was interested enough to prolong our charming interview with personal questions. Miyako yawned, delicately covering her mouth with a dainty hand. Soon she'd be too tired to be any use.

"I need the hoshi no tama you guard for me." No point beating around the bush.

My abruptness didn't seem to bother her, despite the famed Japanese preference for indirectness. Daiyu was a dragon: I figured she didn't bother with chitchat.

"Which one?" she asked.

"All of them."

"Really?" Her face became more animated. "Are you finally going to kill the meddlesome little foxes? A kitsune or two would make a tasty treat."

"My plans need not concern you. Only my wishes."

She bowed, a sullen look on her face. "I was only asking. I don't have many opportunities for conversation down here."

She hulked to her feet, and Luce's sword arm twitched reflexively, but she only lowered herself back into the water and headed out into the lake. I watched until her dark head disappeared under the water, but I saw no movement at the waterfall. The entrance to her cave must be below the waterline.

Luce eyed the sky, a worried look on her face. The clouds covered the horizon now, so we couldn't check on the sun's progress, but it was light enough to see colour returning to the world.

"I hope she doesn't forget what she's doing and fall asleep in there," she muttered.

"Relax," I said, though I felt far from relaxed myself. "Why do you always assume the worst?"

"Because that way I only get pleasant surprises, not nasty ones."

"Here she comes!"

A dark bun, held in place by a long, lethal-looking hairpin, rose from the water, soon followed by the rest of Miyako's head. Did she walk on the bottom of the lake or was she swimming? Her progress seemed too smooth for swimming.

My hopes that she might be fully human now were dashed as she heaved her hideous bulk up onto the shore and approached the teahouse. Between her soft white hands nestled a carved wooden box. I eyed it doubtfully. It wasn't very big. Did it really hold the hoshi no tama of all the kitsune?

She placed the box on the window sill and bowed, scattering drops of water from her hair.

"Is that all of them?" I asked.

She opened the box to display its contents, which gleamed with yellow light. It was like looking at a box of golden eggs.

"This is all you gave me. Thirty-five hoshi no tama, and the one you took before makes thirty-six."

That would be Kasumi's, which Daiyu still held in Sydney. It would be up to Kasumi to secure that one.

Were there truly only thirty-six kitsune left in the world? Kasumi had said they'd been hunted almost to extinction, but I hadn't realised quite how dire the situation was. No wonder the children were so carefully guarded. They'd be worth their weight in gold.

"Thank you."

I took the box and stepped back hurriedly, anxious to be out of the jorogumo's reach. But she only smiled, as if my fear of her was only her due.

Then she lifted her head, sniffing the air. "Someone comes."

Faster than I had imagined the bulky spider body could move, she melted away from the window. I turned, just as Akira crested the rise above the lake. It was bright enough now to see him clearly, and his brows drew together in anger at the sight of Luce.

"What are you doing?" he asked. "Why do you spend so much time with this wyvern?"

We moved up the path to meet him, conscious of the jorogumo lurking somewhere among the ornamental bushes. I didn't like to turn my back to her, but I had no idea where she'd gone. Hopefully back to her cave to sleep. There was no sign of her, not even a ripple on the lake's still surface.

"I had business to attend to."

"Here?" His gesture took in the lake, now catching the orange glint of the sky as the sun rose. Then his gaze fell on the box in my hands. "Is that the hoshi no tama?"

He looked up, not quite suspicious yet, but aware something strange was going on. Luce moved casually to place herself and her sword between the two of us.

And of course Blue's potion chose that very moment to expire. I felt a peculiar ripple run over my body, from my head down to my toes, and saw Akira's eyes widen in shock. He roared in baffled fury, and leapt forward.

Luce's swing nearly took off his head, but he managed to avoid it by rolling to the side. That didn't turn out to be such a great move. Two monstrous hairy legs darted out of the bushes and snared him. His roar changed to a squeal of surprise.

Luce and I fell back as Miyako reared to her full height, her beautiful face contorted into a vicious snarl. Her legs worked to roll him in webbing, but he had a knife out, and was hacking at her and the webbing. When the terror of the moment wore off, he would think to take trueshape, and then she'd be in trouble.

Even as I thought that, the spider body convulsed. At first I thought he'd stabbed her, but then I saw it was the other way around. She had a stinger on the back of her abdomen, like a bee's, and she'd curled her body to bring it into play. As it withdrew from his back, venom dripped from its point.

Maybe Luce had got it all wrong, and it wasn't the jorogumo's fangs but her stinger that dragons needed to worry about. How effective would the poison be? It wasn't the full du recipe, but it might slow Akira down enough for Miyako to drag him into the lake and drown him.

"Think he's toast?" I asked as we backed slowly away from the struggle.

"If we're lucky. Let's not hang around to find out."

When I looked back from the top of the rise, they had reached the edge of the lake. Akira had both arms free and was hacking furiously at Miyako's legs. One of them dragged at an odd angle, but she was still determinedly pulling him toward the water. A gap in the clouds showed the sun three-quarters above the horizon. If he could hold on until she was forced into fully human form he would make it. Was it wrong of me to cheer for the spider?

Luce and I dashed up the path to the house. Things would get ugly fast now I no longer looked like Daiyu. The first guard who saw us spent a second too long in confusion. He didn't know who I was, but had seen Luce in Daiyu's company before, and didn't realise she was hostile until an instant before her sword took off his head. His gun was only half out of his holster when his body thudded onto the verandah.

We raced along the verandah to the west wing. A servant girl shrieked and dropped the bowl she was carrying at the sight of Luce's gory blade. It rolled on the wooden floor with a clanging that sounded loud as a gong. No doubt it would soon summon guards to investigate. We left her screaming in our wake. Speed was our best option.

Luce didn't bother opening the door when we arrived at the kitsune living quarters, but leapt straight through the paper screen. The woman inside sat up from her bedroll with a small squeak of alarm at the sight of us.

"Quickly!" said Luce. "Find Toko."

The woman scrambled to her feet, and I noticed she was fully dressed, in dark pants and shirt, ready to go.

"Follow me."

We hurried down the corridor after her. She shouted something in Japanese—probably "time to party!"—and doors flew open as we passed. Toko appeared in one, and his eyes lit up at the sight of the box I carried.

"You did it."

I shoved the box at him. I could hear guards calling to each other outside. "I hope you're ready to go."

He nodded, and hugged the box to his chest. "We need nothing more than this. We are ready."

A child whimpered, and was quickly hushed. He opened the box. A sigh of relief rippled through the assembled kitsune at the sight of their hoshi no tama softly glowing. Eager hands reached out to receive them, and the box was soon empty.

An angry roaring outside penetrated the solemn hush in the corridor.

"Who is that?" Toko asked.

Damn. Sounded like the jorogumo had come off second-best after all. "That's Akira. Get ready to fight."

CHAPTER TWENTY-SIX

"I have a better idea," said Toko. "May I?"

He reached out before I could guess what he meant and plucked several hairs from my head, passing them out among his kin. A young woman did the same to Luce.

I'd seen a kitsune transformation before, but it was still fascinating to watch. Each kitsune placed the stolen hair on their own head, then held their precious hoshi no tama up to their face and breathed in its shining yellow aura. As the golden light suffused them their features changed, and just like that, there were three new Kates and three new Luces standing there, dressed identically to us.

It was quite the experience, being able to see yourself from the outside like that, but I had no time to decide if my arse really did look big in that. While I'd been focusing on my own clones, the other kitsune around us had changed too. All but the children were now dressed as guards. One even looked like Akira.

"Toko?" I asked, a little hesitant, even though they hadn't moved.

"Here," said the Akira one.

"You guys have been busy." It must have been difficult to obtain a hair or personal possession of so many people, particularly here, where the kitsune threat was so well known. Whoever had stolen a piece of Akira must have had nerves of steel. Dragons were very careful of their personal effects. I couldn't imagine the danger they must have faced to get it. "What now?"

"Now the games begin." Toko gave a fierce grin, and it was the pleasantest expression I'd ever seen on Akira's face. He nodded to one of the Kate and Luce pairs and they ran out onto the verandah.

I heard the real Akira's shout of rage and the sound of a gun being fired. I winced. As if that was the signal, the kitsune scattered, leaving one pair of "guards", Toko, Luce and me.

"This is going to be interesting." Luce's grin matched Toko's.

We hurried down the corridor toward the main wing of the house. Two guards still stood there, keeping stoic watch against marauding kitsune, though their attention was clearly on the distant shouts and occasional gunfire. They stiffened to surprised attention at the sight of Toko.

"What are you doing here, fools?" he barked at them in irate Japanese. Luce obligingly translated for me. "The kitsune have escaped while you guard empty rooms. Go join the hunt!"

"At once, master." They both bowed low, and before they could straighten again Luce and one of our pretend guards bashed them into unconsciousness. We stepped over their crumpled bodies and moved on.

"Where to?" Luce asked.

"The garage. We must get you to the airport. Nowhere in Japan will be safe for you after this."

That suited me just fine. The sooner I got home, the sooner I could be reunited with Lachie. And then there was just the coronation to get through. The endgame was close.

We hurried through empty rooms and past anxious servants who bowed deeply to Lord Akira and watched him escort his captives, whoever they were. If they wondered what had become of Daiyu they kept it to themselves.

Hakawa appeared, flanked by a pair of guards.

"Lord Akira." He bowed. "I can't find Lady Daiyu."

"She has already gone ahead," Toko grunted. "I go to meet her. Wait here until we return."

"As you wish, my lord."

"Stop them!" shouted a familiar voice from the garden. The screens were open. The real Akira, looking a little worse for wear since the last time we saw him, stumbled toward us. His kimono was ripped and smeared with blood, and there was something not quite right about the way he moved, as if he was having trouble coordinating the movement of his limbs. Shame the jorogumo venom hadn't finished him off, but it had certainly had an effect.

"My lord!" Hakawa, open-mouthed, stared from one Akira to the other.

"Arrest that imposter," Toko commanded. "He is a kitsune."

One of the guards with Hakawa started toward Akira. Akira's problem was that, at the moment, Toko looked more like the real Akira than he did himself. Toko was dressed immaculately, drawn up to Akira's full haughty height, whereas Akira himself was slurring his words like a drunkard and covered in filth. There was nothing like being dragged backward through the bushes by a ravening spider-woman to mess with your outfit.

Akira backhanded the guard out of the way. "You fool! *He* is the kitsune."

He dropped his ruined kimono. The air around him shimmered and a red dragon stood in his place. Oops. Looked like the old taboos were out the window in Japan as well as Sydney.

The dragon drew in a deep breath. *Shit.*

"Incoming!" I reached for trueshape. "Get out of the way!"

I slammed into trueshape, smashing screens and bursting through the roof with a roar. Luce and the kitsune ducked behind my bulk as the red dragon let loose a blast of dragonfire. It rolled off my scales, no more than the pleasant warmth of the sun on a summer afternoon, and licked hungrily at the paper screens. They went up with a whoosh.

Hakawa and his guard burned bright as torches. They had time for one scream before their charred bodies collapsed.

"Go!" I urged Luce, my voice booming above the crackle of the flames.

She went, dragging the kitsune with her, and I leapt out into the garden to face the red dragon. My tail lashed the neatly raked pebbles and sent them flying.

"Who are you?" he growled, but his eyes were having trouble focusing. The jorogumo venom was still bothering him.

"Your new queen."

I pounced on him, but he collapsed even before my claws touched him, his eyes rolling back into his head. He shimmered back into human form, leaving me feeling rather stupid, like an elephant who'd just made a big deal out of defeating a mouse. I took human form too, and snatched up his filthy kimono to cover my nakedness.

I hesitated over his body for a moment. His face had a better colour than when he'd first staggered out of the garden, and the wound to his arm was healing over. I should probably kill him now while he was still helpless. Leandra would have done it in a heartbeat.

I shrugged and jogged off in the direction Luce and the kitsune had fled. I had a plane to catch.

CHAPTER TWENTY-SEVEN

The kitsune already had the motor running when I arrived.

"Thank God," said Luce as I fell into the back seat of the black sedan with her. "I was just about to come looking for you. What happened to Akira?"

"He's enjoying a nice rest in the garden." I rubbed one bare foot vigorously. After running across the frozen ground my feet were so cold I couldn't feel them. I dragged the thin kimono a little more firmly around myself, thinking longingly of my thick winter jacket.

"You should have killed him."

I let my head fall back against the headrest with a sigh. "How did I know you were going to say that?"

"Because it would have been the smart thing to do, and you know I'm right."

"Next time, then."

She rolled her eyes at my flippancy. "I hope there is no next time."

But if there is it will be all your own fault, her unimpressed face said.

"What was wrong with him?" Toko asked. He had taken his own form again as soon as the car rolled out of the front gate, and watched me now from the front passenger seat. "He seemed ill."

"Miyako attacked him," I said. "Got him with her stinger."

"Ah." He eyed me with disapproval. "Lucinda is right. You should have killed him. The jorogumo's venom will not slow him for long."

I sighed. I'd just managed to break the captive kitsune out of their prison and saved their leader from death by dragonfire, and still no one was happy. Everyone was a critic. "We don't need long. It's only an hour to the airport. We'll be in the air in no time." I looked out the window. It was full daylight now. The jorogumo would be asleep, if she'd survived her encounter with Akira. From the state he'd been in, I'd guess she had.

"Where are the rest of your people?" I asked Toko. "Did they all make it out?"

"We will rendezvous with them after we see you safely to the airport. I did not see any bodies, so I hope they are all safe."

I hoped so too. There were so few of them left.

"And then where will you go? Where is safe for you now?"

An unexpected smile lit his face. "Anywhere is safe, now we have our hoshi no tama back. We can be anyone. Daiyu will not trap us so easily again."

One day I would have to get the story from Kasumi of how she'd trapped them in the first place. Perhaps they'd willingly walked into her clutches, as loyal servants to the throne, and found their powers stolen and abused. If so, she would live to regret it. Nobody needed an enemy who could take on any form. If she survived, Daiyu would be forever looking over her shoulder. They might make good servants, but kitsune were bad enemies.

"I'm glad. One more thing, if you will. I made a deal with your daughter, that I would free her people if she would free my son." I nodded to Luce and she passed her phone across. "Please tell Kasumi it is done."

He dialled the number, then spoke in rapid Japanese.

It's done, Luce said into my mind. I'd forgotten I still had the compulsion on her. *He told Kasumi we'd held up our end of the bargain. He said to take Lachie and get out of there before Daiyu discovered what we'd done.*

Thank God. I felt as if a weight had been lifted from me. Lachie would soon be safe with Garth. After that there was little to do but watch Tokyo slide by past the window and count the hours until I would see Lachie again. Luce rang our pilot and instructed him to file a flight plan for Sydney and get ready to leave.

At the airport the car rolled onto the tarmac. Our small plane shone in the morning light, the dragon on its side seeming to breathe a fiery welcome. Toko got out of the car and bowed to Luce and then to me, his face grave.

"We kitsune owe you a debt that can never be repaid. Know that you have only to call and we will be there for you."

I bowed back, but then I gave in to my feelings and hugged him. Bowing just wasn't the same. And he looked like he could do with a hug.

"Thanks for all your help," I said.

He smiled, though his eyes glittered with tears he would never admit to. "Thank you, for saving the children. We have a future again because of you."

Well, I was all for saving children. Especially my own. I waved as he got back in the car, and stood there until he'd driven away.

"Coming?" asked Luce.

"You bet." I turned and bounded up the stairs to the plane. The smiling stewardess greeted me in her prettily accented English. "Welcome aboard."

"It's good to be back." I settled into one of the comfortable lounges, and Luce sat opposite me.

"Can I get you a drink before we take off?"

"No. Just tell the captain we're ready, please." I couldn't wait to get into the air. Only eight hours to Sydney. Eight hours before I could hold my little boy in my arms again.

She was still smiling at me, and I'd half-turned away, when I caught the movement of her arm out of the corner of my eye. I thought it was a knife. I launched myself out of my seat and landed on Luce. We sprawled across the seats together.

The stewardess's hand slammed into the back of the seat where I'd just been sitting, unable to stop her momentum in time. She shrieked with rage and lunged at me again. I had time to see that it wasn't a knife but a syringe before Luce dumped me unceremoniously on the floor and closed with the woman. She twisted the woman's wrist until the syringe fell from her nerveless hand, and punched her in the face.

The stewardess went down like a sack of potatoes. At the same moment the cockpit door slammed open and someone fired three shots straight into Luce's back.

"Luce!" I scrambled toward her, the floor vibrating beneath me as the plane taxied out to the runway. She was still on her feet, though she sagged against the nearest seat for support as she faced the man holding the gun.

Akira.

How had he gotten here so fast? He must have flown. There was no sign now of his fight with the jorogumo. The gun didn't shake as he pointed it at Luce. Outside the tarmac flashed past as the plane picked up speed, the engines roaring.

"Shoot me again," Luce said, pushing herself upright with visible effort. "That tickled."

"I think I will." He sneered at her. "And then there'll be no one to protect your precious mistress. There's no room for her here to take trueshape, and I'm prepared for her this time."

He held up his free hand. It held another syringe, just like the first. This was getting old fast. Every man and his bloody dog had a damned syringe full of du these days.

He fired another round and it tore into Luce's chest. I cried out as she fell forward.

So did he, for she took trueshape as she fell toward him and breathed right in his face. She hit the floor, but he didn't move, a look of surprise frozen on his face. The sudden thrust of acceleration as the plane left the ground buckled my knees, and I lurched against a seat.

A weak chuckle came from the floor. "Fear breath. Gets them every time."

My hand closed on the syringe the stewardess had dropped. Akira's eyelid twitched, but that was the only thing he could move. Wyverns could shoot a venomous mist from their mouths that paralysed anyone within range.

Clearly Akira was in range.

I stalked up the sloping aisle toward him, murder in my heart.

"Luce?" I said.

"Uh-huh?"

"It's next time."

I plunged the syringe into his chest and watched in satisfaction as the killing du entered his body.

CHAPTER TWENTY-EIGHT

I fell to my knees beside Luce, ignoring the death throes of the Japanese man. There was blood everywhere; all over Luce's ruined clothes, smeared all over her scales, and much too much still leaking from her changed body.

At least being in trueshape would speed up her healing. A bullet hit the carpet as I watched, forced out by the healing process. Just as I'd feared, it was silver. So there would be silver fever to contend with as well as the damage from the gunshot wounds themselves.

I snatched up her torn shirt, wadded it up and pressed it hard against the wound on her chest. That bullet must have grazed her heart at least, if not gone clean through it. There was a lot of blood. My hands shook. Shifters healed fast, but this? Some things couldn't be recovered from, even by shifters. If her heart was too damaged …

I couldn't even get to the wounds on her back. Her trueshape was too heavy for me to budge in my human form, and her wings got in the way, rammed up against the seats where she'd fallen. The plane was still climbing, its sharp angle adding to the awkwardness. She was barely conscious, her body shutting down everything to focus on healing.

"Come on, Luce," I urged under my breath. "You can do it."

Another bullet rolled out from under her wing. That was a good sign, at least. I lifted my makeshift bandage. The blood flow had slowed to a sluggish welling, but her scaled chest rose and fell in short, panting breaths.

Still, I felt I could leave her long enough to hunt up a first aid kit, and I found one in the well-equipped kitchen. Akira lay still when I returned, his face swollen beyond recognition. No one had appeared from the direction of the cockpit. Either they trusted Akira to handle the situation or, more likely, his last order had been to stay where they were. Though they weren't his thralls but Daiyu's, she would have ordered them to obey him in her absence.

I bandaged Luce as best I could, given the obstacles of wyvern anatomy, keeping a wary eye on the poisoned barb on the end of her tail. She twitched a couple of times as I worked, and moaned. I didn't want that thing twitching anywhere near me. Wyvern poison wouldn't kill a dragon but it wouldn't exactly be a walk in the park either. We had enough worries without that.

The stewardess stirred as I finished tying the last bandage, so I grabbed some tape and more bandages and got to work tying her hands and feet. Her face was a mess; Luce certainly hadn't pulled that punch. Her nose was broken and one eye was swollen shut. She glared at me from the other one and hissed something in Japanese which didn't sound at all complimentary. Since I didn't have Luce to translate I just smiled sweetly and heaved her into a chair. That was probably more consideration than she deserved, but she was getting underfoot.

I swiped Akira's gun from where it had fallen. He wouldn't be needing it again, that was for sure. The stewardess's eyes widened, and she began yelling. Damn. Should have gagged her too. I swung the gun round to point at her, but before I could say a word she stopped mid-yell and slumped to the side.

Hell, I wasn't that scary, was I? I moved closer, frowning. Her head lolled on her shoulder as if someone had just removed all her neck bones. I tapped her lightly on her undamaged cheek, and then slapped her harder, but got no reaction. Weird.

Still, I had better things to do than worry about fainting stewardesses, so I stepped over Akira's body and headed for the door into the cockpit. The plane was still climbing, and I had no idea where Akira had us heading. Time for a course adjustment.

No one had locked the door behind Akira. I turned the handle and shoved the door hard, ready with the gun. Or as ready as someone can be who's never fired one before in her life. Leandra had always left such things to the hired help, and guns had never been a part of my life as Kate, but these guys didn't need to know that.

But my dramatic entrance was wasted on the pilot and co-pilot. They were both slumped in their seats, as out of it as their friend the stewardess.

"Shit."

I dropped the gun and hurried to the first man. His pulse was strong, but there was no waking him. Slapping, yelling, shaking—nothing worked. The other man was just as unresponsive, but his pulse was weaker and more irregular. If it were just the stewardess, I could put it down to panic or something, but all three of them in the same state? That looked suspiciously like something else.

An alarming array of lights and gauges blinked and waved at me from the console in front of the two pilots. None of it meant a thing to me. Outside, grey skies rushed toward us, a featureless wall of cloud. Still the plane climbed.

That could be a problem. What happened if it never levelled out? Did it just keep climbing until there was no longer enough oxygen? Until the engines ran out of fuel? Until we hit the moon and came bouncing back?

Okay, maybe not that last one. I knew nothing about jets and how they worked, but I knew they worked a whole lot better when both pilots weren't unconscious. A stream of increasingly excited demands for a response issued from the radio. Whoever was on the other end was probably also getting worried about our irregular flight path.

For a moment I toyed with the idea of taking Luce and jumping out. Akira was right; there wasn't enough space inside the plane for me to take proper trueshape. If I tried, there would be catastrophic results for the plane, and I could get myself seriously tangled in the wreckage. If I was feeling brave I could just jump out in human form and take trueshape once I was in the open air. But Luce was still in her own trueshape, and there was no way I could pick her up while I was in human form. Even assuming I didn't black out the minute I left the plane. We were probably at some deadly-to-humans altitude already.

So bailing was out. Besides, if I bailed, what would happen to the three unconscious thralls? Leaving them here to die seemed kind of cold-blooded.

Okay, so no bailing. And taking the controls and flying us safely back home was definitely out. So that left reviving the pilots.

I'd already established that slapping and yelling made no difference, so I laid my hands on the head of the younger of the two and closed my eyes. Inside his mind I found him wandering, lost and bereft. Gently I coaxed him toward me, guiding and cajoling. His mind was damaged, torn loose from its guiding light, and I worked to mend it, rebuilding connections, soothing the hurt.

I don't know how long I stood there, lost in his pain. It couldn't have been very long, but it felt like an eternity before I secured him to me. His eyes snapped open, wide with wonder.

"Mistress." He bowed deeply in his seat.

Now that I had him enthralled, we could have communicated through our bond, at least in a basic way, but as it turned out he spoke English. I suppose he had to, as a pilot. Thank goodness for small mercies.

"Yes," I said. "Are you well?"

"I felt her die." He frowned at the remembered pain.

How long ago had Toko made that call to Kasumi? She hadn't wasted any time. My stomach clenched into a tight knot of apprehension. She'd better not have allowed her desire for revenge on Daiyu to jeopardise my son. Not when I was so close to getting him back.

Because clearly there had been some A-grade revenge going down. The only reason for Daiyu's thralls to have all collapsed into unconsciousness was the sudden severing of the bond with their mistress. Daiyu was dead, presumably at the hands of a certain vengeful kitsune. Just another reminder that kitsune made great allies but really sucky enemies.

So now I had a co-pilot at least. I left him to get on with flying the plane, gritted my teeth, and dived into the mind of his companion.

This was harder going. This man's mind had been blown apart by the loss of Daiyu. Grimly I set about finding the pieces. I hated having thralls, yet here I was again, adding to their number.

Or at least trying to. Even in my trance-like state, I could feel sweat trickling down my face at the effort. It was like trying to piece a shattered mirror back together with plasticine, clumsy and awkward. And I couldn't even find all the shards of his mind. It was as if he was resisting me, kicking missing pieces under the furniture where I couldn't see them. As if he wanted to die.

At last I had to give in. I came back to myself and looked down at the grey hairs, the wrinkles on the slack, unconscious face. This man must have been enthralled to Daiyu for a long time. The death of his mistress had driven him beyond my reach. There was no way to put him back together.

Even as I watched, his breathing became fainter. There was no struggle; he just slipped away.

The co-pilot looked at him uncertainly, then up at me for guidance.

"Looks like you're on your own. Do we have enough fuel to get to Sydney?"

"Of course, mistress. That is our destination."

Well, that was something, at least. Akira must have been planning to deliver our corpses to his lover. I left the cockpit and went to check on Luce. There was no fresh blood on her bandages, and she was breathing more easily, but her scaled face had an odd colour to it. Silver poisoning. Four bullets would have her out of action for a while. Thank God she wasn't a werewolf, or she'd be dead already. But no other shifters suffered the extreme reaction to silver that werewolves did.

I flopped into the seat next to the stewardess and eased into her mind, feeling the strain. Putting people back together was hard work, and after the excitement of the last few days all I wanted to do was put my head down and get some sleep.

Thankfully this woman was not as far gone as the older man, not even as much of a challenge as our other pilot. Once she was awake I untied her and got her to help me shift Luce into a more comfortable position. Then I settled down, the hum of the engines lulling me to sleep.

I woke once and saw that Luce had recovered her human form. Her face was flushed and sweaty with silver fever, but it was a good sign that her body had eased out of trueshape. The stewardess had covered her with a blanket and slipped a pillow under her dark head. I watched her for a while until sleep overtook me again. I was too tired to plan what came next.

But there'd better be a reunion with my son in the very near future, or all the kitsune magic in the world wouldn't save Kasumi.

CHAPTER TWENTY-NINE

There's nothing like the feeling when Sydney appears out the plane window, the familiar buildings, the deep blue waters of the harbour. Even the horrible, traffic-choked roads look better from the air when you're arriving home, especially when the sun's just gone down and all the streetlights are twinkling, marking the roads with strings of orange lights. Home. This place was it, whichever house I happened to be living in this week, because the people I loved were here. Lachie was here, waiting for me. I refused to contemplate anything else. I'd see his sweet pointed face again, and get to wrap his skinny body in my arms. And all the members of my crew I'd grown so close to over the past crazy few weeks would be waiting: Steve, the big half-Maori who looked so scary until he smiled, Dave with his determination to feed me up, sad Mac with her brave pink hair, and, of course, Garth.

Garth. Just the thought of him made my heart speed up a little. I stared out the window as the plane circled in for a landing. So close now. Soon, I could feel the sheltering warmth of his arms, lose myself in those moody grey eyes. But first: Lachie. He'd only been stolen a few days ago, but it felt much longer. We were still catching up on all the months we'd missed when I'd thought him dead. He'd changed so much in the time we'd been apart. His face had thinned out, and he'd gotten taller, though the curls were still as wild as ever. I couldn't bear for him to do any more growing up without me.

We bumped down onto the tarmac, the engines roaring. Luce was awake, strapped into the seat next to me now.

"You okay?"

She looked awful, trembling and grey, clutching a sick bag in one hand, just in case. Silver fever had her in its grip. Wyverns, like dragons, didn't suffer too badly from silver poisoning, but a couple of days of violent illness followed by several more of general misery was the usual. Add to that the drain on her body of repairing the damage from the gunshot wounds, and Luce was in for a bad few days.

"I'll live." She pressed her lips together, as if risking any more words might encourage another bout of vomiting.

The plane seemed to taxi forever. Impatient, I undid my seat belt and jumped out of my seat, almost twitching as I waited for the stewardess to open the door. Clear skies and a welcome rush of heat greeted us, and I stood on the top step, shading my eyes against the glare from the lights, breathing in that distinctive airport smell of kerosene.

A limousine waited on the tarmac, a familiar hulking figure lounging against it, arms folded. It did my heart good to see that lazy smile again, but his wasn't the face I was most interested in seeing. Where was Lachie?

As I hurried down the stairs, the car's back door was flung open and a small figure leapt out.

"Mum!"

My feet hardly touched the ground as I closed the distance between us and caught him in my arms. I buried my face in his curls and took a deep breath of his beloved scent. Thank God he was safe. My eyes stung with happy tears as my body relearned his scrawny shape: the way his head just tucked under my chin, the feel of his skinny arms wrapped around my waist. He was the sun my world revolved around.

"Hey, Monster!" I blinked away the tears before he saw them. "It's so good to see you again."

Talk about the understatement of the year. But my heart was too full to tell him everything it held. I'd lost him once, and I never wanted to go through that agony again.

I held him away from me, checking him over. There were shadows under his eyes, as if he hadn't been sleeping well, but he appeared unharmed. Just as well. Nothing on earth could have saved Jason if he'd let harm come to this precious boy.

"I'm glad to see you too. I didn't like those people with Dad. Everyone kept talking in Japanese and there was nothing to do there except watch TV."

I kissed his curly head. "I thought you would have loved that. Since when have you not liked watching TV?"

"Yeah, but not *all* the time. And the food wasn't half as good as Dave's cooking."

"We'll have to get some more of that into you. You're so skinny! Have you grown?"

He drew himself up taller and eyed my shoulder, then ran a hand from the top of his head to see where he came up to on me. The angle at which he moved his hand wasn't even close to horizontal, and out of the corner of my eye I saw Garth grinning, but I kept a straight face. God, I loved this boy.

"Yeah, I think I might have."

Car doors slammed as Steve and Mac joined Garth. I grinned at them all over Lachie's curly head. "Well, I'm sure Dave will be pleased to hear how highly you think of his cooking."

"He already thinks he's God's gift to cuisine," Mac said. "His head will get so big it'll explode."

"We can't have that. Steve might have to cook then."

"You're doomed," said the big half-Maori, with that slow grin that lit his whole face. "I can't cook for shit. Good to have you back, boss."

"Good to be back. Give Luce a hand, will you? She's hurt."

He moved off, and Garth raised an eyebrow, his grey eyes sharp. "Did you have much trouble?"

His eyes roved across my body, checking for injury, though he didn't stir. He still leaned against the car, arms folded across his chest.

"Nothing we couldn't handle. Relax."

He snorted. "Look at me. I'm relaxed. I've never been so relaxed."

"They say sarcasm is the lowest form of wit, you know."

"Is that so?"

His lip curled, and an urge to bite it shot through me. Damn, but he looked good. With his arms crossed like that, his muscles bulged enough to make Jean Claude van Damme jealous. I turned Lachie toward the car and gave him a gentle push, my hands lingering on his narrow shoulders. I wanted to keep touching him, to reassure myself he was real.

"Everything all right here?"

"Just peachy. Daiyu's dead—"

"I figured that when her thralls went catatonic on me. What about Jason?"

"Far as I know he's still alive and kicking. Kasumi's gone inside to handle the paperwork. You can ask her when she gets back."

Shame. I looked a little guiltily at my son. Was it wrong to wish a horrible fate on his father?

"Any progress on the negotiations?"

I'd left Mac and Yarrow in charge of liaising with Valiant. My sisters seemed to be on board with the idea of sharing the domain of Oceania in principle. The issue was in carving up the cake.

"Mac's been tearing her hair out."

"We're getting close to an agreement," Mac said. "Hope is holding out for a bigger slice of the pie, but I reckon she's weakening. Said she wants to talk to you about it, though. Doesn't like dealing with a lowly werewolf."

"Figures."

Dragons and their self-importance. These girls weren't even twenty, but they'd been brought up to believe the sun shone out of their own arses. I suppose I should be amazed that Mac had made any progress at all.

A familiar figure headed across the tarmac toward us, her strides brisk and purposeful. The red tips of her black hair waved in the light breeze, like fireflies buzzing around her head. If she'd been disguised as an official before, she'd given it up in favour of her own black-clad form. It was like a uniform for her. Must get hot sometimes. One day I'd like to see her in a sundress, or a pair of shorts, just for kicks. Probably wouldn't recognise her.

I turned as the stewardess cleared her throat at my elbow. She offered me the carved wooden box that had held the hoshi no tama with a small bow.

"Oh, yes, we have some new recruits." I took the box from her, wincing a little at her swollen face. "Send a car for them when they're finished here, would you? And get this poor woman some medical attention."

Garth nodded, finally unfolding his arms. He opened the back door so Steve could help Luce inside. Kasumi reached us, her eyes glued to the box I held.

"Is that—?"

For answer I lifted the lid, showing her the empty interior, its dark silk indented with the shapes of the glowing yellow balls it had so recently held.

"All safely restored to their owners."

She drew a sharp breath, then looked up at me, her dark eyes swimming.

"You have freed our people. We can never repay you."

Her hands were actually trembling as she reached out. I placed the box gently in them.

"Seems like you made a pretty good down payment already." I nodded in Lachie's direction. He was chatting animatedly to Mac, probably about Lego. "Thank you for rescuing my son."

She gave me a fierce grin. "And for killing Daiyu?"

"That too." That hadn't been part of the arrangement, but I'd be lying if I said I was sorry she was gone. It certainly made my life easier. And it was about time we had a win.

"The wolf was concerned at the risk to the boy." She cast her usual aloof glance at Garth, all sign of tears gone. "But I was careful. He was never in danger."

"I'm very grateful."

Garth had a mulish look on his face. It was pretty much a permanent fixture when Kasumi was around. These two had never liked each other. But it lifted my heart to hear he'd had the same concerns for Lachie that I'd had, and I gave him a warm smile. His answering one nearly sucked all the air out of my lungs. God, he was gorgeous.

It was fortunate they'd brought the limo. I'd never seen it before, so it must have been one of Elizabeth's. There could be anything lurking in those massive garages of hers. She'd probably had a fleet of them, knowing her. Steve drove, and Mac sat up front with him, which left Garth, Lachie, Luce, Kasumi and me in the back. There was still enough room for a phone and a small bar, not that any of us were drinking, though Lachie gave it a wistful glance. Probably hoping for something sweet and fizzy.

"Tell me what's been happening," I said as we left the airport behind. I had Lachie on one side and Garth on the other. My two favourite guys in all the world. "How's Blue going with those glasses I ordered?"

"Blue's gone." Garth's muscular thigh pressed against my leg made it hard to concentrate. I was hyper aware of him. "Took the glasses he was making with him, too, though he didn't manage to find the original pair."

"Gone? Gone where?"

"God knows. I sent a couple of guys to check that cave of his but there was no sign of him."

"Damn." There would be a lot of shifters at the coronation that I didn't trust, and being able to check that everyone was really who they said they were would have been handy. At least we still had the original pair, but one pair wasn't going to go far enough. "Slippery little bugger. What did he have to run off now for? Was he drinking again?"

"Not that I saw."

"You know what he's like," Mac said, turning around to join the conversation. "He can't stand anyone telling him what to do."

"Sorry," said Steve. His dark eyes met mine in the rear-vision mirror. "I should have kept a closer watch on him."

"It's not your fault. There's been a lot going on."

I sighed. We'd just have to manage. God knows it wouldn't be the first time our plans had had to change at the eleventh hour. It was practically tradition.

"Where are we up to with the negotiations on territories?"

Mac filled me in on the details. It sounded like Valiant was well and truly on our side; she was pushing her sisters just as hard as we were to agree on the proposed split, which would see her with New Zealand as her territory.

"You've done a great job," I told her. "Let's just hope the death of Daiyu doesn't put us back at square one."

Kasumi stiffened. "What do you mean?"

"Well, we can't leave Japan without a queen, or one of the other queens will just annex it. Probably Xu." It would make sense for the Chinese queen to take over the Japanese domain, not only because of geographical proximity, but because Daiyu had been her sister.

"The kitsune will not stand for another foreign dictator," Kasumi warned, a scowl marring her pretty face.

"I realise that." Toko had left me in no doubt of the kitsune's desire for autonomy. "But that's dragons for you. None of them will respect the kitsune's wishes, and then there will be bloodshed and upheaval. But I could annex it myself, and not interfere in the local politics, other than making sure the male dragons toe the line."

The scowl only lifted slightly. She didn't seem to like that idea much better, but it seemed the best solution in the short term for the Japanese shifters. And the kitsune had already worked with me, and declared themselves eternally in my debt. I was sure we could work something out.

"So what's the problem?" Garth asked, ignoring Kasumi.

"I suspect my sisters will object to me taking a whole new domain and still insisting on keeping New South Wales out of Oceania." And there was no way I was giving up Sydney. "They may even think that the Japanese domain ought to be added to the pot to be shared out."

Kasumi glowered even more ferociously at that suggestion. Even Mac looked disconcerted, probably seeing all her good work hammering out an agreement disappearing down the drain.

"You never know," I consoled her. "Maybe they won't see it that way." Yeah, and pigs might fly. "Let's hope it doesn't derail our agreement."

CHAPTER THIRTY

Three days later Hope was only half-convinced, but we were out of time. All the overseas queens had flown in for the coronation, and I wanted them out of my domain again as soon as possible. I felt like a minnow holding a party for a pack of hammerheads. I didn't want to give them time to decide I'd taste good on the menu.

In a private room at the Hilton Hotel I faced my sisters. Faith was missing, of course, but it was the first time we'd all been together since the night at Gideon Thorne's mansion. Let's hope the evening ended a little better than that one had.

They wore evening gowns again, and looked serenely beautiful, even if one or two were a little hot under the collar. Hope had grudgingly agreed to accept dominion over Indonesia, but she was still unimpressed about my annexation of Japan.

"The Philippines are closer to Indonesia than they are to Japan," she said. "And your precious kitsune can't possibly have any interest in them. I can't see any reason you should have them too."

"The Philippines have been a part of the Japanese domain for centuries."

"So?" She arched one supercilious eyebrow at me, looking so much like Faith it was as if Faith were still with us. "This whole deal is breaking with tradition. What difference does one more thing make?"

She had a point there, but I'd had enough of the petty demands of entitled dragons.

"Let's see how you manage Indonesia first. Then we can talk."

She might find she was busy enough with what she had. Not that dragons, even young ones, had a very good concept of what was "enough". Greed was practically a defining trait.

"Moving on ..." She might cause trouble for me down the line, but that was a problem for future Kate. Today I just needed to get through this damn coronation. I nodded to Steve and he turned on the big TV he'd set up in the room. The screen showed us a view of the ballroom downstairs, where eight thrones had been set up in a large circle. In six of those thrones a queen waited, with her retainers grouped on chairs behind her. It made for quite a crowd. Two thrones remained empty. One supposedly would be mine. The other was Daiyu's.

My gaze was drawn to the Chinese queen, Daiyu's sister. She wore white, the Chinese colour of mourning, in patterned silk, and her dark hair was piled high on her head. It was impossible to tell what she was thinking, but her black gaze strayed frequently to her sister's empty throne.

All the queens would have heard by now that Daiyu was dead. They all had their spy networks and news travelled fast. They might not be clear on the details yet, but that wouldn't matter. Each one of those six dragons would be busy plotting already how to turn the event to her advantage. My coronation held little interest compared to the opportunities that had just opened up. They probably couldn't wait to get stuck into their backstabbing, murderous games. It was a wonder they were still here.

In the centre of the circle of thrones, the crown of Oceania rested on a plush cushion atop a small circular table. The cushion seemed a little over the top, but Luce had assured me that a certain amount of pomp and ceremony was expected, so pomp and ceremony had been laid on. Privately I thought the crown itself was garish enough without the cushion, encrusted as it was with rubies as big as eggs. That sucker was going to be heavy. Thank God I didn't have to wear it any more after today.

A second table stood next to the one bearing the crown, but it was draped with a golden cloth which covered several intriguing bumps. This part wasn't regulation, and I could see the French queen frowning at it, no doubt wondering what was underneath that cloth. Traditionally the queen to be crowned was surrounded by the other queens for the coronation. Each touched some part of the crown as it was raised and settled on the new queen's head. Must be kind of awkward. Today the program would work a little differently. The French queen would find out soon enough what was under that cloth, and the part it would play in my highly unorthodox ceremony.

"You ladies will wait here with Garth and your attendants until we're ready for you." I was counting on Garth to keep them in line. He wasn't the type to be cowed by imperious teenagers. "I need to have a chat with the queens first. Deliver a few home truths."

Valiant smiled. "That will be fun to watch. Can we get some popcorn?"

I liked Valiant more and more as I got to know her. She had a sense of humour, and that was pretty unusual in dragons. They were normally too pompous to laugh at anything other than the total destruction of an enemy. She seemed a little more human in her thinking. Hopefully that was a good sign for our future partnership.

"I'd better get down there. They look like they're getting restless."

Garth walked me to the door. "You know you look hot in those glasses."

I was wearing Blue's goblin glasses, just in case. There were a lot of shifters in the queens' entourages, and I didn't want any nasty surprises.

"I look like a librarian."

His breath tickled my ear as he leaned closer, sending a shiver through me. "A really hot librarian."

"Idiot."

I headed for the ballroom with a grin still on my face. I expected some argument from the visiting royalty—probably just for the sake of arguing—but no real objection to my plans. The queens would probably think I was weakening the domain by splitting it, and see opportunity for themselves in that weakness. Being dragons, it wouldn't occur to them that we sisters might band together to support each other.

The lift doors opened on the ballroom floor, and I nodded to the guards stationed outside the doors. Thralls of mine mostly, with a backup of hired trolls. Two of them opened the double doors, and I paused in the doorway for effect. At least I hoped that my sisters would work together. That was the plan. I was confident of Valiant, and probably Virginia, Justine and Prudence too. Not coincidentally, all the younger ones. They were realistic enough to know their chances of going it alone weren't good, and pretty enthusiastic about the idea of holding some part of a smaller domain rather than dying in the proving. Hope, as the oldest now, had a better opinion of her chances in a proving. Not a high enough one to think she could beat me, which was why she'd reluctantly agreed to the plan in the end, but perhaps high enough to harbour some backstabbing plans of her own later. I'd have to keep an eye on her.

The assembled queens all rose at my entrance, as protocol demanded. This was their first look at the new human-tainted queen. Some of them wore crowns even more preposterous than the one waiting for me. Maria del Fuente wore a golden monstrosity that towered above her head. It looked like half the Incan treasures had been melted down to make it, and my ruby-encrusted effort looked positively mean in comparison. Lucky dragons were strong. That thing would have snapped the neck of a human wearer. It was hard to believe this woman headed one of the great fashion houses.

"I greet you in the name of Oceania," I began, sticking to the traditional script for the moment, "and welcome you as its new queen by right of proving. Elizabeth Anne is no more, and I claim her throne as my own."

Six pairs of eyes watched me. I met them all in turn. Some were calculating, some looked bored. Xu held mine in challenge.

"Where is our sister, Daiyu of Japan?" she asked.

As if she didn't know. But I was happy to spell it out for her.

"Daiyu is dead." Probably in a body bag on its way back to Japan right now. None of the Japanese contingent were here. I could just imagine the turmoil that would be going on over there right now, with the kitsune scattered, and no young queenlings to fight out a proving. The Japanese dragons would be running for cover if they knew what was good for them, hoping that when the dust settled and their new mistress showed up they might be able to crawl into her new court.

Xu pinned me with an accusing glare. "Did you kill her?"

"I wasn't even in the country when she died."

"Don't play games with me. You ordered her death."

"Rubbish. It was her own harsh treatment of the kitsune that led to her downfall. One of them turned on her."

"Really?" Maria drawled. "And where were you? It seems an unusual time for a new queen, as yet uncrowned, to be taking an overseas jaunt."

She smirked, as if she'd managed to catch me out. Well, I had news for her, the evil old lizard. I was not going to be intimidated by these creatures.

"As it happens, I was in Japan." Her superior smile faded. She hadn't expected me to admit it. "Helping to liberate the kitsune. And no, I didn't order Daiyu's death, but I'm not at all sorry for it. If she'd stayed home and minded her own business, I wouldn't have gotten involved, and she'd still be alive. She was here trying to steal my throne, so I'm happy to return the favour. Happy to return it for anyone who tries that stunt on me, actually."

Ooh, you'd think I'd hurled a firecracker into the centre of the circle of thrones. They all stiffened at the threat. No one looked bored any more.

"So I consider Japan mine by right of conquest. Any objections will be met with force."

Makeda, whose domain covered the whole of the African continent and stretched into the Middle East, spoke up. "You're a forthright little thing, aren't you?"

"I see no point beating around the bush. Japan is mine, and I'm prepared to defend it."

Xu's eyes narrowed to furious black slits. "But can you hold it?"

"Ask the kitsune. I think you'll find that they won't tolerate any interference from the other domains."

And stick *that* in your pipe and smoke it, lady.

Xu seethed quietly, having no answer to the problem of the kitsune. The Chinese queens had always looked at their smaller neighbour with greed, anticipating the day when they might incorporate the little domain into their larger one. She'd probably thought it was a done deal now her sister was out of the way, but the kitsune were a thorny problem indeed.

The French queen, Celeste, waved a languid hand, as if the disposal of one of the eight great domains of the world was merely a side issue. Perhaps it was, for her. She may have started as the French queen, but she now held all of Europe, including Great Britain, plus most of Scandinavia. Despite competition from the North American domain, hers was probably still the wealthiest of all of them. A tiny little domain like Japan was barely a blip on her radar.

"So you claim two domains?" she asked. "I fail to see how you can hold even one of them after the hornet's nest you have stirred up among the humans."

"We should kill you just for that," Xu spat. "And now our names are known!"

"That wasn't my doing," I replied, in the mildest tone I could manage. Xu was a serious pain in the butt. "I would hardly release a list that had my own name on it."

"I have had nothing but paparazzi and people yelling in the streets since the news broke," said Maria, looking at me with distaste. "If you had not flaunted yourself so brazenly on New Year's Eve, this would never have happened."

New Year's Eve had hardly been my fault. With Valeria taking off with Lachie in her clutches, I'd had no choice but to pursue her, but I refused to explain myself to these bitter old women. They had no dominion over me, and I was not going to offer excuses with my tail between my legs.

"What's done is done. Dragons were seen, the names were released—it's pointless to play the blame game now. The world is changing, and we have to change with it."

That didn't go down well. The world had been organised to suit them, after all, and they weren't interested in giving up any part of their cosy arrangements, thank you very much. There was even some murmuring from the entourages assembled behind each queen.

I strode to the second table and grabbed a handful of gold fabric.

"And speaking of which …" With a flourish a magician would have been proud of, I whipped the gold fabric aside. No rabbits underneath, but six brand-new gleaming crowns. The murmuring grew louder. I let them exclaim for a moment, turning on the spot to check out each queen. Xu glowered at me, but the others looked intrigued.

"You may have heard that Elizabeth laid a second clutch, which produced a further seven royal daughters." Of course they'd heard it; it had probably been the talk of the dragon world since that particular bombshell had been revealed. "One of those has since died, but my remaining sisters and I have agreed to share the domain of Oceania between us."

Forget polite murmuring. An uproar greeted this announcement.

"You can't be serious," Maria said when the noise died down enough for her to be heard. "How can seven of you share one throne?"

And why haven't you killed these upstarts already? said her shocked expression. I could tell she thought less of me for not finishing my sisters off. It was the dragon way. Each of these women had arrived at her throne drenched in the blood of her sisters. They couldn't conceive of anyone wishing to do anything else.

"We're not planning to share the one throne. We will divide Oceania between us, and each take charge of our individual pieces."

"But you will be the overqueen, I assume?" said Celeste. "With each of them reporting to you?"

Nope, definitely couldn't imagine anyone voluntarily giving up power. Their certainty made me quail a little. Was I kidding myself? Could we really make this work, my sisters and I? I'd only known them for a week, after all. How could I really trust them to keep their word?

"There will be no overqueen." I put some firmness into my voice. If I couldn't believe the idea myself, how could I convince anyone else it would work? "Oceania will simply be split into seven smaller domains. Each of us will rule independently, just as you all do."

"But it won't be as we do, will it?" Maria said, poisonously sweet. "Oceania is already the youngest and least of the domains. If you divide it, it will be as nothing."

And ripe for the taking, said the gleam in her eye. I looked around and saw the others had reached a similar conclusion.

"We may rule independently, but together we will be strong."

"Well, if your heart is set on it, far be it from us to try to talk you out of this mad scheme." Maria shrugged prettily, as if she were doing me a huge favour. She looked around at her fellow queens with a knowing smirk. They all nodded, except for Xu.

The message couldn't have been clearer. *It's your funeral.* None of them thought we could make a go of it, but they were more than happy for us to make the attempt. It made it easier for them to step in and wipe us out.

"Excellent," I said, as if I wasn't well aware what they were thinking. "So there will be a change in the usual arrangements for the coronation. There are six of you, and seven of us." I paused to let that idea sink in, but I doubt they saw any threat from seven young, untried queens. "That works out nicely, doesn't it? One of you will have to double up, but you can all crown one of us, as a sign of our unity."

Unity, my foot. And how I managed to keep a straight face while saying it, I don't know, though none of them seemed bothered by the irony. I signalled to Mac, who was waiting by the door. She nodded and ducked out.

"My sisters will arrive in a moment, and I can formally introduce them to you."

I wondered what my sisters had thought of the proceedings they'd just watched on their screen. The queens' reaction had probably come as no surprise to any of them. They were well versed in dragon history and politics. They wouldn't exactly have been expecting an enthusiastic welcome.

I was pleased. Things could have gone much worse. No one had stormed out, and Xu hadn't challenged me on the spot, as I'd half-feared. Guess her sisterly love didn't extend too far. She would have killed Daiyu herself if Daiyu hadn't seen an opportunity in Japan and fled China.

I heard a commotion in the foyer outside the ballroom. My sisters arriving. The other queens heard it too, and rose, eager to get their first look at the weaklings who had agreed to share rather than fight. They couldn't possibly be real dragons.

They'd be easy to take down, and then Oceania could be plucked like a ripe plum. Despite the earlier comments about Oceania being young and not particularly wealthy, I could see a calculating greed in their eagerness.

But it wasn't my sisters. An explosion ripped through the room, and the doors blew off their hinges. Men with guns poured into the room and started firing. Fools! What were they thinking, bringing guns to a fight with dragons? And then I felt something sting my bare arm. When I looked down a dart quivered there, sticking out of my flesh.

Dart guns?

A wave of nausea hit me. For crying out loud, not again. Bane leaf was supposed to be a rare poison. Lately it seemed every Tom, Dick and bloody Harry had a stock of it. Either that or du. At least it wasn't that. Hey, things could be worse! I felt an inappropriate giggle bubbling in my chest. Was this any time to come over all Pollyanna? My vision blurred, and everything seemed to happen in slow motion. I saw Xu fall to the floor, writhing and foaming at the mouth. Maria slumped in her seat, her eyes rolling back in her head.

And I saw a dart whiz around the corner of a throne to take Celeste in the throat just as she was beginning to shimmer into trueshape. What the hell was this? Darts that could fly around corners?

My knees gave way, and I subsided onto the floor, my stomach lurching horribly. The glasses fell off and I felt too weak even to pick them back up. You'd think, given the number of times I'd been poisoned with bane leaf lately, that I might have built up some immunity by now, but no such luck.

I curled around my heaving stomach and saw, through the blurring haze of illness, a man march into the ballroom. His troops had fanned out, making sure that their darts found everyone in the room. The air was filled with the sounds of screaming and retching. Guess we'd soon find out which shifters bane leaf was fatal for. How had this happened? Where were the guards I'd left outside? Who were these people?

I squinted at the man, forcing my bleary eyes to focus. His murky aura said he was a goblin, and as he approached I recognised his dark face. Patel. Damn. No wonder the darts could swerve in mid-air. Goblin magic. They were spelled to find their target, no matter what. Hadn't the little weasel died in the building collapse at Taskforce Jaeger HQ? I'd certainly had my hopes up. And now he turned out to be a mage. I reached for trueshape, but the effort brought the contents of my stomach hurling onto the floor. I collapsed into a heap. Standing up just seemed an impossible challenge.

Around me the screams were fading, replaced by whimpers and the soft sound of crying. I shut my eyes. Someone was repeating "no, no, no" over and over again. It wouldn't be one of the queens, nor any of the dragons who'd come with them. This felt much worse than the time Kasumi had stabbed me. I'd just started to wonder if maybe bane leaf could be fatal to humans in strong enough doses when my body gave up the struggle and I blacked out.

CHAPTER THIRTY-ONE

When I woke, Patel was standing over the body of Xu, admiring his handiwork. Not all the shifters were down; his men surrounded the ones who were still standing, covering them with real guns now, not dart guns. It was remarkably quiet in the ballroom, and I wondered how long I'd been out. Why had no one responded to the noise of the door blowing out and the subsequent screams? Had they secured the whole hotel? Taskforce Jaeger must have thrown everything they had into this mission.

I stared blearily at Patel, wondering how it had come to this. The taskforce could only have existed for a few weeks at the most. They'd escalated from investigations to wholesale slaughter at breathtaking speed. Surely the government couldn't have authorised this? I knew people were scared by the revelations of shifters in their midst, but this seemed way out of proportion. And Patel was a shifter himself. It didn't make sense.

He moved to check out Maria, collapsed on her throne. She was still alive, though probably not for much longer, judging by the look of her. Sweat ran down her pale face, and her lips stood out starkly blue against her skin. She groaned as I watched, and shifted her head restlessly.

Patel considered her, scrawny arms folded. No white lab coat today; he wore dark clothes, as if he fancied himself some kind of ninja, though he wasn't armed that I could see. As he stood there, he absentmindedly pushed his glasses up onto the bridge of his nose, and the action tickled at my memory. A terrible suspicion took hold of me.

Trying not to draw his attention, I looked around for my own glasses. They'd slipped off when I fell. I groped around on the floor until I found them. Fortunately they were still in one piece. I slipped them on and suddenly Dr Patel sprouted a mop of dirty orange hair, and a face I knew all too well replaced the Indian doctor's features.

"Blue! You bastard!"

He grinned and came to crouch at my side. "Hello, Kate. How are you? Feeling a bit off, perhaps? What a shame."

"I can't believe it." Although I could, actually. It made a twisted kind of sense when I thought about it. He'd never hidden his dislike of dragons. But to actually join the humans in hunting us down! "What the hell are you doing?"

"Ridding the world of a great evil," he said. "We'll all be so much better off without you lot lording it over everyone and treating us as disposable serfs." He waved a hand that took in the bodies on the floor and the general destruction. "This is just the beginning. Oceania will be the first dragon-free domain, but the others will follow soon enough when they see how much better off we are without the lizards."

I convulsed, trying to bring up something when there was nothing left in my stomach. The pain in my gut was so bad it was like giving birth all over again. I could hardly think through the agony.

He laid a comforting hand on my shoulder. "Don't worry, it shouldn't be much longer. I'm a little surprised you've lasted this long, actually. I distilled the brew until it was extra strong. Used up my whole stock of bane leaf, but it'll be worth it."

No way. No *way* was I dying here, covered in vomit, and letting this dirtbag win. I tried to find trueshape again, but the pain blocked me. It felt as if the connection between the parts of myself had been severed, and a hard knot of panic formed in my breast. *Calm down*, I told myself. *You're immune to bane leaf.* I had to believe it was still true. It was the ace up my sleeve, because Blue hadn't been around for that revelation.

"And then what? Who are you going after next, once the dragons are all dead?"

He shrugged. "I doubt I'll need to go after anyone. Now the names are out there, I can leave it to the humans to take care of."

The list. Of course. No wonder there'd been so many shifters from Oceania on that list, and only the overseas queens and a handful of other prominent people. Blue had given them the list. They were all the names he knew.

"You bastard. How long have you been working for Taskforce Jaeger?"

He grinned, baring his sharp teeth at me. "Haven't you figured it out yet? I thought you were smarter than that. Taskforce Jaeger wouldn't exist without me. I started it."

"But why? You're a shifter too. People are dying already out there. How could you do that?"

"I'm just a goblin. Hardly even a person in a dragon's eyes. What's the point of being a shifter at all when you get so little respect?" He leaned closer and whispered. "I'll let you in on a secret. It's a shit world out there unless you're on top of the heap. No one likes goblins—not even other goblins. And mages are kept like animals, whipped into working."

There was something really offputting about his intensity. I shrank back, as if his hatred would infect me if he got too close.

"That's why I've decided to aim high," he said in a more normal tone. "Time to be top dog for a change, see what it's like not to be everybody's bloody whipping boy."

He looked at me as if expecting a reaction, but I had no idea what he meant. I could hardly focus on him, lost in the grip of the pain that engulfed me, much less figure out his cryptic utterances. He was going to have to call a spade a spade.

"What the hell are you talking about?"

He blew out an impatient breath, ruffling the lank orange hair of his fringe.

"Let me spell it out for you, Kate. I'm going to cut that funny little stone out of you. You know the one, right? It sits on your rib, just over your heart, and it lets you change into a dragon."

My channel stone? What the hell?

"I tried using Faith's, but there was something wrong with it. Or maybe there's more to it. Maybe the anaesthetic we used on her interfered with the magic, or maybe it only worked in your case because Leandra had been poisoned with bane leaf first."

"But ..." But he hated dragons. Was he talking about making one by stealing my channel stone? I was lost.

"See, I was trying to be nice, knocking Faith out before I cut it out of her." His face twisted as he pulled his shirt aside to show me a small scar above his heart. "But it ruined everything. It didn't work. It's just a lump of useless rock."

Holy hell. I'd seen that scar before, back in the goblin's cave. The guy was a certifiable lunatic. He thought that just shoving a channel stone into his chest could make him into a dragon?

"So I won't be making that mistake again. I'm afraid you'll have to be awake for the whole experience when I cut it out of you."

Except I wouldn't be pushing my essence into the thing before it left my body, if it came to that. He'd never be a dragon.

"If you hate dragons so much, why do you want to be one?"

"I never said I hated dragons." He readjusted his shirt to hide the scar. "I just hate the fact that they can push me around. Even you, with all your pious worrying about the poor shifters I've betrayed to the humans—you're just as bad as the rest of them. You used me, same as all the others. 'We'll tell your family where you are, Blue. Work for me or else, Blue.'"

He pitched his voice high in a childish imitation of mine. "Not so caring then, were you? Well, now it's my turn."

"Was that your whole reason for creating Taskforce Jaeger and starting this vendetta against shifters?"

"You sound like you don't approve. Never said I was Mother Theresa either."

"Seems a bit short-sighted." The pain in my gut had eased in the last few moments. I hope it didn't occur to him that I was taking an awfully long time to die. "Won't the humans come gunning for you next?"

He waved his hand dismissively. "It'll all die down soon enough. And you'll notice that *my* name wasn't on that list."

Someone behind me cleared their throat. I lay still, not wanting to give away that I now felt well enough to roll over and see who it was.

"Sir, I think we have a problem."

I recognised that voice. Wilson, who'd led the Taskforce Jaeger raid on Thorne's house. I'd assumed he was the commander of the taskforce, but apparently not.

"What?" Blue's voice was sharp.

"We don't seem to have enough dragons here."

Blue spun on his heel, checking the circle of queens, then letting his gaze rove the rest of the room, over dead male dragons and other assorted shifters.

"You told me they were all assembled! I specifically said to wait until they were all in the room!" He turned an accusing glare on me. "Where are your sisters?"

He sprayed me with spit with the word "sisters". I wiped my face, and his eyes widened as he saw the ease of my movements. Yes, I was feeling a lot better. So much so, in fact …

"Find them, you idiot! And give me that dart gun!"

He snatched the gun out of Wilson's hand, but he was too late. I surged to my feet, reaching for trueshape as I went, and felt the blessed thrill of union as the parts of my soul rushed back together. Blue screamed, a high-pitched wail that held the death of all his hopes.

The scream cut off abruptly as I bit him in half.

CHAPTER THIRTY-TWO

I felt the impact as dart guns hissed out their deadly little missiles, but they fell harmlessly off my scales. I swung my great head round to glare at the offending men, and they backed away, trembling. They huddled together against the far wall, no longer so sure of their superiority. Numbers were nice, but manpower meant nothing up against dragon power. One of them unloaded a handgun into my chest, but the bullets had no more effect than the darts had.

Behind the mass of terrified taskforce men, the wall exploded, spraying them with bits of plaster board. The lights died abruptly, and large bodies shouldered their way into the room through clouds of dust and bits of ripped-out wiring. Large dragon bodies, glinting silver and golden and copper in the half-light from the foyer behind them. My sisters had decided to join the party.

I spat the two halves of the goblin's corpse out, and saw the glitter of silver in the remains of his chest, peeking out from beneath all the blood. Silver veins on a black stone. Faith's channel stone, stolen by this imposter. My blood boiled, and I turned to the soldiers, a song of vengeance singing through my veins.

What followed was a bloodbath. With seven dragons in the room, the soldiers stood no chance, and I lost myself in the pleasure of ripping into my enemies, feeling their blood spurt in my mouth and run down my chin. Some of the other shifters joined the fray too; they had no love for these men who had killed their queens. I saw a leshy turn into a bear and tear a man's arm off, gun and all, and a wolf leap for the throat of another who was trying to fight off two mermen.

All too soon, there were no more enemies to face, and I came out of my killing frenzy. That wolf was Garth. Now I recognised his night-black coat, and felt a fierce pride in the blood coating his muzzle. He was a killer, same as me. Our eyes met across the room and he gave me a wolfish grin.

As the dust settled my sisters gathered in a loose semicircle around me, crouched low, tails still lashing. The ballroom was big, but with seven full-sized dragons in it and a crowd of shifters and corpses, it was almost cosy. Most of them were golden like me, though one—Charity?—was silver, and Valiant had such a red tinge to her gold it could hardly be called gold any more. More like rust.

Valiant held a body between her front feet, and chewed absently on its leg. It was Wilson.

"We could have used him," I said, my voice reverberating in my chest and coming out in a deep growl. "Someone needs to report back to the government on the folly of attacking dragons."

"Sorry," she growled back, and my lips curled back in a snarl of amusement. She wasn't sorry at all. I guess I wasn't either. The corpses would probably be just as effective as a deterrent.

"You looked like you needed a hand," said a golden dragon in Hope's voice.

They must have seen what happened on their TV feed and hurried down to help. Of course they would have missed the part where I turned dragon and chomped Blue, but there was no need to be ungracious. We needed to build a working relationship, after all, and this had been an excellent bonding exercise. The family that slays together stays together.

"I had it pretty much under control by the time you got here, but I appreciate the assistance."

The black wolf trotted past the crouching dragons, with no apparent concern for the size of the jaws looming over him. He sniffed my bloodied claws, gave them an exploratory lick, then settled himself comfortably between my front feet.

I glanced down at his furry trusting head and felt a wholly undragonlike rush of love.

"Time to shed your fur and get to work, wolf," I said. "You can't laze around like that. We've got a lot of clean-up here."

He rolled his yellow eyes at me and began the bone-crunching contortions to shift back to his human form. The other dragons watched him like cats watching a mouse, and I rose, a warning rumble vibrating its way up from my belly as I stood over him.

Valiant tore her eyes away and made an effort to refocus our sisters' attention. Everybody's bloodlust was still up. Time to talk them down.

"Do you think this is all of Taskforce Jaeger?"

I surveyed the mess of corpses and body parts scattered over the bloodied floor.

"I'd say so. Seemed like this was a big step in the goblin's plans. He would have wanted to make sure of it."

She cocked her giant bronze head at me, and I realised most of my conversation with Blue had probably taken place after they'd left the suite with the TV feed, so I filled them in on what had been said. That distracted them from the vulnerable werewolf completely.

They were all shocked; Hope seemed positively outraged.

"He meant to make himself a dragon? The *only* dragon?" The spurs on her golden head trembled with anger as her gaze swept the room. "Is there anyone else here who'd like to see the end of the dragons?"

The assembled shifters hurried to assure her that no, they were all very happy to bend the knee to dragonkind. Maybe they were even sincere. Certainly no one was brave, or foolish, enough to say otherwise.

"Looking on the bright side, this gives us some ammunition in the PR war," I said.

"What do you mean?"

"When word of this gets out, the government will have a huge scandal on its hands. A taskforce they set up to investigate goes totally rogue and starts conducting secret experiments and killing shifters. And word is *definitely* going to get out."

A naked man stood now between my feet. He still smelled of wild wolf and blood, but he looked like a Greek statue come to life, all strong muscled limbs and sculpted torso. The urge to take human form and jump those gorgeous bones nearly overwhelmed me as bloodlust surrendered to plain old garden-variety lust instead. Only the knowledge that it would be a bad idea to expose my weak human form to six riled-up dragons gave me the strength to hold back.

"You want to be careful how much you say about those secret experiments," he said, nodding at the top half of Blue's corpse. The channel stone had disappeared beneath the blood now, but I knew what he meant. The fewer people who knew the secret of dragon transformations the better.

"I think we can manage something suitably incriminating without giving too much away." I gave him a gentle nudge, which still managed to make him stumble. "Go and put some clothes on before I *eat* you."

He grinned at me, and I saw a promise in those clear grey eyes. Later. We could both be as predatory as we liked when this was over. A thrill ran through me, right down to the tip of my tail, which lashed in anticipation.

I turned to the remaining shifters, who'd gathered in a wary knot to one side of our discussion.

"I'm sorry for the death of your queens. Now there are six more empty thrones in the world. And here before you are the last remaining queens to fill them."

A short silence greeted this thought. A voice came from the back of the group, safely anonymous. "What if we don't want to live under a queen any more?"

Hope and Charity shifted restlessly, but I rumbled at them until they quietened.

"That's a good question. Maybe some of you agree with the goblin, and think that dragons should be left to die out." No one was brazen enough to nod, but I daresay a few of them were thinking it. "If that's what you think, let me just pose you one question: if there are no queens to rule, who will control the male dragons?"

I said nothing else, just let them stew on that. Male dragons left to their own devices were so territorial they became monstrous—well, even more monstrous than normal. It was not unusual for lone males to turn rogue and go completely mad, laying waste to vast tracts of land and killing everything they could find. It hadn't happened in modern times, but all those tales of knights being sent to slay ravening dragons hadn't sprung out of people's imaginations. An unchecked male was a very dangerous beast. Only the soothing influence of the queens kept them in check. It was why male dragons usually took a place at court; they felt the pull to be near the queen.

"It would be a bloodbath," said the leshy who'd been fighting as a bear.

There were murmurs of agreement from all sides, and the twitching tails of my sisters settled to the floor again.

"Good. Then all that remains is to decide which queen takes which domain. When you have had time to bury your queens you may send a delegation to me, and we will discuss the most suitable distribution of domains."

My sisters eyed me, some speculatively, others with a more resentful gleam in their eye, but no one questioned my right to dispose the dragon empires of the world as I saw fit. Sometimes it was good to be the queen.

CHAPTER THIRTY-THREE

Morning sun slanted through the gap under the half-closed blind and fell on the clothes abandoned on the floor, making a trail from the door to the bed. I grinned and snuggled down under the sheet. My partner grunted sleepily and flung a muscled arm around me, pulling me closer.

Last night had been my reward for all the crap I'd had to put up with in the last couple of months. Last night and the night before that and the night before that … Obviously I needed a lot of rewarding.

I'd thought the negotiations over the division of Oceania had been bad, but they were nothing compared with the bickering over which sister got which of the vacant thrones. Between the jostling for prime real estate from my sisters, and the manoeuvrings of the interested parties in each domain, it had been enough to try the patience of a saint. And clearly I was never going to be a candidate for canonisation.

We'd managed to settle some of the disputes early, which had fooled me into thinking this might be simpler than I'd feared. Valiant had laid claim to South America straight away. She said she'd always been fascinated by that part of the world. Of course it didn't hurt that Spain was part of the package. Charity, rather surprisingly, had gotten quite chummy with two male dragons from Africa, and her decision to take the African throne seemed to make all parties happy.

The problem was Europe, Celeste's old domain. Head and shoulders above the others in terms of riches, it was the most fiercely contested. At one stage Hope and Prudence almost came to blows, and in the end it was only settled when I threatened to pull names out of a hat if they couldn't come to an agreement another way. The European male dragons and some of the higher shifters eventually chose Prudence over Hope, which I can't say broke my heart.

I annexed Japan into Oceania, which made sense geographically. Japan had always been a tiny domain, and it only existed separately for historical reasons, which were hardly relevant any more considering the Japanese line had died out years ago.

I rolled over and burrowed my face into the crook of Garth's neck. He smelled of wolf and wind and blood, as he always did, that wild scent that was part of his nature, but he also smelled of sex and hard-earned sweat. I took a deep breath of him. I could wake up next to that smell every day.

"Whassa time?" he grunted.

"It's still early. Go back to sleep."

For answer his arm tightened around me, and the other hand buried itself in my hair. Yes, it had been an interesting few weeks. It was a wonder we'd found any time for ourselves amid the madness. Our revelations about Taskforce Jaeger had almost brought down the government, and had forced a change in prime minister. He'd stepped down with bad grace, then watched, scowling, from the back bench as his successor rescinded his controversial anti-shifter legislation. The new guy was a vast improvement. He'd invited me to become the official representative of the shifters, and I'd given my first official press conference last week.

Luce had helped me write my speech, which was still being replayed all around the world.

"We have always lived among you," I'd said, doing my best to hide my nerves. This was a big deal, and first impressions were so important. I'd worn a simple shift dress in a dark green that complemented my eyes and set off my auburn hair. Nice, but not too dressy. I wanted to look like an ordinary person. "We always will. Nothing has changed except that now you know about us. We are you. Your child's kindergarten teacher, your dentist, that helpful mechanic at the local garage. Were you scared of the woman on the checkout at the supermarket before? Of course not. There is nothing to fear but fear itself."

I was quite proud of that speech, and I thought Roosevelt wouldn't mind if I appropriated one of his best lines. It seemed to fit the circumstances so well.

Of course things weren't going to be as easy as all that. There was still a large and vocal number of people who thought we should all be burnt at the stake. You didn't have to look too far to find some nutter calling down God's wrath on the unholy, but an encouraging number of people seemed to be coming around to the idea of peaceful coexistence with the monsters.

The fashion industry was in mourning for Maria. The fact that she'd been a dragon didn't stop the tributes from pouring in, and the many heads of fashion houses talking about the great loss to the world of haute couture. In fact, it didn't seem to bother them at all that she'd been a dragon. It seemed only secondary to the consideration of her talent as a designer.

I pulled back from Garth, giving myself room to admire his hard body. His sculpted chest was thick with hair, as were his arms and legs. Werewolves always had a lot of body hair. Just as well pretty smooth-skinned boys weren't my thing.

His eyes opened, and his aura blazed with orange fire as he dragged himself fully from sleep. Like a wild animal, he seemed to have a sixth sense that told him when someone was staring at him.

"What?" His tone was gruff, but his lips curved in a welcoming smile. Those lips were full and oh-so-kissable, I was discovering.

"Nothing. Just admiring the view."

"View, my arse."

"I'm happy to look at that too. You might have to roll over, though."

He growled, but he was still smiling. He looked ten years younger when he smiled, and he was smiling a lot these days. It was as if the goblins had stolen grumpy Garth and left this grinning changeling in his place.

"I was thinking about Jason," I said.

He cocked one eyebrow. "Why? You fancy a threesome?"

"Get your mind out of the gutter." I swatted at him, but he caught my hand and started trailing kisses up my arm. "I made sure to tell the girls all about him." It had been a full and satisfying account of all my ex's many character flaws. "There's no way any of them could take him in, is there?"

"You asking me or trying to convince yourself?" His grey eyes sparkled down at me as he paused in his kiss trail.

"Bit of both. I can't imagine that he'd manage to fool one of them, but you know what Jason's like. He can be very charming when it suits him."

"Forget him. He'll probably go into real estate in some pokey little town and fleece rich divorcees out of their money."

The thought was cheering. Not for the rich divorcees, of course, but the idea of Jason reduced to a salesman to make ends meet held definite appeal.

Garth had kissed his way to my shoulder, where he was distracted by my hair, drawing strands of it across his face, nuzzling into it.

"I've always had a thing for redheads, you know. Can't believe I'm waking up next to one in my bed every day."

I smirked up at him. "*My* bed."

He gave me a challenging stare, then laughed, a sound of mingled joy and disbelief. "Our bed."

"Yes." I liked the sound of that. "Our bed."

Our bed. Our lives, together now. I felt at ease with him in a way I'd never experienced with Ben. Garth not only accepted me for who I was—dragon and all—but rejoiced in it. The fierce pride and love I saw in his eyes when I took trueshape was a reflection of my own when I saw his wolf. Ben had never accepted me as a dragon, but with Garth there were no reservations. We were two predators together, glorying in each other's strength and ferocity. Right for each other.

If only he'd been a dragon. Wolves lived no longer than humans did. Neither did half-breeds, who always inherited their human parent's genetics, so Lachie was fully human. Whereas dragons … I pushed the thought away. It was unbearable that I would outlive both Garth and Lachie, probably by centuries. That future would destroy me.

Live in the now. I reminded myself of that every day, seeing Lachie off to his new school. *Live for today.* So many joyful moments. My mother's face when she realised her own daughter was the infamous queen of Sydney, oh, and by the way, her grandson wasn't dead either. Meals around the kitchen table with the crew. Nights with Garth. *The present is all we have.*

And the present was pretty damn hot, even if it had a shocking tendency to argue. I met those warm grey eyes and smiled. To think I'd ever found this man frightening. He was my joy, from his greying buzz-cut hair right down to his toes.

"I could eat you," I whispered into his ear, then gave his earlobe a playful nip.

"I'd like to see you try." He threw me onto my back, pinning me down with his naked body.

"Hold that thought." I wriggled out from under him, feeling the loss of his warmth as I slipped out of the bed. "I'll be back in a minute."

He lay back, arms behind his head, and watched me as I crossed the carpet to the en suite. I shut the door and hurried through using the facilities, eager to return to him. As I washed my hands I leaned forward, checking myself in the mirror. I looked tired, which was hardly surprising given the events of the last few weeks. The delicate skin under my eyes was so grey it looked bruised. I needed to get some more sleep.

I couldn't help grin at my own reflection. More sleep? What I was doing instead of sleeping was way more fun.

And then I saw something else … Surely it couldn't be—? I leaned closer to the mirror, eyes widening in shock.

"Oh, my God!"

My shriek brought Garth slamming into the bathroom, stark naked but ready to do battle on my behalf.

"What's wrong?" His gaze darted around the small room, as if he expected to find an assassin lurking in the bathtub.

With a sharp tug, I had it in my hand. My eyes filled with tears, but they were tears of relief, and I was still smiling as the tears welled over and rolled down my cheeks.

"I found a grey hair."

"So?" He took the hair from me and dropped it on the floor, then enclosed my hands in his big ones. "I know I said I liked redheads, but really I don't care what colour your hair is."

A single grey hair. Such a small thing, but such a momentous meaning. He wasn't seeing it, but I knew what it meant, and my heart filled with joy.

"Dragons don't get grey hairs. Not until they're centuries old. But humans do, even twenty-nine-year-old humans."

He frowned at me, still confused.

"I'm unique among dragons, in that I have a human body. Sure, now it's stronger and faster and has enhanced senses, blah, blah, blah, but it's still basically human. That means—"

My voice shook, and I had to swallow hard. "That means I'm only going to have a human lifespan."

It was so enormous, I felt as if I'd just been handed the world's greatest gift. I beamed at him through the tears, but Garth stared as if I'd lost the plot entirely.

"And that's a good thing?"

"Of course it is! I'm not going to outlive you and Lachie!"

"Okaaay. Most people would be kind of happy to have the lifespan of a dragon."

"Would they? Really? Sure, it sounds good on paper, but imagine seeing everyone around you die, while you go on and on into the centuries alone."

"Well, I can see this causing a few problems with your sisters down the line. Another domain to fight over." He shrugged. "But if it makes you happy …"

He was right, there could be problems when it came time to pass my domain on. But I had big plans, and hopefully by then my sisters—and the whole shifter world—would be used to a different style of rule. I meant to introduce a council to share my rule, with representatives from the main shifter groups. In time I hoped to persuade my sisters to do the same. Lessening the stranglehold the queens had on power would go a long way towards reducing the general resentment toward dragonkind.

Yes, big plans, and only a human lifespan to implement them. But I had a good team at my side, starting with this man.

"It does." I threw my arms around him. "It makes me very happy indeed."

"Then if you're finished in here, come back to bed and make *me* happy."

I scrubbed the tears from my cheeks. "You can't boss me around, I'm your queen."

"Yeah, you're the boss. Whatever. So you can be on top."

THE END

If you enjoyed this trilogy, don't miss the prequel, *Moonborn*. You'll find out how Garth became a werewolf, and what he did to get himself exiled from his pack.

For updates on new releases, plus special deals and other book news, sign up for my newsletter by visiting my website, www.marinafinlayson.com.

Reviews and word of mouth are vital for any author's success. If you enjoyed *Twiceborn Endgame*, please take a moment to leave a short review where you bought it. Just a few words sharing your thoughts on the book would be extremely helpful in spreading the word to other readers (and this author would be immensely grateful!).

ALSO BY MARINA FINLAYSON

MAGIC'S RETURN SERIES
The Fairytale Curse
The Cauldron's Gift

THE PROVING SERIES
Moonborn
Twiceborn
The Twiceborn Queen
Twiceborn Endgame

SHADOWS OF THE IMMORTALS SERIES
Stolen Magic
Murdered Gods
Rivers of Hell
Hidden Goddess

For a full listing of books by Marina Finlayson, please visit the Books page on her website, www.marinafinlayson.com/books.

ACKNOWLEDGEMENTS

Thanks once again to my beta readers: Mal and Mal, Peter, Geoff, Chris, Pauline and Christine. Your feedback helped make this a better book and I'm very grateful to all of you. Thanks also to Lachie for his advice on airports.

ABOUT THE AUTHOR

Marina Finlayson is a reformed wedding organist who now writes fantasy. She is married and shares her Sydney home with three kids, a large collection of dragon statues and one very stupid dog with a death wish.

Her idea of heaven is lying in the bath with a cup of tea and a good book until she goes wrinkly.